I0713714

Searching for Home

Vanessa E. Kelman

WORD COLLAGE PUBLISHING

Cover photograph © Trace Hudson / Pexels

ISBN 978-1-961761-06-3 (KDP print edition)
ISBN 978-1-961761-08-7 (Ingram print edition)
ISBN 978-1-961761-07-0 (KDP ebook edition)
ISBN 978-1-961761-09-4 (Ingram ebook edition)

Chapter 1

Addy felt like she'd been running forever. Her lungs ached, struggling to breathe in the cool, damp air. It had to be less than a mile now. Surely it hadn't been this far when she was driving, though, of course, the miles had passed in a blur through the car's windows. Time had flown, too, as the darkness had descended.

Addy paused a moment, bending over to rest her hands on her knees and suck in a few lungfuls of air. It didn't help that she was weighed down by her duffel bag. She thought about slowing her pace, but she knew between the fast-approaching night and the crispness in the air she would be chilled to the bone in no time. She had started at a walk and had nearly frozen. Besides, the faster she got to civilization, the better. She was not one to enjoy nature in bright sunlight, never mind misty moonlight. One wolf's howl, and she would be a goner.

She was right about the distance, and less than a half hour later she was walking into a town center, panting and wiping sweat from her brow. It wasn't late – a glance at her watch said it was barely 8 – but not much appeared to be open. It looked like a small town, quaint, with a few stores and restaurants, and houses dotting the distance with squares of light. She supposed if it was day that she would see a cute little post office, children pouring out of a little red schoolhouse, and a playground filled with mothers pushing tiny tots in swings. She felt as if she'd walked into a 1950s sitcom.

Spotting a diner that boasted 24-hour service, she turned her steps in that direction. She could really use a cup of coffee.

A bell above the door jingled, and a waitress gestured toward an open seat at the counter. Addy slid onto the red vinyl seat, placed her duffel bag on the floor by her feet, and grabbed a menu from behind the napkin holder. A moment later the same waitress flipped the coffee cup in front of her and picked up a glass pot from the percolator.

"Coffee?"

"Please."

The cup was poured, and the waitress disappeared for a moment or two before returning, pencil poised above a pad.

"What can I getcha?"

Suddenly ravenous from her run, Addy's eyes flitted over the menu. *Get the salad, Adelaide.* She could hear her mother's voice as clearly as if she were in the room. *Add grilled chicken if you must, but don't you dare get anything else.* Addy sighed. "Chicken Caesar salad, please." She placed the menu back where it belonged. Her mother wouldn't approve of the Caesar dressing, but Addy was tired of bland salads with plain chicken. *A girl must watch her figure.*

"Coming right up."

As she waited, Addy sipped her coffee and looked around the diner. It looked as she had expected. A family sat in the corner, eating ice cream sundaes. A young couple sat at the other end of the diner, by the window, gazing adoringly into each other's eyes. All that was missing was – nope, here they came.

As Addy turned back toward the door, a group of high school-aged boys burst in, laughing and chatting up a storm. From the attire, Addy gathered they were a sports team, and by the ball one of the boys was tossing into the air, she deduced it was basketball.

The waitress who had been helping her greeted the boys with a smile. "Did we win, guys?"

"Creamed 'em." One of the boys shouted with a grin.

The waitress whooped. "Then pie's on the house."

The young men piled into a couple of booths in the center of the diner, and the waitress showered them with attention, handing out thick slices of pie and glasses of water. By the chorus of "Thanks, Mags," Addy surmised that the waitress's name must be Margaret, or some derivation thereof. Funny how she hadn't even thought to ask. Or look at a name tag. Or something. She really used to be more observant – and more outgoing – than this. Maybe the stress of the past few months was taking its toll.

She could hear her mother scolding her again. *Adelaide, you've got to get your head out of the clouds. What are you doing here? In the middle of nowhere, with people you don't know, in a town you don't even know the name of?*

Pine Valley, Addy argued back in her mind. *The boys' shirts said Pine Valley Panthers. The town must be Pine Valley.*

And have you ever heard of it?

Addy closed her eyes and took a deep breath. She was arguing with her mother in her head. She was really starting to lose it. Never mind that her mother had died seven years earlier. Addy could still picture her as clearly as if she were sitting on the next stool over. And it was scary to think she still had that much control over her. But, even if it was just a voice in her head, that voice did have a point. What was she doing here?

She had set off looking for somewhere, anywhere, where she could get a fresh start. She had figured on driving as far as she could, then finding some city she could disappear into. New York had been her first idea, but it was so stereotypical she had resisted and kept going. Maybe Boston would be okay.

Instead, her car conks out in the middle of the country. Not even the country. A freaking forest. Trees everywhere. She didn't even know if she was right next to somewhere or in the middle of nowhere. Running five miles proved it was the middle of nowhere. The size of this town she found was further evidence. Maybe she should ask about a car repair place. Though it was probably too late for any of them to be open. She supposed she'd have to find a place to crash for the night. She would ask "Mags" when she returned with dinner.

Once the pie was dished out, the waitress disappeared into the kitchen and reappeared with Addy's salad. The mere sight of it made Addy's mouth water, and she dug in with barely a second's thought. She would ask after she ate, which didn't take more than five minutes. *Well, that was ladylike.*

"Goodness, you must have been starving."

Addy looked up to find the waitress staring in amazement at her empty bowl. Addy shrugged. "I guess I was."

Mags gave her a thoughtful look. "You new here?"

"Just passing through. My car broke down a few miles that way." Addy gestured.

"Tough break. Not a good place for it to stop. You walk all this way?"

Addy shrugged again. "I ran. It was too chilly to walk."

"No wonder you're hungry. Can I get you something else?"

The pie looked delicious, but Addy resisted. "No, I'm okay. It does look like I'm going to need a place to crash, though. Are there any hotels around here?"

Mags thought for a moment. "No chains. But the Jacksons run a little motel on the other side of town. Or there's a B and B the next street over."

"Do you by any chance have phone numbers for them? So I can see if they have a vacancy?"

Mags laughed. "They have vacancies, trust me. I think the only time they book up is if we're hosting the sports championships, and that only happens once every few years. You shouldn't have a problem with either one. Might want to check the motel, first, though. Nate and Joanna, who run the B and B, lock up kind of early."

"How far of a walk would it be? You said the other side of town."

Mags thought a bit. "Maybe fifteen minutes. Town's not that big, and it's not on the outskirts." She gave a few quick directions, which Addy scrawled on a napkin.

"Thank you for your help."

"No problem. Good luck with your car."

Mags left the receipt and went to check on the other patrons. Addy took a last sip of coffee, tucked a few bills under the check, and stood up. She wasn't looking forward to any more walking or running tonight, but she would be grateful for a soft bed and warm blankets. Just knowing she would be spending the next fifteen minutes in a cool mist made her shiver.

Bundling up the best she could in her jacket, Addy set out for the motel. Though it was dark and damp, at least now she had a few street lamps to light her way.

Her initial impression of the town remained, though the buildings were a bit more modern than she had expected. Maybe the school would be a bit larger and updated than a single-room house. It didn't take long, though, to come across the motel. A dozen or so units side by side, an open sign flashing in the window of the nearby office.

Addy entered the empty office and rang the bell that lay on the counter. A moment later a middle-aged gentleman greeted her with a warm smile.

"Looking for a room?"

Addy nodded. "Please."

"How long will you be staying?"

Addy paused. "Uh." She had no idea how long it would take to get her car up and running. "I don't really know. My car broke down. I need to take it to the shop, and I don't know how long it'll take."

"Not a problem." The man smiled at her. "You can stay as long as you need to. I'll put you in one of our best rooms." He grabbed a key off a board behind the counter, then gestured for her to follow him.

The overhang protected them from the rain that had started to fall, though a light mist still made its way under. Addy shivered again, glad she didn't have to be out anymore tonight.

They stopped in front of one of the middle units, and the man handed her a key. "Here you go. My name is Ed. My wife's name is Sylvie. She'll probably be the one manning the front desk in the morning if you need anything. Or you can hit the front desk button on the phone, and it'll ring us right up." He smiled again. "Have a good night."

"Thank you." Addy returned the smile and watched the man retreat back to the office before opening her room door. As she stepped inside and flipped on the light, she found a surprisingly comfortable room greeting her. Nothing fancy, but it wasn't as tacky as she had been expecting. The phone wasn't rotary. The TV was a flat screen. And the bedspread was a modern pattern, subtle flowers spread over a pale green background. Tossing her duffel bag by the desk chair to her right, she kicked off her shoes, then collapsed on the bed.

After a few moments of sheer exhaustion, Addy acknowledged that she should probably get up, get out of her damp clothes, and climb under the covers. And ten minutes later, she was in heaven, letting the weight of the blanket lull her to sleep.

Maggie wiped off the counter and said good-bye to the couple who had just finished their dinner. The diner had quieted down after the basketball team left, and now only the lovestruck couple remained by the window, reluctant to go home. Maggie didn't mind. It was nice to have company, even if they were wrapped up in their own world.

Running a 24-hour diner could be lonely sometimes, in the wee hours of the morning, when few, if any, customers came in. Many times she had thought about changing her hours to those of a "normal" restaurant. But then someone would come in who needed her: Ann, the single mother whose kids periodically stayed with their dad, leaving her alone and lonely; Matt, the high school kid whose parents didn't understand him and his ridiculous smarts; Katie, who was torn between wanting to grow up and leave and wanting to stay curled up in safety; Pete, who just plain got lonely. They came to her late at night, when the rest of the town was quiet and still, unsure what to do with themselves, needing a sympathetic ear and a comfortable stool to sit on. She gave them pie and hot cocoa, talked to them about the latest news or gossip, and let them just enjoy some company for a bit. And she knew that if she changed her hours, they wouldn't have anywhere to go. So she dealt with her own loneliness and relieved theirs.

It wasn't so bad, not really. She had some college kids helping her in the kitchen for most of the night, and they kept her company. A lot of the time they were wrapped up in their schoolwork or video games, or some other such thing, but they didn't mind talking to her once in a while. And really, what else did she have? A lonely apartment instead of a lonely diner? At least here she had the possibility of seeing another soul.

At this point, she didn't even sleep much. It wasn't often her mind let her rest soundly. A few hours sleep tucked between the breakfast and lunch hours, with a couple extra hours between lunch and dinner, usually sufficed. What she had to think about, she had no idea. But it never failed: the instant her head hit the pillow, her mind would start wandering, thinking about the customers who had come in that day, the latest happenings in town, the bills that needed to be paid, or the latest shipment she expected to receive. Today it would probably be the young woman whose car had broken down.

If she was honest with herself, it was probably a subconscious attempt to think about anything other than what she should really be thinking about: her life and the meaninglessness of it all. How many times had she thought about selling the diner and leaving this town? How many times had she longed to meet someone she could spend her life with? She had long given up on the dream of having children. She was pushing 60 now. She should be having grandchildren, not children. But she still had other dreams – of seeing the world, having someone hold her close at night. She wanted to feel like she had a purpose beyond running a diner in a tiny little town, waiting for someone who needed her to come in at two in the morning. She supposed, if she was really honest with herself, she just wanted to feel loved, needed, *complete*.

But instead her mind thought about everyone else, and everything else, so she wouldn't focus on the depressing reality that was her life. And she was so busy avoiding the truth that she couldn't sleep.

My, she was being philosophical tonight. Maggie finished wiping the counters, then made her way around the diner, straightening menus, filling napkin dispensers. She had to keep herself busy. It wouldn't do her any good to get depressed. It never did. She would still be Maggie Devin, plain Jane with a head full of dreams that would never be.

With a sigh Maggie tossed the cleaning rag into a bucket of soapy water and wiped her hands on her apron. It was time to do the nightly drawer count. She wouldn't see many, if any, more people tonight, and this way she would know if she had to lock any up. You could never be too careful, even in a podunk town like Pine Valley.

Chapter 2

Addy opened her eyes to find a strange popcorn ceiling above her. It took a moment to remember where she was, and when she did, she groaned. City girl Adelaide Rogers was stuck in the middle of nowhere in some tiny little town that probably didn't even have a repair shop. She would probably have to go to a town miles away, get her car towed, spend a ton of money she didn't want to spend, and sit and wait.

With that kind of day ahead of her, she opted to spend a few more minutes snuggled under the blankets. At least the bed was comfortable. It had done her sore muscles good to sleep a few hours. Next she would crawl to the shower and let the water beat down on her, washing away her tension. For now, anyway.

An hour later she was locking the door to the motel room. As she stepped into the daylight, she was amazed at how warm it was. The chill that had been in the air last night was gone, replaced by bright, warm sunlight. Even the rinky dink motel didn't seem that bad. The brick walls were clean, the light fixtures clear of bug build-up, and the sign touting the motel's name was bright and modern. Even the parking lot was free of leaves and dirt.

Not knowing where to go, she decided to stop in to the motel office. She would probably need a phone book or something. Did they even still make phone books? Maybe she should just search on her phone, though she wouldn't know how far away anything was. Addy sighed and pulled open the door. The woman behind the desk looked up and greeted her with a smile.

"Good morning, Dear."

"Hi. I was hoping to get a phone book or something? I need to find a place to take my car. It broke down last night."

"Oh, yes, Ed was telling me about that. But you don't need a phone book. Just walk a few blocks that way, and you'll run right into Mike's." She gestured toward her left.

"Oh. Okay." Addy stuck her hands in her jeans pockets. "Thanks."

"Any time."

Addy went the direction the woman had pointed and looked around as she strolled. With the improved weather, she found herself relaxing. If she had her car, she could go for a drive, roll the windows down, let the breeze blow through her hair. Not that this would have been her chosen destination, but that was a moot point. Who knew how long it would be before it was up and running again? And who knew how much it would set her back? She did not want to dip too much into her savings. She would need it when she left. But she would cross that bridge when she came to it. First she had to get the car going. Then she could think about leaving.

Mike's was a small shop, but obviously busy. Both bays were full, with techs working away. Two other cars sat in the parking lot, service tags hanging from their rear view mirrors. And the guy at the counter was on the phone when she walked in. At least this time she remembered to check the name tag. And she found herself face to face with Mike, who she could only surmise was the owner.

He looked up when she entered and held up a finger, asking her to wait. She did so patiently, looking around at the surprisingly well-lit and clean waiting area. It seemed to be a full-service shop, with sample tires lining the wall on her right, a price board hanging behind the counter in front of her, and informational guides presented on a display by the front door behind her. She could see in to the bays through a large window to her left, and in the corner between the bays and the front door were a few chairs, along with a table covered in magazines and a TV airing the news.

Mike was talking automotive gibberish, but she could hear an appointment being made before he hung up the phone and turned his attention to her.

"Hi there. Sorry for the wait. What can I do for you?"

"Hi. My car broke down outside town, and it looks like I'm going to need a tow. And get whatever's broken fixed. Any chance you're available?"

"Sure. Give me five minutes to get things lined up."

"Okay. Thanks."

Four and a half minutes later, Addy was in the cab of a tow truck, driving in the direction she was pretty sure her car had ended up. She hadn't seen many landmarks in the dark, but she remembered the diner, and the street leading up to it. Ten minutes later they found her car, pulled to the side of the road, looking forlorn all alone.

"If you don't mind, I'd rather just tow it to the shop before examining it. It's a lot easier when I can get it on the lift if I need to."

"Sure. That's fine."

Mike hitched the car to the back of his tow truck, and they were heading back before she knew it.

It was so quiet out here, Addy mused. The trees muffled whatever noise there was, leaving only a few rustles and soft chirps from birds. And once they re-entered the town, Addy was surprised to see how many people were bustling on the streets, driving every which way, and filling up the sidewalks. Yet no one seemed to be angry or frustrated, just going quickly on their way, greeting others as they passed.

The feeling of being in a sitcom intensified. It was surreal here, so seemingly peaceful and friendly. It made her wonder what was hiding under the surface. What secrets did Pine Valley hold?

Maybe she was being too cynical. Maybe her past had just made her too hard, too pessimistic. Maybe there were still some good, friendly, honest people in the world.

Stopping her musings short, she turned to Mike. "So, how long do you think it'll take to diagnose the car?"

Mike shrugged with one shoulder. "I should be able to get 'er open this afternoon. I'll have a better idea once I get under her hood. You said she just died?"

"Yeah. I was driving along fine, then the power just cut off."

"Huh. Could just be a fuse. But I'll check it out." He glanced her way, and for a moment their eyes connected. His were a deep blue, and while she couldn't completely read him, she saw honesty in their depths. "Are you in a hurry?"

It was Addy's turn to shrug. "Not really. I don't have anywhere specific to be."

"Where you coming from?"

That was a loaded question, though he probably didn't know it. Where was she coming from? A broken home, with a domineering mother and a father who had run off years ago. Failed relationships, with the latest beau deciding after three years that she didn't fit his new executive image. Failed jobs, with nothing clicking just right, despite numerous attempts to find that perfect career. Deep, utter loneliness, and a feeling of never belonging anywhere. But she answered simply "the D.C. area."

"Wow. What brings you up here?"

"Uh." Running away? "Just looking for a change, I guess."

Mike laughed. "Well, Pine Valley is definitely a change. No big city politics here."

Addy gave a polite smile. "No, I suppose not."

"So where you headed? Up to Boston?"

"That was the thought." Addy sighed. "I had decided to take the scenic route. It didn't exactly go as planned."

Mike laughed again. "No, I guess it didn't. Though, I'm sorry, I probably shouldn't laugh at your misfortune. It's nice up there. A little busy for my tastes, but it's a nice change of pace once in a while."

They pulled into the parking lot for the repair shop and stepped out of the truck.

"So I guess just call my cell phone when you've had a chance to check it out."

"Will do. Like I said, should be sometime this afternoon. I've got a couple we're working on now, but as soon as one's done, I'll pop the hood."

"Sounds good. Thanks."

She watched him a moment as he started unhooking the car, then decided to move on. Where to, she didn't know. There were only so many places she could go. A faint rumbling in her belly reminded her, though, that she should probably start with grabbing a bite to eat. Not knowing where else to go, she headed back to the diner.

It was a lot busier today. Middle-aged men in plaid shirts lined the counter, nursing cups of coffee and assorted breakfast treats. It appeared a few business transactions were going on, as booths were filled with people in suits – suits in Pine Valley? – looking official, despite their smiling faces. There were a few older couples enjoying a leisurely breakfast. What appeared to be a mothers' club, with several young women and assorted strollers clustered around a couple of tables that had been pushed together.

Addy didn't know where to sit, not wanting to take up one of the few free tables, but not wanting to wait for a spot at the counter. After a moment's contemplation, she opted for a small table by the kitchen.

Grabbing the menu from behind the napkin dispenser, she questioned whether she wanted to stick with her typical egg-white omelet or if she wanted to comfort herself by getting a platter of French toast. *Don't be ridiculous, Adelaide. Think of all the carbs in that.* Addy sighed, but with a mischievous smile to herself decided to get the French toast. With a side of bacon. She had been getting a lot of exercise over the past couple of days. And she would be working it off today, too.

Maggie greeted her with a friendly smile. "Looks like you survived the night."

"I'm a survivor." Addy returned the smile.

"I hope Ed and Sylvie were good to you?"

"Of course. The motel was fine."

"I'm glad. What can I get you?"

Addy recited her order, a little butterfly of excitement low in her belly, then sat back as Maggie left to submit it. She must work long hours, Addy mused, to have been working the late dinner crowd last night, and the breakfast group this morning. Addy wondered if she had been here all night.

What must it be like, she wondered, to sit in a nearly-empty diner in the middle of the night? In a town this small, it couldn't be that busy. Was it even worth it? Did she ever go stark raving mad, pulling her hair out in the abominable loneliness? It crossed her mind to ask, but Addy dismissed the thought. It really wasn't any of her business.

Instead, she turned to look out the window. While it was a nice day, she had no idea how she would fill it. Already her feet were tapping, and her fingers were twitching. She had to do something, go somewhere. But she was stuck. What did they do around here except eat?

As she sat gazing out the window, she felt a presence behind her and saw a shadowy figure in the glass. Her heart quickened, her feet stilled, and she straightened her spine.

"Hi."

It took her a moment to turn. A man stood at the edge of her table, hands folded in front of him. "Hi." Her voice held a question, wondering who he was and what he wanted.

"I'm Bill." He held out a hand, but she paused before taking it.

"Hi, Bill."

"What's your name?"

Another pause. "Addy."

"I like that name."

"Thank you." The question was in her voice again.

"Maggie said your car broke down. I'm sorry."

"It's okay."

"If you need a ride someplace, just let me know. That's my Toyota out there." He pointed to where a 1998 Toyota Corolla sat in the parking lot. "It doesn't look like much, but it does the job."

"Uh. Thanks, but I'm okay."

He shrugged. "Okay. Just let me know. How long are you staying here?"

"I don't know. It depends on how long it takes to fix my car."

"Oh. I hope they fix it fast, but you can still stay as long as you want to."

"Thanks."

There was a moment of silence as they stared at each other. She waited for him to continue, wondering why he had approached her, but he didn't seem to have anything else to say. After a moment he stepped back and said "okay, then. I guess I'll see you around."

"Bye."

Addy watched Bill leave, a look of puzzlement on her face. He was a strange character, but he seemed harmless. Regardless, she wouldn't be taking him up on the offer of a ride anytime soon. Though if she had to stick around very long, she may be singing a different tune. Already she was bored, and she hadn't even been here a day.

Maggie arrived a moment later with her breakfast. Just watching the pat of butter melt on top of the French toast made her mouth water. But Maggie paused before leaving her to eat.

"I hope Bill wasn't too much of a pain."

Addy shook her head. "No, he was okay."

"Good. He's a nice enough guy, but he's a little funny. Doesn't quite understand what he should and should not do and say."

"That's okay. He seemed harmless."

"Yeah, he is." She gave a curt nod, then returned to the kitchen for more platters.

It didn't take long for Addy to devour her breakfast, though she savored every bite. *What were you thinking, Adelaide? Any more meals like this, and you'll be packing on the pounds. Then who will want you?*

It occurred to her as she was sipping her coffee, trying to push that little nagging voice of her mother's out of her mind, that she didn't even know why she was watching her weight. Because she needed a husband? Because she wanted to impress people?

Her mother had always hammered in the thought that she had to be slim, elegant, to attract a man. And she had usually stuck with it, careful with her weight and appearance. But so far the only men she had attracted were people who cared only about how she looked. Take Jack, for example. She had been pretty enough to attract his attention, and hold on to him for a few years. But as soon as she started showing her real personality, and expressing interest in being more than arm candy, he had tossed her to the curb. Did she really want to be tied to someone who only wanted to be with her because she was thin and pretty?

Maybe it wouldn't be so bad to be fat. Then she would know who really liked her for her personality. If they even stuck around long enough to learn her personality.

Addy chuckled to herself. Boredom did not agree with her. If her only entertainment was picturing herself obese, she really needed to find something to do.

After a moment, though, her smile faded. What *was* she going to do with her time? It was easy while she was driving to focus only on the open road and the song on the radio. She was driving, and that was all she had to think about. But without the steering wheel beneath her hand, she didn't know what to do with herself.

She supposed she should start thinking about what would happen once she stopped driving, when she got to Boston or wherever she decided to stop. She would have to find some kind of job, some place to live. What would she do, in a strange city all by herself, with no idea who she was or what she wanted out of life?

But she didn't want to think about that. Thinking about that would mean having to make decisions, real decisions, and having to think about the empty, hollow feeling inside. The feeling she did her best to ignore. The feeling that kept trying to sneak its way to the forefront of her mind.

Addy took a deep breath, then reached for her coffee cup, anxious for something to do. She stopped when she realized it was empty. Refusing to think about the metaphor, she instead took another deep breath and looked up to catch Maggie's eye. A moment later the waitress was at her table.

"More coffee?"

Addy shook her head. "No, just the check."

Maggie nodded, then pulled out her pad and ripped off the slip.

"What do you do for fun around here?"

Maggie put her pen to her lip and thought a moment. "Not much, really. Some people are into nature, and there are lots of trails and paths for hiking, a stream for fishing. There's the park for the little ones. Mini golf and bowling next town over. And a movie theater about 20 minutes away."

"20 minutes driving, I assume."

"Yeah, sorry."

Addy sighed. "Looks like I'm in for a long, boring wait."

"There's a library in town. They sometimes have events going on, or you can read or hop on a computer, of course. And I think there might be one of those concerts in the park tonight. But I'm not sure. That might be tomorrow."

"Seems a little chilly for a concert outside."

Maggie shrugged. "Not much to do around here, as I mentioned. And people love an excuse to get together. So as long as they can bundle up, events go on. They're usually pretty well attended."

"Far cry from the city, that's for sure."

"You a city girl?"

"Yeah. D.C. Always something going on. I think I might go crazy here."

"Some people prefer a slower pace. And you get used to it, but probably not in the time you'll be here."

"Probably not."

"Sorry, Sweetie." Maggie shot her a sympathetic look.

"It's okay." She took a quick look at the check, fished a few bills from her wallet, and handed them to Maggie, who tucked them into her apron pocket.

"Good luck."

"Thanks. I'll probably be back for lunch." She grinned.

"I guess I'll see you then." Maggie returned the grin, then went off to help other customers.

Addy pushed her chair back and stood up, a feeling of defeat washing over her. A minute later she was back outside. At least the sun was warm, and it wasn't raining. The day definitely would have been worse if it was still cold and wet like the night before. This morning the residual raindrops on tree branches glistened in the sun, and the smell of fresh air and damp dirt filled her nostrils.

Not sure which way to head, Addy took a right out of the diner doors, in the direction of the playground she had seen. Kids were running around, and a couple of moms were chatting on a bench as their kids played. The swings were mostly empty, probably because their sling seats had small puddles from the rain. Addy made her way over and tipped one, watching the water droplets slide to the ground. Then she brushed the rest of the seat with the sleeve of her jacket and sat down. How long had it been since she had been on a swing? *What are you, five years old?* The voice in her head made Addy sigh, and she closed her eyes. She gave herself a little push off the ground and began pumping her legs. The sun-kissed wind felt glorious against her face, and she moved her legs faster, feeling her body get higher and higher. After a couple of minutes she let herself slow down and come to a stop. Her chest felt heavy, and tears were stinging her eyes.

After a moment, Addy took a deep breath, brushed the tears from her eyes, and stood up. The moms on the bench were looking at her from the corners of their eyes; she could tell. She forced a smile to her face and left the playground. Where to next?

The library was nearby, but it looked like it wasn't open yet, so Addy just kept walking. Next to the library was a community center, but it looked like the only people going inside were senior citizens, so she opted not to check it out. As she continued, she took in the sites and sounds that made Pine Valley. The town center was a far cry from D.C., that was for sure. While there were cars on the roads, those roads were considerably narrower, and there was no angry honking or yelling. Pedestrians dotted the sidewalks, going in and out of small retail shops, offices, or a cafe. It didn't look like any chain businesses existed in Pine Valley, but that seemed to suit it.

A bit further down the main road Addy saw a single-story building identified as town hall, with a police department attached to one side. It stood at an intersection, and Addy remembered that if she headed down that side street to the left she would end up back at the motel. A volunteer fire department sat across the side street, with a young man and woman in front of the building, taking advantage of the sunshine by washing a fire engine.

Since she knew what lay in the direction of the motel, Addy opted to turn right and see where that took her. She found herself in a neighborhood filled with quaint houses and their corresponding yards. While some yards were more picturesque than others, it appeared for the most part that the residents of Pine Valley took pride in their lawns, gardens, and homes. She didn't see anything that could be described as rundown or grungy, but everything looked lived in, loved. She saw an occasional adult weeding a garden, an occasional child laughing and running around. A small pang of envy stabbed Addy in the stomach. What would it be like to live here, to grow up here? She had spent her childhood in a sprawling colonial home, with a pristine lawn that she wasn't allowed to play in. To be honest, she hadn't done much playing at all. Her mother had insisted that she be well behaved, learn good manners, and keep her clothes neat and tidy. When her father had left them, the home had been downsized, but the expectation had remained the same, with the added pressure to take care of her appearance. The older she got, the more demanding her mother had been. *It is not demanding to expect one's daughter to be the best she can be,* Addy's mother defended herself in Addy's mind. *To be respected and successful, you must put your best foot forward at all times. If you want any respectable man to take you seriously, you need to show him your take yourself seriously.*

Addy sighed, then took a deep breath. She had left D.C. to try to break away from that life, to have a fresh start. But it would appear her mother had decided to join her on this road trip. Would Addy never be free of her?

At the next intersection, Addy saw the bed and breakfast Maggie had mentioned on her right. Not wanting to venture too far from the center of town, she opted to turn right and hopefully loop back around. After a few more minutes of walking, she spotted Mike's automotive shop at the next corner. She took a moment to get her bearings. If she turned right here again, that should take her back toward the center. Maybe the library would be open by now, and she could at least sit down. Her legs were getting tired. It had been a while since she had done this much walking.

Passing by the auto shop, Addy glanced over. Her car was still in the parking lot, waiting to be looked at. Since Mike had said he probably wouldn't get to it until the afternoon, she wasn't surprised, but she had been hoping he would get to it early. The sooner she was out of this quiet little town, the better.

After passing a bank and a grocery store, Addy found herself back at the library. Seeing a couple of people walk inside, she turned toward the front door and stepped inside, as well. Addy hadn't spent much time in libraries, but this one was definitely smaller than what she was used to. Still, it seemed friendly and inviting. She saw shelves full of books and DVDs, a play area for children, and a reading area by the front windows. A few computers sat in study corrals forming an island to her left. Unsure what to do with herself, she approached the main desk, behind which sat two middle-aged women.

"Hi, I'm not from around here. Can I still use a computer?"

"Of course," one woman responded with a smile. "Let me get you a guest pass, and we'll get you logged on."

A couple of minutes later, Addy was sitting at one of the computers, but she still wasn't sure what to do with herself. She checked her email – all junk – and ventured over to Instagram. She could see people she used to know living it up at nightclubs and parties, dressed to impress with drinks in their hands. That had been her life, too. Maybe one day it would be again. But did she want that?

Unsure how best to pass the time, Addy zoned out to TikTok for a while before getting bored with that, too. This was ridiculous. She could feel her leg bouncing up and down of its own accord, and her fingers were starting to twitch. She needed to *do* something.

Addy logged off of the computer and headed toward the reading area near the front windows. She saw a few racks of magazines, so she perused the offerings, selected a couple to read, then sat in one of the plush chairs. It didn't take long to realize that the magazines that used to hold her attention no longer did so. The hottest celebrity gossip and latest fashion trends just didn't seem very important. Had she really been so superficial? Or was that just what she had been conditioned to want?

She put down the magazines and gazed out the window. From her vantage point she could see friends greeting each other, people bustling to and fro, entering doctors' offices, shops, and back to their cars. She wondered what their lives were like. Were they happy? From their clothes she could tell that most weren't concerned with the latest fashion trends, though they looked respectable and appealing. They seemed down to earth, sensible. Then again, she could just be making generalizations. Surely everyone else had their lives together, lives that were significantly more meaningful than her own.

Geesh, get it together, Addy. This time it was her own voice that broke her thoughts. Here she was, on a beautiful fall day, free as a bird to build the life she wanted. No, she didn't have a place to live or a job, but she had her health, a decent amount of money in the bank, and a good head on her shoulders. It had taken her a while, but she had found the courage to break the pointless monotony of her life. She was strong, even if she didn't often feel like it. Why was she being so pitiful?

Giving herself a mental shake, Addy put the magazines back on their racks and left the library. It might be too early for lunch, but she could stop in at the cafe she saw and grab a cup of coffee. She crossed the street and entered the small shop, the scent of coffee and freshly baked muffins greeting her.

A few people stood in line, but the line moved quickly, and Addy was served promptly. Though the baked goods were tempting, she resisted, more out of concern for her wallet than her waistline. She found a seat by the window so she could once again watch the world go by, but this time she had the added benefit of listening in to conversations around her without looking obvious. Though she wasn't usually one to eavesdrop, it would be nice to think about someone else's life for a while.

Conversations flowed, with people coming and going while Addy sat there. She felt like she was in another world, and she was convinced that if she hadn't had the coffee to keep her awake she would have drifted into dreamland. Maybe she should have just headed back to the motel and slept the day away. This was much more enlightening though.

As Addy sat sipping her coffee, she heard friends updating each other on love lives, new hobbies, and how their kids were doing in school. She heard grandparents brag about grandchildren, newly-retired men chatting about up-coming travel plans, and a couple chatting with a realtor. She heard laughing and whispers and an occasional baby cry. She heard life moving all around her. No, the conversations weren't all happy and upbeat, but they were all real, and Addy soaked them all in.

When an hour had passed, Addy stood up, stretched her legs a bit, and tossed her coffee cup in the trash. Then she left the cafe and made her way back down the street. She stopped at the town green and sat in the gazebo there for a while, watching life go by. While she was still feeling unsettled and lost, her body had slowed enough that she didn't feel the need to squirm or tap or move. She closed her eyes, letting a cool breeze lift her hair off her shoulders. The sun felt warm on her face, and she tilted her head back to catch the rays before the sun moved too high and cast her in shadow. Taking a deep breath, she listened to the birds in the trees, the cars driving past, and the rustling of squirrels scurrying past. Just as she was feeling soothed into a near sleep, her stomach grumbled, and her eyes flew open. Must be lunch time.

Checking her cell phone, Addy saw that it was almost noon. She stretched her arms and legs and stood up. At least eating would give her something to do, though she had been surprised to find herself enjoying the peace of a quiet morning.

Though she had passed an Italian restaurant in her meanderings, Addy opted to head back to the diner. The casual atmosphere there appealed to her, and sitting at the counter would mean she didn't have to feel awkward sitting by herself again.

Maggie greeted her when she entered the diner. Seeing an empty seat at the counter, Addy made her way over and sat down.

"Coffee?"

Addy shook her head. "No thanks. Just water to start."

"You got it."

As Maggie filled up her water glass, Addy perused the menu. Should she play it safe or get what she really wanted? *You splurged enough at breakfast, Adelaide. Walking does not make up for the number of calories you consumed. Stick with the salad.* "What can I get for you?"

"Burger and fries, please."

"Coming right up." Maggie scrawled her order on a pad, then ripped off the paper and stuck it on a carousel resting on a ledge by the kitchen. After greeting a couple of other customers and taking their orders, Maggie made her way back over to Addy. "So how was your morning?"

"Quiet."

Maggie laughed. "No surprise there."

"Actually, it wasn't bad. Once I settled into a groove and slowed my own pace, it was fine. Just took a little getting used to. I'm usually on the move."

Maggie nodded. "I hear ya. It's definitely an adjustment from city life."

"You ever lived in a city?"

Maggie shook her head. "Nah. But I've seen them on TV." She grinned. Addy smiled back.

"Just like I've seen small towns on TV. It's like an episode of Gilmore Girls here."

Maggie laughed again. "Not quite, but I catch your drift." A bell dinged, and Maggie turned to grab Addy's meal. Placing it down in front of Addy, she said "enjoy," then grabbed the water pitcher and went off to check on other guests.

Addy sat for a moment, staring at the burger. When was the last time she had eaten a burger? With a bun, no less? And fries? Two big meals in one day. She wasn't sure if her body would rebel or rejoice. With the first bite of a fry, though, her tastebuds were definitely rejoicing.

She tried to savor her meal, not only to enjoy the experience, but also to make it take longer. She wasn't sure she could handle many more hours of sitting and people watching. Once the burger and fries were gone, she decided to really go all out and order a piece of pie. Maybe she shouldn't be spending the money, but in her strange state of limbo and passing the time, she was feeling relaxed and comfortable for the first time in a long time. A piece of pie wouldn't break her. She was just polishing off the last bite when Maggie came over to check on her.

"My, it looks like you were enjoying that."

Addy nodded. "I cannot tell you the last time I had a piece of pie. I'm honestly not sure if I ever have."

"You're kidding me."

Addy shook her head. "Nope. My mother always encouraged me to keep my slim figure, and the people I hung out with all did the same, so dessert was a rarity."

"Well, I am honored to have served you your first slice of pie."

"Thanks." Addy took a drink of water, then sat for a moment.

"Can I get you anything else?"

Addy shook her head. "No, that should do it." She reached for her wallet, took a glance at the receipt Maggie put down on the counter, and fished for some bills. Counting out the cash she had left, she found she was a bit short. With a sigh she took out her debit card. She had hoped the cash would last longer. Maybe she shouldn't have had that pie after all. After signing the card slip, Addy slid off the stool and, waving good-bye to Maggie, headed out the door.

She was just figuring out her next destination when her cell phone rang. Seeing a Connecticut number, she figured it had to be the auto shop. She accepted the call and put the phone to her ear. "Hello?"

"Hi, Addy; it's Mike."

"Hi, Mike." She took a deep breath. "What's the damage?"

"Well, it looks like a couple of fuses blew. I was able to replace them easy enough, but I can't for the life of me figure out why they blew."

"Is the car running?"

"Yeah. It's working now. I just can't say for how long."

Addy bit her lower lip. "Think it'll make it to Boston?"

"You can try. I wouldn't be surprised if you had future issues, though. You may want to look into replacement."

Addy's heart sank. That was not what she wanted to hear. Though she supposed if it would at least make it to Boston, she wouldn't really need a car after that. That's what subways were for. "I'll think about it. Is it ready to pick up?"

"Whenever you want."

"Great. I'll be over in a few minutes."

Destination determined, Addy headed to the right and resumed walking.

Maggie watched Addy with a twinge of jealousy. She had seen her pick up the phone outside the diner, and she could only assume her car was ready. Looked like Addy would be leaving town.

Though their interactions had been brief, Maggie felt as if she'd found a kindred spirit in Addy. The only difference was, Addy was going places. And Maggie was stuck in her same rut. What would it be like to just drive off and leave it all behind? Would Boston hold more opportunities for her, too?

Sadly Maggie had to acknowledge that she would likely never find out. She wasn't exactly rolling in dough, and she wouldn't know what to do with herself, anyway. All she knew was how to waitress and run a diner. And if she was going to do that someplace else, she might as well stay here where she knew she would be successful. Was a change of scenery worth the risk of a move?

Maybe what she really needed was a vacation. Maybe she just needed to stop staring at the same four walls for a week or two. She could go on a cruise or something, see a bit of the world. Then at least she could say she had been somewhere. Maybe that night, instead of wallowing as she waited for customers, she could look at some travel websites. It didn't hurt to at least look.

Chapter 3

Mike tried to look busy while he waited for Adelaide Rogers to come in to pick up her car. It was a shame she was leaving town. She was the first woman he'd been attracted to in quite some time. Maybe it was because he didn't see new people very often, but he had figured he would have found someone to spend his life with by now. He was in his thirties, and he would consider himself reasonably attractive. Though he wasn't wealthy, he ran a successful business, and he was comfortable. He had a sense of humor, was perhaps slightly above average in the intelligence area. He had a lot to offer a woman. But there was always something missing.

He felt that something with Addy. Though it hadn't lasted long, he had enjoyed their brief conversation. She was beautiful, yes, but he could tell she had a good head on her shoulders. She wasn't a bimbo. And that was definitely a requirement for him. He needed to be able to carry on an intelligent conversation with a woman. Why would he want to spend his life with someone he couldn't talk to? Who was only with him so he could afford to take her shopping? It had never made sense to him. Sure, he'd like her to be nice to look at, but she didn't have to be drop-dead gorgeous. It was much more important to have something between her ears.

But it didn't matter. Maybe Addy was the woman for him, but it didn't matter. She was leaving, and he would probably never see her again. Why put himself out there? Much better to just let her float out of his life, forget she ever existed, and look on to the next possibility. Pine Valley was small, but it wasn't tiny. There were a lot of people here, and new people came through on occasion. Some decided to stay. It was a great place to raise a family: quiet but not stifling, good school system, surrounded by beautiful nature. It had a decent economic balance: enough jobs for many of its residents, and enough businesses to appeal to residents by way of shopping and necessities. They didn't have to drive an hour to go grocery shopping or anything. And by having everything right here, they were able to flourish as a small microcosm of the world. They had options outside, but they didn't have to go out unless they wanted to.

The one thing they could use, Mike had to admit, was more entertainment. Even if Addy was staying, where would he take her on a date? They could go out for dinner, he supposed, but beyond that they would have to leave town. And a city girl like her probably wouldn't be amused by mini golf or bowling, or hanging out at the local bar. Would she be willing to sit in the cold and hear a cover band on the town green? Or a lecture at the library? Probably not. They would have to take a drive. Which he was okay with, but it could get expensive if they had to leave town whenever they did anything.

Maybe it was better she was leaving. Then he wouldn't have to worry about impressing her.

She walked through the door just as he was thinking about going into the garage to do something else. He had been beginning to think she wouldn't show until later on. But in she walked, a vision of forced confidence with undertones of sadness and courage that he respected but also pitied.

"Hey, Mike." She sounded casual and laidback, but her fingers started drumming the counter as soon as she approached.

"Hi. Let me grab the keys."

"Okay."

He grabbed a packet of paperwork and handed her the keys.

"How much do I owe you?"

He went over the paperwork with her, and Addy handed over her debit card.

"Was there any kind of sign I should have recognized? Just so I know if it happens again?"

"Not really. Fuses had blown. It's just like in a house. When the fuse blows, the power just shuts off. There isn't really any kind of warning. And without knowing what caused it to blow in the first place, I can't tell you how to prevent it."

"So it could happen again at any time?"

Mike nodded. "In theory, yeah. And maybe it's just me, but when I test drove it after the repair, I just got this feeling in my gut. The car didn't seem reliable anymore. I've driven these cars before, and they're good cars. But I felt almost like it could die at any time."

Addy sighed, and her shoulders sank.

"I'm sorry. I know that's not what you want to hear. I just wanted you to be prepared."

"I know. And I guess it's good to know. But it's not good news."

"I know. I wish it were better."

They stood in silence for a few moments, just staring at the car out of the window. Mike hemmed and hawed for a minute. She seemed reluctant to leave, but maybe that was just because of the car troubles. Still, maybe he should take a chance. Maybe he would regret not taking a chance.

"So, Addy..." He let his voice trail off.

She looked up at him expectantly.

"I know you'll be leaving town now. But if you ever happen to be in the neighborhood again, I'd love it if you look me up. Maybe we could go to dinner or something."

Addy's eyes widened in surprise. "You're asking me out?"

Mike shrugged with one shoulder. "It was just a thought."

"That's so sweet."

Mike knew what that meant. That meant "no," but she was letting him down easy. "It's okay."

She paused for a moment, then said "I'd love to."

Really? He felt like a kid at Christmas. "Great. Well, here's my card if you're ever around."

"How about tonight?"

It was Mike's turn to be surprised. "I thought you were leaving?"

Addy shrugged. "I will. But it's better to start a trip in the morning, don't you think?" She gave him a small smile.

He smiled back. "Yeah, that sounds like a good idea."

"So, tonight?"

"That would be great. Where are you staying? I can pick you up."

"At the motel." Addy gestured in its general direction.

"Okay. I'll pick you up around six?"

"That would be nice."

"I'll see you then."

She got into her car and drove off after a final little wave. He watched her go, then did a little shimmy of a victory dance.

When he walked back toward the shop, the techs were watching him and laughing.

"Get back to work."

"Yes, boss," one said with a fake salute and a grin.

Mike couldn't keep the smile off his face.

Why had she done that? Addy couldn't for the life of her figure out why she had suggested dinner that night. It would have been easy to say "sure, maybe if I'm passing by one day." It never would have happened, and she wouldn't have hurt his feelings.

But maybe that's why. It never would have happened. And Mike seemed like a sweet guy. The look in his eyes had been hopeful, even though he tried to act nonchalant. Hadn't she just been telling herself she needed to find someone who liked her for her, not just because she looked decent? Maybe Mike would be different.

But what if he was? It's not as if she was moving to Pine Valley. She was not cut out for this kind of place. She needed action. She needed people. She needed to have something to do, other than sit in a diner pondering the banalities of her life. She did not need to fall for a guy in a place like this. Because then she would feel bad about leaving.

And she had to leave. She was anxious to leave. She wanted to get to Boston and start her new life. The life she hadn't figured out yet but was excited about.

So why had she done that?

Addy kicked herself during the ride back to the motel. Then she kicked herself as she threw herself on the bed. Now she was back to square one: what was she going to do for the rest of the day? But at least now she had her car. She could drive to the next town if she wanted, catch a movie or something. Maybe a shorter test drive would be a good idea, given the state of her car. If something happened, she would have a trusty mechanic close by.

Or she could up and leave anyway. She didn't owe Mike anything. She could tell him she had changed her mind. She could just leave and not tell him anything. But did she want to be that person? She didn't think she did, though she had to admit the thought was tempting. Then she could just forget this little blip on her journey and get back to her real life.

Chapter 4

By God, he was nervous! Mike couldn't remember the last time he had been nervous on a date. Then again, he could barely remember the last time he'd been on a date. But no matter, he was nervous. And excited. And about to lose his cool if he didn't calm down.

It might be cheesy, but he had picked up a single rose to give to Addy. He clutched it in one hand as he pulled up beside her car in the motel parking lot and walked up to the unit with the light on in the window. He wiped his sweaty palm on the leg of his slacks before knocking on the door, then stepped back to wait.

The wait seemed lengthy, but he held himself back a bit before knocking again. His hands got sweaty again. Was he being blown off?

Mike was contemplating getting back into his truck when the door swung open and a frantic Addy with dripping hair greeted him.

"I am so sorry. Movie ran late. I was in the shower. Come in. I'll just be a minute."

Mike entered the room awkwardly and sat on the desk chair by the front window while Addy re-entered the bathroom. A few minutes later she came back into the room and smiled.

"Sorry about that. I promise I'm usually more put-together. There were some technical difficulties at the movie theater, and the movie cut out, and, well, long story short, the movie got out about 45 minutes later than I thought it would. I had to race back to get ready."

"It's okay."

Addy looked at the rose in his hand, slightly wilted now from being clenched in his sweaty fist. "Is that for me?"

"Oh. Yeah." He held it out for her and stood up. "Sorry."

Addy had the good grace to look bashful. "That was nice of you. I'm sorry this evening has gotten off to such a weird start."

"It's okay. Are you ready to go?"

"Sure."

She locked the door, and they climbed into his truck.

"So where are we headed?"

"I made reservations at an Italian place in town. Nice, quiet, great food."

"Sounds good."

Silence fell, and Mike tried thinking frantically for something to talk about. The night was going to be a disaster. Two minutes in, and they had already run out of things to talk about?

"So what is it that you do?" he finally came up with.

"Do?"

"You know, for a living."

"Oh. Nothing at the moment."

"Nothing?"

"I guess you could say I'm between jobs."

"Oh. That's right, you did say you were looking for a change. What kind of work do you want to do?"

Addy laughed. "If I knew the answer to that, I'd be a whole lot happier."

He chanced a glance at her. "You don't know?"

Addy shrugged. "I've had some ideas, but so far nothing has panned out. And now I'm tapped out of ideas. I haven't figured out what to try next."

"What have you tried so far?"

Addy sighed. "Well, let's see. I've done a bunch of clerical work. I've worked retail. I tried my hand at acting. That was interesting. Did a little waitressing." She closed her eyes. "I don't know. I've lost track at this point. I feel like I've tried everything. All I know is that nothing has felt meaningful, or like what I was meant to do." She opened her eyes and turned to him. "I know that probably sounds corny. I should probably just suck it up and get a job – any job – and figure it out."

"I don't think it's corny at all." He met her gaze for a moment. "I don't think life's worth living if you're not doing what you want to be doing. As for me, I love what I do. I've always been a car nut, and I love taking things apart. And I enjoy the challenges of running my own business. But I've had jobs I didn't like, too. I know what it's like to not be happy."

Silence fell again, but it wasn't as uneasy.

"What do your parents do?"

"Uh. My parents aren't exactly in the picture."

"Oh. I'm sorry."

"No, it's okay. My mom died a few years back. She was a secretary. She bounced from political candidate to candidate, whoever was paying the most and gave her the most exposure. I tried for a bit, but it wasn't my cup of tea. My dad ran off when I was going into middle school. I hardly remember him."

Mike didn't know what to say. He hadn't intended to open a can of worms. He focused on pulling into the restaurant parking lot and finding a spot to park.

"He's probably the reason I have trouble with men. Well, actually, they're both probably the reason. My mom raised me to be a trophy wife. And when I tried to be myself, it didn't work out so well. It hasn't worked out so well. To be honest, I think that's what happened to my mom, but I don't know for sure. I just know she always wanted me to be pretty, and thin, and find a successful man."

"I can't imagine that would be a very happy life, just being someone's arm candy."

"It isn't."

Mike pulled into a parking space, then stepped out of the truck and moved to open the door for Addy. But she was already on her way out by the time he got to the other side of the truck.

"Sorry," she said.

"It's okay." He grinned. "Just trying to be a gentleman. But I guess I should have known from the way the conversation was heading that you're an independent kind of woman."

"Yeah. That tends to get me into trouble."

"Well, rest assured, I don't have a problem with it. But I do like to do nice things. Will you allow me to open the front door for you?"

"Sure."

He made a grand production of yanking the door handle and sweeping her into the restaurant. She responded to his efforts with a grin. "Thanks."

"Any time." He returned the smile.

They were seated promptly and took a moment to linger over the menus. By the time they ordered, Mike felt that perhaps the evening wasn't going so badly after all.

The evening was a disaster. Oh, Mike was a perfect gentleman. He was sweet, and understanding, and seemed to accept her. But that was the problem. She didn't want to like him. She wanted to find a reason to cut the night short and leave town without regrets. And it wasn't looking like that was going to happen. *You should have canceled.* Her mother's voice was back. *What were you thinking in the first place? A mechanic, Adelaide? He will never be able to give you the life you deserve, regardless of where he lives. Don't even get me started on the town. You should have just left without a backward glance and left this whole ridiculous experience behind.*

She didn't want to think about her mother. It didn't matter what Mike did for a living. He was a good man, and he deserved better than her ditching him. Maybe she could just treat this as a rebound date. It hadn't been that long since she had broken up with what's-his-name. Maybe this would simply be her re-entry into the dating scene. She could get her feet wet, regain a sense of self, and be prepared for her arrival in Boston. Sitting up a little straighter, Addy gave Mike a smile and did her best to get through the night.

He could sense he was losing her about the time dessert arrived. She was distracted and didn't seem to hear him when he asked questions.

"Everything okay?"

"Hmm? Oh, yeah, everything's fine."

"Okay."

Silence fell, and he sunk a spoon into his tiramisu while she picked at her cheesecake.

"Did I say something to offend you?"

"Of course not. Why do you ask?"

"You just seem to have gotten quiet all of a sudden. I thought we were having a good time."

Addy sighed. "We were. That's the problem."

"Um. Okay?"

"I'm leaving for Boston, Mike."

"I know."

"So what are we doing here?"

He didn't know how to answer that. He had just wanted to enjoy her company for a little while longer. "Having dinner?"

She shot him a pointed look. "You know what I mean."

"I know." He leaned back and released a sigh of his own. "I don't know. I guess I just thought we could have a nice evening together. You seemed like someone I would like to know better. You didn't have to say yes. Actually, I didn't expect you to say yes."

"I probably shouldn't have."

"I didn't force you to."

"I know."

Silence fell again.

"I guess I didn't want tonight to go well. If I had said no, and I left, then I would have felt bad. So instead I hoped we wouldn't get along, or you would have some horrendous habit or personality trait that I couldn't stand, so I could leave with a clear conscience."

"I take it I don't?"

"Not that I know of." She gave a small grin. "Yet."

"Well, you can be upset, but I'm glad about that."

"The problem is: I like you. And I didn't want to."

"I like you, too."

"But I'm leaving."

"Do you have to?"

She seemed startled by the question, and almost shocked that he would ask. "Of course."

"Why?"

She gave it a moment's thought, but when it appeared she couldn't find an explanation he would accept, she settled on "because."

It wasn't acceptable. And maybe he shouldn't push, but what, really, did he have to lose? She would leave no matter what. "I guess I just don't understand why. You don't have a job waiting for you. I don't get the impression that you have friends or family waiting for you. I don't think you even have a place to live lined up. So why are you in such a hurry to get there?"

Her face fell then, and he felt bad, but something compelled him to keep pushing.

"I know it's a lot more exciting, but what does Boston have that Pine Valley doesn't?"

He could see tears welling up in her eyes. He hated seeing women cry. But he didn't want to cave. He had to know what was going on in that pretty head of hers.

"If you're looking for a change, this is a heck of a lot bigger than moving to another city, where you'll just get lost again. You can be someone here. You can make something of your life here."

"You wouldn't understand."

He could barely hear her, and he softened his voice as a response. "Maybe I wouldn't. But I definitely don't now. And I'd appreciate it if you'd explain it to me."

Addy sighed, and it took her a few moments before she spoke. "I would suffocate here. I need things to do. I need to be occupied. I can't just sit in one place. I need to be in the city, where there are options and people and places to go."

"I admit Pine Valley can be on the quiet side. But it's not as if you can never go anywhere. You're not confined to your home, or to the town."

"I know that. It's just..." Her voice faded.

"Just what?"

How could she tell him that she needed to be distracted? That if she wasn't distracted, her mind would start drifting into uncomfortable places, like thinking about how meaningless her life was, how miserable she was? How could she explain that in the city at least there was a chance she wouldn't die alone? That if she kept busy and went out, that she could surround herself with people and not feel so alone?

He let her sit in silence for a bit, let her nibble at the cheesecake she suddenly didn't really want. She was grateful, but, really, she didn't owe him any explanations. Who was he to question her choices? Yes, it had been a nice date, but that didn't make him her husband. He had no say in how she ran her life. Or ran from her life, as the case may be.

"I'd like to go home now."

"You don't have a home."

The instant the words left his mouth, he regretted them. And when he saw the tears well up again, then the anger flash in her eyes, he knew he had just undone any progress he might have made.

"No," she spit out. "I may not have a home now. But I will. In Boston." And she stood up, grabbed her jacket, and left the restaurant.

By the time Mike flagged down the waiter, paid the bill, and joined her, she was shivering on the sidewalk out front. He stopped beside her.

"I'm sorry. That was uncalled for. I don't know why I said that. I don't know why I said any of it. We were having such a nice evening, and I shouldn't have pushed. I'm sorry."

When she didn't respond, he mumbled "I'll get the car" and proceeded to his truck. After she was safely buckled into the passenger seat, he drove on. It was a silent drive back to the motel, and he had barely come to a stop when she stepped out of the truck, slammed the door, and went into her unit.

Well, he told himself, at least he could say he had tried. He had tried to get her to stay, and he had tried to apologize. Of course if he hadn't stuck his big foot in his mouth, he wouldn't have had to apologize. And if he hadn't pushed so hard, maybe he would have had a better shot at keeping her around.

Now she would go to Boston, just as she had said she would, and he would be kicking himself for being such a jerk. And he would be back to looking for a special someone amongst the tiny crowd that was Pine Valley. Or maybe he would be forever alone. Who knew? All he could say was that Addy had been someone special, and he had blown it.

Addy barely made it through the door before the tears started falling.

She couldn't decide, however, if she was mad, sad, depressed, disappointed, or a combination of it all. She couldn't decide if she liked Mike or thought he was a jerk. She couldn't decide if she should have told him everything that had been running through her mind, or if she was grateful she hadn't opened up that much to him.

What she did know was that she felt horrible. And she wanted the feeling to stop.

She had learned long ago that drinking didn't make the pain go away. She was a somber drunk, and she usually felt worse. The one thing that had always helped, though, was being around other people. Then she couldn't dwell on the mix of emotions swirling through her. She could forget her problems. And she wouldn't be alone, at least for a little bit.

In a place as small as Pine Valley, she didn't have much hope that she could find a place to surround herself with people. But she knew that there would be at least a person or two at the diner. So she got up, washed her face, and grabbed her keys and purse on her way out the door.

Maggie could tell something was wrong the minute Addy walked through the door. At the very least, she had though Addy would have left hours ago. But here she was, the faint sheen of unshed tears in her eyes, and a fake smile plastered on her face.

"Hi, Maggie."

"Hey. I'm surprised to see you. I thought you left this afternoon."

"Slight change of plans. But I'll be leaving in the morning."

"Did you want some dinner?"

"No, thanks. I've already eaten. But I could go for a cup of coffee."

"Sure thing."

Addy sat at the counter while Maggie pulled out a mug and poured. Addy was the only one there at the moment, and Maggie was glad. Addy obviously needed to talk, and perhaps a good old-fashioned heart-to-heart would help.

Despite Maggie's best efforts, however, Addy seemed determined to keep her lips sealed. And when a young couple came into the diner, Addy made her excuses, purchased a muffin for breakfast the following morning, and said good-bye.

Maggie was at a loss. Though she didn't know Addy well, she was sure a little girl talk would have helped. But Addy had remained clammed up. Instead, Addy had seemed to be searching for some kind of distraction, something to take her mind off her problems.

Not that Maggie could blame her. She didn't want to talk about what was on her mind, either. She could see the appeal in keeping it all bottled up inside. But experience had taught her that she couldn't keep it bottled forever. Eventually it would explode.

Maggie was starting to get to that point herself. Though her life wasn't horrible, she was definitely disgruntled, and had been for a while. She needed a change. And she needed it soon. If not, the tension would cause her to explode, and she pitied the person who was there to witness it.

Maybe she should put the diner up for sale. It wasn't the first time she had had the thought, but maybe she should actually do something about it this time. While it was on the market, she could tie up loose ends and try to figure out her next course of action. And when it sold, she would take it as a sign that it was time to move on to bigger and better things. If it never sold, well, then, that was a sign, too. Though she hoped it didn't come to that.

She ran the idea over and over in her mind as she wiped off tables for the night, counted the drawer, and waited for more people to come in. What would it be like to not be chained to this building? To be able to do what she wanted, when she wanted, where she wanted?

Her thoughts drifted back to the time when she had taken over the restaurant. The previous owners had been an elderly couple, and they were anxious to retire. She had been helping them out during the summer and after school since she was sixteen. They begged her to take over. Actually, they hadn't had to do much begging. Her prospects were few. She couldn't afford to go to college or move out of town. Her parents just wanted her to get married so she would leave their house.

The diner had seemed a wonderful option. There was an apartment in the back, so she wouldn't have to live with her parents anymore. But she didn't have to worry about shackling herself to the first man that paid her the time of day, either. She could do her own thing, be her own person. And she would be the boss. She could run things however she wanted to. She could make changes she thought were long overdue. And she would have a purpose in life, even if that was only to feed hungry, lonely people.

She had enjoyed it for a while. But she had also thought that eventually she would meet someone to spend her life with. She had thought at least some of her friends would stick around, not go to college and never come back. She hadn't expected the little apartment in the back to feel like a prison sometimes, with her in solitary confinement as the rest of the world lived their lives.

She still enjoyed being her own boss, but it did have its trying moments. She was fortunate to be blessed with good, loyal staff, but she could do without the bills. And the health inspections. And the chores, the constant cleaning, and the cranky customers.

Still, she acknowledged it could be worse. She had a roof over her head. She had a little bit of money set aside for the day she finally did retire, whenever that might be, though not as much as she might like. She wished she had more people to talk to. Her employees were primarily high school and college kids, and she had nothing in common with them beyond the diner. Some of her patrons were pleasant, and loyal, and liked to chat. But those were customer-server relationships, not real friendships. Did she even have real friends at this point?

It really was time to move on. She had run this restaurant for over 30 years. And she was tired. She needed new challenges, new excitement. And she couldn't do that as a waitress at a diner.

Why was it that whenever Addy tried to escape her problems, they always ended up finding her? The visit to the diner had been a nice, if brief, reprieve. But the moment she was alone in her car, the doubts and depression came back tenfold.

Enough, she told herself. She was going to Boston in the morning, and she had to focus on the future, not on the past. She couldn't dwell on the disappointments. She had to focus on the possibilities that a new beginning would bring. With the briefest burst of energy, she got together the few items she had unpacked, brushed her teeth, and got into her pajamas. As she climbed into bed she tried to focus on the big city life she was hoping for: tall buildings, bustling crowds, shopping plazas and museums. A place where she could dance all night, sleep all day, and reinvent herself. Into whom, she wasn't quite sure. But someone great. Someone wonderful. Someone whose life wasn't so miserable.

Chapter 5

The next day dawned bright and cool. It would be a great day for a road trip, and Addy threw her duffel bag in the car before heading to the motel office to check out.

Sylvie was at the desk and greeted her with a smile. "I take it your car's all set?"

"For now. Mike said it may conk out on me at any time, but it's running for the time being."

Sylvie's face took on a worried look. "Oh, dear. Well I hope it gets you where you need to be."

"Me, too."

Addy signed her credit card receipt and bid Sylvie farewell.

"Come back anytime," Sylvie said with a wave and a smile.

Addy smiled back but made no promises. After the night before, and the whole experience really, she wanted to leave Pine Valley and never look back. She climbed into her car and turned the key in the ignition. The car flared to life, and Addy buckled her seat belt. After a moment the dashboard lights and radio flickered. Addy's heart fluttered. It couldn't die again. Not now. But after the one flicker everything seemed to be fine. Addy breathed a sigh of relief and backed out of the parking space. She would be glad when she was back on the highway.

Mike saw the car drive by the shop on its way out of town. It was hard to miss, since he had been staring out the window all morning, spacing out, reliving the night before and kicking himself over and over. But now that he saw the car pass, he could officially say it was over. She was gone, out of his life, and he could move on.

Funny how a couple of days could really screw you up. His head was a muddled mess, when before he had been clear-headed. A bit lonely in the love department, maybe, but overall happy with his life. And now? Well, now he was kicking himself over a woman he hadn't known existed two days ago. What a mess.

What he really needed was to focus on his business. His bays were full again, and he had three more cars waiting to be worked on. Maybe today he would get down and dirty and let one of the other guys run the counter. He could use something to occupy his mind.

His friend Ben was willing to swap places, but he wasn't letting Mike down easy. "There'll be someone else, Mikey. You knew her what, a day? I can find you someone even better."

Mike shrugged. "No biggie. I'm over it."

"Sure you are." Ben patted him on the back, then went to the counter to answer the ringing phone.

Mike was grateful for his shop, and the great guys he had working for him. They were reliable, motivated, and they did good work. It wasn't often that cars came back for the same issue. And in a town as small as Pine Valley, they had a surprising amount of work. He supposed it was because so many people commuted out of town for work. More wear and tear meant more damage that needed repair. That kept him in business. And people around here weren't the kind to get a new car every few years. They found something decent and ran it into the ground. More years on the road meant more business, too. And being the only repair shop in the area helped even more.

It wasn't often Mike actually did the repairs these days. He was so busy with the bookkeeping and appointment setting that he let the techs do what they did best. He didn't really mind. But every once in a while he wanted to get his hands dirty. He wanted to figure out what was wrong with something and fix it. And today was one of those days. He needed a problem to solve that didn't involve his love life.

Maggie half expected to see Addy that morning, but no such luck. She saw the car drive by, and Addy didn't so much as glance in her direction. But Maggie tried to shrug it off. Addy certainly didn't owe her anything. And Maggie had bigger fish to fry, no pun intended. She had picked up a "for sale" sign the previous day, and she was debating when to put it up. She was going to start slow and see how the sign worked. At the very least she expected to be the subject of a bit of gossip for a while. She wondered what people would say. Would they think she was moving away? That she was sick? That she had met someone special? It really didn't matter. Though she was friendly with others in town, she, like Addy, didn't owe any explanations or excuses. She was a free woman who was capable of making her own decisions.

If the sign didn't gain any interest, or if she got a serious offer, then she would discuss the situation with a realtor. But she really didn't want things to happen too fast. She still didn't know what she was going to do once it sold. What would she do for money? Where would she live? Would she stay in Pine Valley? Would she travel the world? Would she just pick up and go somewhere new, start a new life? She had started looking online to get ideas, but so far nothing had clicked for her. Nothing felt right.

When Maggie took over the restaurant, it had felt like the right decision at the time. Sure, it was the best option given her few, not very desirable, alternatives, but she had also felt drawn to the decision. She knew she was making the right choice, that it would be the right path for her. And so far she hadn't gotten that feeling about any of the ideas she had come up with. Maybe she was naive to think that she would.

Maggie liked Pine Valley. It was where she had grown up, and it was a great place to live. She was seriously considering staying. But she had to consider the fact that she was still hoping to find someone to share the rest of her life with. And if she hadn't found that person in Pine Valley yet, what were the odds that she would in the near future? And that meant she would have to leave, at least for a while. But where would she go? She knew nothing about the world. Her trips out of this little town had been few and far between, and they had been to places like the beach, or other touristy places that didn't hold appeal for her in the long term. The beach sounded nice, but they were so crowded, and she certainly couldn't afford anything that would offer a private patch of sand.

But unless she found other employment, she couldn't really afford anything. Her savings would last her a little while, but certainly not forever. Most of the money she had earned had gone back into the restaurant, doing repairs and renovations, buying new equipment. She had had enough to live comfortably, and to build a bit of a nest egg, but it wasn't enough for her to retire yet. Of course she would have whatever money the business sold for, but it would likely be a while before she would even want to retire. She would quickly grow bored if she just sat around and didn't work. And that opened up a new can of worms: what would she do for a living? She had never gone to college. She had barely graduated high school. All she knew – all she had ever done – was work in this diner. And while she had learned a lot in the process, it didn't open up too many opportunities for her.

Maggie was a mess. Throughout the day she kept going over the same things in her mind, and when she counted the cash drawer at night, she wasn't any closer to making a decision. And because she felt in limbo, she hadn't even put up the "for sale" sign. Was she making a mistake? Should she even consider selling the diner? What if she fell flat on her face? She was too old to be starting over. She was too indecisive to take that step.

And that, she decided, was her problem. She lacked confidence. She couldn't even believe in herself enough to know that she could make the right decision. Maybe it was time to change all that.

In the middle of counting the drawer, Maggie took a deep breath, reached under the counter, and pulled out the "for sale" sign. Before she could second guess herself, or talk herself out of it, she walked to the front window and tucked the sign in the corner. Then she went back to the register and finished counting her drawer.

It was a beautiful fall day. The air was cool and crisp. The trees colored the world around her. And Addy's favorite song had just come on the radio. Things seemed to be going her way. For once.

It wasn't much longer to Boston. She had seen signs even before she had reached Pine Valley. And as the signs got more frequent, and the exits started popping up, she found herself battling butterflies in her stomach.

This was it, she told herself. This was her goal, her mission, her end result. She could be entering the city where she would spend the rest of her days. It was a sobering thought, but not necessarily a bad one. This could be her happy place. She could find the career of her dreams here. She could fall in love here. She could start a family here. And it would all start with this: driving into the city and finding a place to live.

Of course she would have to stay in a hotel for a couple of days. She had to acclimate herself, find out which areas were the best, and see what was available. As long as the hotel had Wi-Fi, she should be good to go. And when she wasn't researching, she would be checking out this new home of hers.

She had to admit it made her nervous. Though she had always been a city girl, there was something intimidating about entering a place with this many people and not knowing a soul. She had no idea what to expect. She didn't know what she would find, who she could trust, or where she should go.

Abby's mind flittered back to Pine Valley, but she pushed the thoughts away. True, she hadn't had that feeling there. But she also had just been driving through. She wasn't looking for people to trust, or a place to settle down. She had wanted to get in and out as quickly as possible. And she had succeeded. Mostly. She had made it through unscathed. Well, almost unscathed. But she wouldn't dwell on the uncomfortable bits.

Since she probably wouldn't be able to check in to a hotel this early in the day, Addy decided to find somewhere to grab a bite to eat. As she ate she could figure out how to spend her day and where to stay for the night. If it was nice, she could stay there until she found a permanent place. If not, then she could head somewhere else the next day.

Content with her plan, Addy looked around. There was definitely no shortage of restaurants. Her choice would really depend on what she was in the mood for. Deciding on a deli that looked good – if the line of people waiting to be served was any indication – she found a public parking lot and made the short trek to the restaurant.

You could learn a lot by listening to people, and, trying not to be obvious, Addy listened in to conversations around her. Most of it was gossip, or work talk, or lovers' spats, but there were tidbits here and there: new restaurants that had just opened, places that were hiring, apartment vacancies. She had no idea where any of the places were, but it was somewhere to start, and she jotted down whatever notes she could.

The wrap and soup didn't disappoint, and Addy spent a few moments after she had eaten to gaze out the window in front of her and watch the people go by. They were all in a hurry, frantically passing each other in their haste. And no one seemed happy. Well, that wasn't true. There were a few people laughing, and a couple looking sweetly into each other's eyes. But most of the people bustling about just looked anxious, as if they couldn't wait to get where they were going but didn't want to actually be going there. Again Addy's thoughts floated back to Pine Valley, where people had looked busy but happy. No one ever seemed anxious or on edge. They were simply moving quickly in the direction they had to head.

Forget Pine Valley. She couldn't tell if it had been her mother or herself scolding her, but it didn't matter. This wasn't Pine Valley. Obviously. She didn't want it to be. She loved the hustle and bustle. She loved the crowds of people moving through the streets, anxiously going this way and that. There was a sense of urgency here. A sense of importance. And you didn't have to look happy to be happy. Perhaps they were just preoccupied with their to do lists, or where they were going, or where they had been. Maybe they were looking forward to exciting evenings, filled with parties and dates and movies and dancing. Once she checked into her hotel, she would search to see what events were going on. Maybe she could find a concert. Or a play. She would hold off on the movies. Going by herself the previous day had been off-putting. She had felt as though everyone were staring at her, thinking how pitiful she was. So she would wait to go again until she had made some friends. She gave it a couple of weeks, if that. Quicker if she ended up getting a roommate, which she would probably have to do. This was a city, and apartments were likely not cheap. Unless she got a great deal or happened to land a high-paying job, she would have to make sacrifices. But a roommate wouldn't be so bad. It would be nice not to be alone. She just hoped she didn't end up with a psycho.

Deciding her lunch break was complete, Addy discarded her trash and headed back out into the chilly fall day. Joining the crowds on the sidewalk, she decided to just walk a bit, to take in the sights and sounds that this part of Boston had to offer. Who knew what she might find?

Chapter 6

It took until the morning rush the next day, but Maggie's sign caused quite a stir. Some asked what was for sale and were taken aback when she said the diner. Some couldn't believe she was doing it. Some thought it was the biggest mistake ever. Some told her it was about time. And some simply ignored it, pretending their morning routine would go unchanged.

Bill was the first to mention anything, as he was one of her first customers that morning. His response was perhaps the most surprising.

"I thought there was something different about you yesterday."

"Oh yeah? What was that?"

"There was something in your eyes. You didn't look happy. You looked kind of sad. And that made me sad."

"I'm sorry I made you sad, Bill."

"I'm sorry you were sad, Maggie."

"Thank you."

"I think it's a good idea to sell the diner."

"Why's that?"

He thought a moment, as he often did before answering. "Because if something makes you sad, then you shouldn't do it. And yesterday wasn't the first time I saw you sad. I thought maybe something had happened to your family, but then I remembered you didn't have any family. And I hadn't heard about anything sad going on in town. So I figured it had to be the diner. So I think it's good that you're selling it."

"Thank you for your support."

"What are you going to do now?"

Maggie sighed. "I don't know yet. First I have to sell the diner, then I can decide what I want to do."

"You should decide now. That way you don't get nervous when it sells. It might sell fast."

"You're right, it might. But it might not. And I don't want to look forward to something that might take a long time to get here."

"At least then you would have something to make you happy."

"I guess I'll have to give it some thought. Would you like to order breakfast?"

Most of her customers were interested but not as in-depth in their questioning. And Maggie found herself thinking about Bill's response throughout the day. He was probably right. She should really figure out what she was going to do once the diner sold. But while she wanted something to look forward to, she was also nervous. Sitting down and deciding was not only difficult; it also scared her. What if there was nothing that interested her? What if she was making a mistake? She supposed it would be better to find out now, rather than after the diner sold. But it would be rather depressing. And she would have longer to think about. If she waited, then she would have hope that a brighter future was just around the corner, even if she didn't know what that future held. Wasn't it better to live in limbo than to be depressed?

Her employees were disappointed in her decision to sell, but they were pretty laid-back about it. Since most were college kids who planned on moving on to bigger and better things soon, anyway, it wasn't a big hit to their life plans. But they were sympathetic when she told them she wanted a change. A couple complained about the potential loss of income. She tried to assure them that the new owners could very well keep all of them on as they were. The conversation dropped after a short time, but Maggie had to acknowledge that she wasn't the only one who would be living in limbo.

Now the night was winding down. It was time to clean up empty tables, count the cash drawer, and start getting things ready for the morning rush. With the nights getting colder, it was less likely she would see anyone. And to be honest, she could use the time to think. She had a lot of decisions to make, even if one of those decisions was to hold off making decisions.

Maggie was just settling down with her laptop when the door jingled, and Mike the mechanic walked in. That was always how she thought of him, even though that was just one of his many titles. She was surprised to find him there. Though he stopped in for lunch, usually once a week, he was not one of her frequent late-night visitors.

"Hi, there, Mike. What can I get you?"

He looked tired, drained, and he collapsed onto a stool at the counter before asking for a cup of coffee. He was in need of a chat; that much was obvious. For someone who was usually so laid-back and seemingly content with life, he looked miserable. Maggie couldn't help but wonder what was wrong. But if she had learned anything through her years as a waitress, it was that people had to open up to her on their own. She could lead them a bit, but nothing made someone clam up like prying.

"So you're selling the place, huh?"

"Yup. I decided it was time for a change."

"Good for you."

When he didn't continue, Maggie decided to talk about herself a bit. Not only could it encourage Mike to talk about himself, but it might also help to say things aloud. It couldn't hurt.

"I've had this place a long time. It's been good to me. But sometimes it's just not enough. Sometimes the status quo needs to get shaken up a bit. I need to try something different. I need to move on with my life."

"It's not easy though."

"No, it's not."

"Do you have any regrets, Maggie?"

"I think we all have some. But I don't think I have any big ones. Overall I'm pleased with the choices I've made."

"Me, too. But I did something stupid, and I'm kicking myself over it."

"We all do stupid things."

"I guess so. I just wish I could change it."

"We've all been there, Mike. Don't beat yourself up over it." She placed a piece of pie in front of him. He looked like he could use pie. And he took a bite without seeming to notice what he was doing.

"It really shouldn't be bugging me this much. I mean, she was leaving anyway. What difference did it make if she left on good terms with me? It's not like anything would have come of it anyway."

So that was why Addy had been upset the previous night. At least she assumed Mike was talking about Addy. Maggie wasn't aware of anyone else leaving town. And certainly no one who could have gotten under Mike's skin so badly. Apparently they had had a falling out. Though what about, Maggie could only speculate.

"I wasn't wrong in what I said. But I know I could have handled it better. I drove her away even faster than she was already going. Maybe if I hadn't we could at least have kept in touch. I mean, Boston isn't so far. I could head up there once in a while."

"And if you did hit it off? What then? Would you move to Boston?"

Mike sighed. "No, I guess not."

There was nothing Maggie could say that Mike didn't already know, so she kept quiet. But after a moment she decided to speak up. Maybe it was because her mind was already filled with life changes, or maybe it was just because Mike still looked so miserable.

"Maybe you should go up to Boston and apologize."

"I did apologize."

"But it's obviously still bothering you."

He seemed to mull it over a moment before he shook his head. "Do you know how big Boston is? I would never find her."

Maggie shrugged. "So wait a couple of weeks for her to get settled in. Then Google her. There's bound to be a bill in her name or something with her new address and phone number."

"Probably not with privacy laws and all that. Besides, she might not even get a phone in her name. She had a cell phone. And if she gets a roommate, everything could be in that person's name."

"Hmm. Sorry. I guess it wasn't a very good idea."

"I do have her cell phone number."

"Well, there you go."

"I don't know if she would want to talk to me, though. Probably not." Mike ate a few more bites of pie. "I could text her, though."

"That way if she doesn't want to talk to you, she doesn't have to. But you could say your piece and know that you did what you could."

"Exactly."

"Sounds like a plan."

"Yeah, it does. Thanks, Maggie."

"Hey, it was your idea."

Mike shrugged and took a sip of coffee. He poked what remained of his pie a couple of times with his fork. Before Maggie could ask if there was something else wrong, a couple walked in. My, wasn't she busy tonight.

This couple didn't need to talk, though. They were wrapped up in each other. After she had served them mugs of hot chocolate and slices of pie, she returned to the counter. Mike was looking at the couple, trying not to look obvious. As Maggie approached, he looked back down at his plate and sighed.

"I thought that would be me by now. You know, with someone else, settling down. I thought I'd be married, maybe have a kid or two."

"You're still young. You've got plenty of time."

"I know. But that doesn't ease the loneliness, Maggie."

"I know the feeling, Mike. You fill your days with friends and neighbors, but you still go home to an empty apartment."

"Exactly. I guess it's hard in a place like Pine Valley, but still. Maybe if I worked somewhere else I would have found someone. But when your entire life revolves around one small town, it's hard."

"It definitely limits options."

"I thought I would settle down with Ginny. You know, my high school girl-friend? But she couldn't wait to get out of here fast enough. Like Addy, I guess." He sighed.

"Have you tried the internet? I hear lots of people meet there now."

Mike shrugged. "Yeah, I've looked a little. It felt weird. How am I supposed to know if I'll have a connection with someone based on an online profile? They could be lying. They could be completely crazy for all I know. I want to be able to look someone in the eyes and know."

"I understand completely."

"Is that why you're leaving, Maggie? To find someone?"

It was Maggie's turn to shrug. "I don't know. I don't know what I'm looking for. I don't know why I decided to sell now. I don't even know if I'm leaving town. I just felt like something needed to change. And I couldn't make any big life changes with this place around my neck."

"It's hard running your business. I mean, even if I did do something crazy like move to Boston, what would I do with my business? And what would I do for a job?"

"You could be a mechanic."

"I guess. But it would be hard working for someone else." He paused for a moment. "I would hate the city."

"I think I would, too."

"There's too many people. I feel like I get lost."

"Sometimes that's the appeal. There's so much to do and see, and so many people to talk to, that you don't have to think about yourself. You can lose yourself in the crowd, in the moment."

"Do you think that's why Addy wanted to go?"

"I didn't know Addy well enough to know."

"She just seemed so unhappy. I think she was already lost."

"Maybe being in the city she didn't have to think about that."

"Maybe." He took another bite of pie. "I tried to get her to stay."

"Is that what you regret?"

"No. I don't regret asking her to stay. But I do regret pushing so hard. We were having a perfectly nice evening, and I went and ruined it. Maybe if I hadn't..."

"But you're going to text her."

"Yeah. I'll text her."

"And who knows what'll happen?"

"Yeah." Mike gave Maggie a small smile. "Thanks, Maggie."

"I hope it works out as you want it to."

"I don't know what I want to happen. I just know I feel really bad about how things ended."

"Then maybe you just need some closure."

"Maybe." He scooped the last piece of pie into his mouth and stood up. "How much do I owe you?"

Maggie waved her hand to shoo him. "Don't worry about it. Consider the conversation payment enough."

"Thanks, Maggie. But you're going to need the money if you leave." He tossed a couple of bills on the counter. "I'll catch you tomorrow."

"Have a good night."

Maggie cleaned up Mike's dishes, then sat on a stool behind the counter. The couple in the corner seemed content, and she had more to think about. Maybe she had to start thinking outside the box.

Barely a day in Boston, and Addy could already feel the blood rushing through her. Her heart was pumping, her mind was whirring, and her feet were moving at the same pace as those around her. It felt good to be back in a city.

Despite her excitement, she had opted to stay in her hotel room the night before. Though there were plenty of things going on, she didn't want to go alone. She had thought about shopping, but she didn't have a place to live yet, and she didn't know how much her job would bring in, so she didn't want to eat up too much of her savings. Instead she watched a movie on TV and browsed job listings.

Though many complained about the economy, she found plenty of places hiring. The problem was: she didn't know what she wanted to do. A lot of the positions were in sales, which didn't hold much appeal. There were clerical jobs, but she had tried that and not enjoyed it very much. There were artsy jobs she wasn't qualified for, and financial jobs she wasn't qualified for, and customer service jobs she wasn't qualified for. With retail she would be too tempted to shop; with fast food she would feel like a teenager. Waitressing was a possibility, but it wasn't easy. She had tried it once and not been very successful. She couldn't figure out how they all knew how to balance so much and carry it so quickly. Or maybe that was just the place she had worked. It was hard to say.

After two hours of searching, she hadn't applied to anything. But she was trying not to get discouraged. It was her first day, and she hadn't really thought about what she should do.

Actually, if she was honest with herself, that wasn't true. She had spent a lot of time thinking about what she should do. She had just dismissed it all. She wasn't good at anything. She didn't have a passion, or a calling, or whatever you wanted to call it. Things she thought might interest her she wasn't qualified for. Things she had already tried didn't interest her. She should probably go back to school, but she wouldn't even know what to study if she did. Nothing clicked for her. It was discouraging and depressing. *If you landed a rich husband you wouldn't have to worry about working.* Her mother's voice was nothing if not persistent. Addy rebutted with a short *but then I would be miserable.*

It was too early to give up.

The hotel offered a free newspaper, and she perused it while enjoying the free continental breakfast the hotel provided. Skimming the headlines, she opted to flip to the comics instead of read any of the articles. She supposed she should be more interested in politics, having lived in Washington D.C. all her life, but it really didn't hold any appeal. It was all just mumbo jumbo to her, a part of life that she would rather just leave to other people. She would rather giggle at the funnies.

She had just finished her first cup of coffee when her cell phone dinged, indicating she had a text message. She paused a moment, wondering who in the world could be texting her. She didn't have any close friends she wanted to keep in touch with, and she hadn't made any friends in Boston yet. Maybe it was just her phone carrier telling her about an offer.

She didn't recognize the number, but it was from Connecticut. Who did she know in Connecticut? Her heart skipped a beat as she read it:

"Hi, Addy. It's Mike. The mechanic from Pine Valley. I know I'm the last person you probably want to hear from, but I wanted to apologize again for how I behaved the other night. I crossed the line, and I'm sorry. I didn't want your last memory of Pine Valley to be a bad one. Good luck in Boston."

Mike. From Pine Valley. Shouldn't he have forgotten about her by now? They had had one date, and she hadn't been that remarkable.

Memories of that night flooded her mind. It hadn't been that long ago, but it felt like a lifetime. Pine Valley was a world away. And he had wanted her to stay there, or at least consider staying there. She had snapped at him. Not her finest moment, but he had gotten her angry. It was a shame. He had been a nice guy. But that was probably why she had snapped at him. The evening had been going too well. She needed a reason to hate him. And he had given her one. Kind of. But now he was taking it back.

She wondered what he was doing. It was early, but not that early. He was probably already at the shop. She probably shouldn't bother him with a response. He was likely busy. But he had taken the time to text her. It was only polite that she acknowledge the message. Right?

Addy's thumbs hovered over the keyboard, unsure what to do. If she was honest with herself, she was happy to hear from him. Yes, they had left on bad terms, but she couldn't really blame him. Perhaps he had crossed a line. Perhaps he had pushed too much, brought up too many good points. Or perhaps he had just been too sweet and needed to show her he could be serious and determined. No, she didn't know him well, and perhaps he shouldn't have said what he did, especially considering how little he knew about her. And yet what he had said hit home. And how could it have hit home if he hadn't gotten to know her, at least a little bit? Had she let him in that much?

Before she could second guess herself, she typed out a quick message to thank him, then sent it. Then she dropped the phone as though it were on fire and turned to the classified section of the newspaper.

Mike hadn't been expecting a response. He just wanted to ease his conscience a bit so he could get on with his life. But he had to admit that when his phone dinged he got a little butterfly in his stomach. The simple "thank you" might not have been what he hoped for, but it was more than he had expected. And he took a deep breath, unsure how to interpret it. Was she simply being polite? Did she forgive him? Dare he reply back? Was that being too pushy again?

Despite the cool morning, he found himself sweating. This was too stressful. Addy was the first woman who had sparked his interest in months. Maybe years. And she had messaged him back.

But she could have just been being polite.

He asked Ben to switch spots again.

She didn't really expect a response back. Still, she was disappointed she didn't get one. Maybe she had been too abrupt. Maybe she should have said something other than "thank you." Maybe she should message him back.

Don't be ridiculous, Adelaide. You wanted to come all this way to Boston to start over, not to get hung up on a mechanic from a tiny town in the middle of nowhere. Get your act together.

Addy sighed. As much as she hated to admit it, this time her mother's voice had a point. Did she really want to be hung up on a guy from Pine Valley? She was a city girl. He was a country guy. They didn't mix. There was no future for them. She would just go on with her plans as if he had never texted her. And she would try to forget he existed.

She had to go out and meet people. Maybe that was what she needed. Maybe she just needed to find someone else, get her mind off Mike. That had been her plan, hadn't it? Then she could focus on the future, not on a tiny part of her past she just wanted to forget.

Chapter 7

The diner was hopping. Maggie didn't know what to make of it. She did pretty good business, but today was ridiculous. It was as if everyone expected her to close tomorrow, and they had to get there while they still could. She didn't really mind. She could use the money. But it was strange, and she couldn't help wondering if it would be the same every day until she sold the place, or if today was just a fluke.

No one brought up her selling. No one asked her about her plans. They were just friendly, hungry people. And she served them the best she could. She just hoped she didn't run out of food.

Maggie kept to herself most days. She saw people in the diner, and she figured that was about as much socializing as she needed. Once in a while she attended an event in town, or took a walk to get a bit of fresh air, but for the most part she took the time she had to herself and spent it in her apartment, sleeping or watching TV. She had always been content with her own company, and while she enjoyed talking to others, she also enjoyed being by herself.

With everything going on at the diner, Maggie decided she needed some quiet. So she decided to take a walk in town between the breakfast and lunch crowds. The cool air invigorated her, and, though she was tired, it revived her a bit so she could clear her head. She was just considering turning back when she saw the first sign. Then the next. And when she looked around, she saw more. They dotted the entire town center, posted to telephone poles.

Signs that said "save the diner."

Though her selling the restaurant had caused quite a stir, it took her by surprise that the town thought it had to "save" the diner. It wasn't closing. It would just be going to new ownership. But perhaps they thought it was inevitable that it would close or undergo such vast changes that it would be unrecognizable. It certainly explained her rush of business this morning. But while she appreciated the concern of the town, she was a little upset, too. Didn't she have the right to make her own decisions regarding her business and her life? She wasn't selling because business was down. She was selling because she needed a change. And she had told that to anyone who had asked.

Disturbed by this new information, Maggie decided to instead head to the office of the local newspaper. She hadn't thought it would come to this, but perhaps it was time she told the entire town her reasons for selling, and how, while she appreciated their concern, it was for naught.

James was the editor of the town paper, and he greeted her with a smile when she entered the office. It was a small, weekly paper, so the staff was small. At the moment he was the only one in the office, and he didn't appear to be too busy, if the cup of coffee and crossword puzzle were any indication.

"Hello, Maggie. How's it going?"

"Let's cut to the chase, James. I think you know why I'm here."

"I heard you're selling the place. A few of the townspeople aren't too happy about it."

"Yeah, I picked up on that. What's with the signs?"

James shrugged. "You got me. I don't know who posted them. When I came in this morning, they were already up."

Maggie sighed. "The diner doesn't need saving. Business was fine."

"The rumor mill says otherwise."

"I'm thinking it's time I set the record straight."

"Sure. You want to write an editorial? I'd be happy to publish it."

"I'm not a writer."

"That's okay. I can help you, if you want. I'm not too busy at the moment."

"Yeah, I noticed." She flashed James a grin, trying to lighten the mood. It wasn't his fault the signs had her agitated.

He laughed. "Yeah. You're the biggest news at the moment. I have Sandy covering a new business opening, and I have Kurt covering a local resident turning a hundred. That's about it."

"Wow. Mary's a hundred already?"

"Yup. Her birthday is tomorrow. Since the paper comes out tomorrow, I thought we'd do a big 'happy birthday' front page."

"I'm sure she'll like that."

"Yeah. But back to your predicament. Why don't you have a seat, and we can get started. Do you want to dictate to me, and I can type? Or do you want to write it yourself, and I'll just be moral and editorial support?"

Maggie thought a moment. "Maybe you'd better type. I work with two fingers, and it'll take me all day."

James laughed again. "No problem." He slid his chair to the computer keyboard and poised his fingers over the keys. "Shoot."

Maggie sighed. "Well, I guess we could start by saying business is fine. I don't get much late night, but throughout the day I get plenty of people. I have a lot of regulars."

"Okay. So something like 'The Pine Valley Diner can still draw a crowd, but the owner wants to sell anyway.'"

"That makes it sound like I'm spiteful or ungrateful or something. I'm not trying to do the town a disservice.

"Okay. So 'The Pine Valley Diner can still draw a crowd, but the owner is dreaming of something more."

Maggie released a breath. "Yeah. After spending the last thirty-some-odd years running a restaurant, I'm looking for a change. I'm looking to start a new chapter in my life."

"That's good." He hammered on the keys a bit. "What is it you want to do? Your public will want to know."

Maggie closed her eyes. "I wish I knew."

"You're selling but don't know where you're going?" He seemed surprised.

"Crazy, huh?"

James leaned back in his chair. "I wouldn't say crazy. Sometimes you just need a change."

"Yeah. I feel like I need to do something. It's almost like my life has been on hold. Don't get me wrong. I've loved running the diner. But there's so much I haven't been able to do because of it. I haven't been able to travel. I couldn't even afford to buy a house if I wanted to. And I don't have much free time. Heck, I don't even get a full night's sleep."

"You want a life."

"Pretty much."

"I can't say I blame you for that one. I know what it's like to run a business, and it's not easy. I can't imagine what it must be like in your case, with the diner open 24 hours. Have you thought about just changing the hours? Maybe it would give you enough change to satisfy you."

"It crossed my mind, but I don't think it's enough. I – " Maggie paused, unsure how much of her thought process she wanted to reveal. "I might leave Pine Valley."

James raised his eyebrows. "We'd be sorry to see you go."

"I'd miss it here. But I feel like there aren't enough opportunities."

"A small town does have limited career choices."

"And love choices."

"Ah. I see."

"I'm lonely, James."

He gave her a sympathetic look. "I get it." He took a deep breath, then looked back at his computer screen. "Okay. Let's get this article written so you can get a life and get the fine people of this town off your back."

"Should I take down the signs?"

"That's up to you. Or you could wait until the article comes out and see how people react. Maybe whoever put them up will take them down themselves."

"Maybe."

They spent the next half hour tweaking Maggie's article before she was content and decided to head back to the diner. As she shuffled through the leaves that covered the sidewalks, her mind replayed the conversation with James. He had been understanding, and he seemed to appreciate where she was coming from. She hoped the article would clear up a bit of the confusion and encourage the public to give her some space.

The thought had crossed her mind that the article might also publicize that the diner was for sale, and make anybody who didn't already know aware. Maybe she would get more interest in buying the business, rather than saving it. It couldn't hurt. James had said he would send the article to some neighboring towns, too, to see if it would generate any interest. Maybe by this time tomorrow she would have an offer. The thought made her nervous, but excited, too. Maybe she would get a life sooner rather than later.

Chapter 8

Addy was bored. And frustrated. And depressed. She still didn't want to go out by herself. Her online research hadn't gotten many leads. And there was nothing good on TV. Even the pay-per-view movies held little appeal.

Addy rolled from her belly to her back on the bed and stared at the ceiling. Boston was supposed to be exciting, a new start. And while she was sure there was plenty going on in the clubs and shops and all over town, she felt isolated from it. She wasn't a part of this city yet. She felt like an outcast, which was ridiculous considering no one she had met so far had shunned or berated her. If anything, they had been friendly.

She had made a few calls to look at apartments, and the people she spoke to had been upbeat and amiable. She was planning on stopping to see them the following day. And, while the few job applications she had submitted had been done online, the postings had been lighthearted and friendly. The clerks at the front desk of the hotel had greeted her with a smile. The staff at the restaurants around her had been pleasant. So why was she so discouraged?

It had been so much easier in D.C. She had her core group of acquaintances, and someone had always been available to go out, whether it was to get manicures or dance the night away at a club. She hadn't had to start from scratch. *You never should have left D.C.*

She was probably just lonely. She was sure that once she started making friends and hanging out with people she would be out every night, or at least enjoying the company of others in her apartment. But what would she do until then?

Addy checked her cell phone for the hundredth time to see if she had any new text messages or voicemails. Which was ridiculous. Who would be texting or calling her? The only remote possibility was Mike. Why did she want to hear from him so badly? It wasn't as if they had a future. Maybe she just wanted some kind of human contact.

Get over it, Adelaide. And get your head out of the clouds. You want to meet people? Then go out and meet them. Since when have you been so meek? I taught you to be confident. Addy forced herself to get up. She would go to the cafe down the block and have a cup of coffee. Maybe there would be a band playing. She had seen a poster, but she couldn't remember what night it advertised. If not, at least she could have a drink and a pastry and get out of the hotel for an hour or two. Decision made, she slipped on her shoes and coat and left the room.

It wasn't even November, but shops in the area were flaunting holiday decorations. Though she didn't really have any family or close friends to spend the holidays with, she had always been invited to a couple of parties. The friends she did have were social butterflies, and she clung to them so she would have company. She wondered what kind of friends she would make here. Would it be the same? Would she have superficial friendships that satisfied her desire for human contact but little else? Or would she have deep, satisfying relationships she could count on?

She didn't usually dwell on the superficiality of her friendships in D.C. She usually focused on her failed romantic relationships, and how they had wanted nothing more than a pretty face. But if she was honest, her friends had been the same way. They weren't the kind of people you turned to if you needed someone to talk to. Addy didn't have any of those. But they could be counted on to know where the hottest parties were, where the best new restaurants were, and what she should wear, say, and do. They had enhanced her pretty face image.

Maybe in Boston she could be more than a pretty face. Maybe she would meet people who actually cared about her. But where would she meet them? She had met her prior friends through acquaintances of her mother, at parties and through introductions. It wasn't surprising the kinds of relationships that had resulted. But where could she meet real friends?

Addy felt as if she were in kindergarten, on the first day of school, wondering who she would meet and what she would do. Would they like her? Would she like them? Would she be accepted?

Shaking her head to get rid of the thoughts, Addy focused instead on the short walk to the cafe. She would walk in, find a seat, get a drink. She would sip said drink either listening to music or watching people go by. And she would try not to dwell on how alone she really was.

Mike usually watched some kind of sporting event after dinner. It didn't matter what; it was really just for background noise as he did paperwork or surfed the web or something. Except for when he hung out with friends on the weekends, his evenings were quiet, subdued. But today he felt anxious, antsy, and he kept reaching for his cell phone.

He wanted to text Addy.

But what would he say? He still had no idea if she would even want to hear from him. And even if she did, he had no idea how to even start a conversation. Texting was such an awkward way to communicate with someone you hardly knew. But it was better than calling. Then he would have to worry about long pauses, and nothing to talk about. At least with a text you could formulate your thoughts. And the other person wouldn't know you were at a loss for words. They could just think you were busy or something. But what would he say?

He supposed he could just say "hi" or something. Would that be weird? It would be simple, to the point. And she could ignore it if she wanted to. But if she wanted to talk, she could just say "hi" back.

Before he could think twice about it, he typed a quick "hi" and sent it off. And a minute later he regretted it. Of all the stupid, pointless, juvenile things to do. What was he hoping to get out of this? It wasn't as if they had a future. He was setting himself up for disappointment. Still, he waited anxiously to see if she would respond.

Surprisingly it didn't take long to get a "hi" back. And Mike couldn't keep the grin off his face.

Addy had just sat down with her mug of coffee and a cinnamon roll when her phone dinged. Though she hadn't looked at her phone yet, butterflies began fluttering in her stomach. There was really only one person it could be. What would he say?

From the meager "hi," Addy guessed Mike was feeling as unsure as she was. Though considering how things had been left, she supposed it was understandable. He probably thought she was still mad at him or something. Should she respond? Hadn't she just been thinking in her hotel room that there was no point?

But he was sweet. And, perhaps more importantly, he actually wanted to talk to her. And in her current frame of mind, that counted for a lot. So she typed a quick "hi" as a response.

The next message came soon after: "how are you?"

Addy smiled and settled into her seat. Real human contact. Before she knew it, their conversation was flowing back and forth. Mostly small talk, updating each other on what had happened in the past couple of days. With texts it was easy to fill up a half hour with snippets of conversation. But by the time Addy had finished eating and walked back to her hotel room, she was tired of typing. So she decided to answer the question "what are you up to tonight?" with a phone call instead.

Mike nearly dropped the phone when it rang in his hand. He had been enjoying texting. It made him feel safer somehow. But they had been texting for nearly an hour, so he supposed it did make more sense.

"Hello?" As if he didn't know who it was.

"Hey."

"You surprised me. I wasn't expecting a call."

"I figured it made more sense. And my thumbs were getting tired." She laughed softly, and Mike's heart beat a little faster.

"Yeah, mine, too."

"I was in a coffee shop when you texted me. But I figured since I was back in my hotel room now, it would work out better."

"So you haven't found an apartment yet?"

"I'm going to see a few places tomorrow. But it's only been two days. I figured I would be in a hotel for a little while."

"And no luck on the job front?" He was reiterating bits of their conversation, but he didn't know what else to say.

"Nope. I don't even know what I want to do yet. But I have applied to a couple of places, just to get my feet wet."

"Yeah, I remember when we had dinner how you were saying you didn't know what you wanted to do."

Silence fell, and Mike scrambled to come up with something to talk about.

"Maggie's selling the diner."

"Really?"

"Yeah. It caught everyone by surprise. Somebody even hung up posters to try and save the diner."

"Just because it's selling doesn't mean it's closing."

"True. I guess they figure it'll be different, though."

"Is she selling because of the money?"

Mike shrugged, then realized Addy couldn't see him. "I don't know. I don't think so. She said she wanted a change."

"I can definitely understand that one."

"Yeah."

Silence fell again, but after a moment it didn't seem so uncomfortable.

"I'm sorry I bothered you, Mike. You were probably in the middle of something."

Mike looked up at the football game he had muted. "Nah. Just hanging out."

"Yeah, me, too."

"Nothing to do up in Boston?"

"Oh, there's plenty to do, I'm sure. But it feels so strange doing things by myself. Hopefully I'll make friends soon and be able to hang out with them."

"I imagine you make friends pretty easily."

"I guess so." Addy sighed. "Just not the right kind."

"What do you mean?"

"The people I knew in D.C. were just people I did stuff with. They weren't really friends. So I knew a lot of people, but I didn't have any close friends."

"None?"

"Not really, no."

Mike felt bad for her. He had grown up with the same group of people he hung out with now. They knew him better than he knew himself. And he knew he could turn to any of them for advice, or if he needed help. He couldn't imagine not having that. "You must have been lonely."

She was silent for a moment before whispering "yeah."

He didn't want her to get depressed. Quickly he tried to reassure her. "I'm sure it'll be better in Boston."

"Maybe. I hope so."

He needed to get the conversation on more secure footing. Grasping at straws, he remembered she had gone to see a movie the day they had had their dinner date, and he asked her about it. That fortunately sent them on a discussion about movies and books and music. Before he knew it, Mike glanced at the clock on the wall and found it was eleven o'clock.

"Wow. We've been talking for three hours."

"Seriously?" She paused, as if she didn't believe him and had to check. "Wow. I didn't realize it was so late."

"Me neither." He realized they should probably disconnect, but he found he didn't want to. Despite a shaky beginning, he had been enjoying their conversation. "I guess we should probably get some sleep."

"Probably. I imagine we both have busy days tomorrow."

"Yeah. I have a bunch of appointments lined up."

"And I have a job and an apartment to find."

"Yeah." Still he lingered, trying to find something else to say. Coming up with nothing, he figured he could at least ask "can I talk to you again?"

"I'd like that."

"Tomorrow?"

"Okay."

Mike fist pumped the air. "Great. So, uh, I can call about eight? Would that work?"

"I think so."

"Okay. So I guess I'll talk to you then."

"Yeah."

"Bye."

"Bye. Oh, and, Mike?"

"Yeah?"

"Thank you."

"For what?"

"Helping me feel less lonely for a little while."

Mike swallowed. "I could thank you for the same thing."

"Good night."

"Night."

Mike disconnected the call, then flopped back on his sofa. Addy. He had just been talking to Addy. He had spent three hours talking to Addy. And, except for a little bit in the beginning, it hadn't been awkward at all. He felt like he was sixteen again, with a crush on the prettiest girl in class. The only problem was: this time the prettiest girl lived two hours away. Was he out of his mind?

Addy had kicked off her shoes and curled up under the covers of the bed while she had been talking to Mike. She had felt warm, and protected. And happy. She had been happy. When was the last time she had been happy?

Tossing her phone on the nightstand, she debated getting up. She should probably change and get ready for bed, but she was afraid reality would set in if she did. Lying here, still warm under the covers, she could hear Mike's voice. And she could hear his laugh. And she could pretend that the weight of the blankets was actually the weight of his arm tossed over her.

And she would get to experience it all again tomorrow. Smiling to herself, she slid even further down the bed, burying herself under the blanket. Was she crazy? Maybe. But definitely a good kind of crazy.

Chapter 9

Business at the diner was still booming the next day. The town paper didn't get delivered until the afternoon, so Maggie was still riding the wave generated from the posters. She would appreciate it while it was there, since she expected things would be much quieter once the article came out. But selling or not, she could still use the money that the extra business had brought in.

Around lunch time James hand delivered Maggie's copy of the paper. The front page was covered with news of Mary Thompson's hundredth birthday celebration, but Maggie found her editorial still had a place of honor on the second page. Though she had read it the day before, she read it again, pleased with the end result.

"Thanks, James. I hope it clears up a few things."

"I hope so, too. Say, while I'm here, mind if I grab some lunch?"

"Of course not. Though I must warn you, we have run out of a couple of the specials."

"No problem. I'll just have a burger and fries."

"Sure thing." Maggie submitted the order to the kitchen, then approached a couple that had just sat down. It had been nice of James to run her article. And it had been nice of James to deliver the paper to her. She had always been fond of James, though they didn't often have the opportunity to interact. He was friendly but didn't overstep boundaries. And, though he knew everything that was going on around town, he wasn't one to gossip.

Too bad he was a little young for her, Maggie mused. There were nearly ten years between them, and, while she could definitely appreciate his boy-next-door good looks, he wasn't likely to want anything to do with an aging waitress who still didn't know what she wanted out of life. Still, she was grateful for his kindness. And she hoped their efforts paid off. She didn't want anyone thinking she needed saving.

Still riding high from the warm fuzzies her conversation with Mike had provided, Addy was grinning as she approached the first apartment she was checking out. She didn't even mind that it was a third-floor walk-up. It would be good exercise, she reasoned, and with her new love of carbs, she could use it. She rang the buzzer her new potential roommate had indicated, then stepped back and waited. As she waited, she looked around. The neighborhood was okay. Not exactly pristine, but she supposed that was to be expected in a big city. It didn't feel unsafe, so that was good. And maybe she could lead a neighborhood clean-up or something. Who knew what the future would bring?

Fifteen minutes later, Addy knew the future would not be bringing this apartment. At least not for her. The apartment was worse than the street in terms of mess, and the woman looking for a roommate had been a bit too laid-back in terms of inviting people into the apartment. While Addy wanted to socialize and make friends, she couldn't imagine living somewhere that had people coming in and out of it at all hours of the night. She was just glad she had learned that ahead of time.

On to the next apartment.

Addy didn't even make it into the next apartment building. As soon as she got off the T she could tell this was not the part of town she wanted to live in. She called the woman to cancel the appointment, then got right back on the T and headed back toward her hotel. Looked like finding an apartment would be tougher than she had hoped. She had one more appointment after lunch, but at the rate she was going that would be a dud, too. Addy sighed and blinked back tears, then took a deep breath to fortify herself. It was her first day looking. Of course it wouldn't be that easy. She just had to take things one step at a time.

The third apartment ended up being the exact opposite. The neighborhood was great, and the woman seemed nice. But the apartment was too immaculate, and the woman had a cleaning schedule that Addy would have to adhere to, a chore-sharing calendar, and the expectation that Addy would have to be as neat as she was. Addy wasn't a slob, but it was all a bit too much. She wanted to feel comfortable in her new home, not afraid to move. She politely turned that one down, as well.

By the time Addy got back to her hotel room, she was feeling discouraged. She had a couple of appointments the following day, but she didn't have high hopes. With nothing to do for the rest of the day until her phone conversation with Mike, Addy turned on her laptop, scoured the apartment listings again, and applied to a few more jobs. It would all work out. It had to. She just had to give it time.

Mike was feeling hopeful and couldn't wait to talk with Addy again. So he had floated through the day, with smiles and his cheerful demeanor back in place. The guys at the shop had teased him, of course, but they seemed glad he at least wasn't moping around anymore.

When he got home, he tossed his keys on the table, took off his jacket, grabbed a beer from the fridge, and settled on his couch with his phone. He didn't even bother putting on the TV. Who needed a game when he would be talking to Addy? When Addy answered the phone, however, he could hear the disappointment in her voice. Apparently her day hadn't been quite as positive as his had been.

"Hey, what's up? You sound like you're about to cry."

Addy sniffed. "Just not a great day of scoping out apartments."

"I'm sorry."

"It's okay."

"You haven't been there long, though. Give it some time. Something will come up."

"Yeah. I'll be seeing a couple more tomorrow."

"There you go, then. It will all work out."

"I hope so."

"How's the job hunt?"

"Even worse than the apartment hunt."

"No luck, huh?"

"Nope. I've applied to some, but those were more just because I need a job. Anything that sounded even remotely interesting I wasn't qualified for."

Mike tried to turn the conversation around, discuss more upbeat topics, but Addy didn't seem to even be listening. After about a half hour he decided to say good night, suggesting they talk again the next evening. Part of him was glad that she hadn't found something quickly. Maybe she would get discouraged and give Pine Valley a chance, instead. But he hated hearing her so dejected. It was as if she had lost all her Addy-ness. So the other part of him hoped she found something soon.

In the meantime, though, it was out of his hands. All he could do was wait and see how things played out. With a sigh he took a last swig of his now-warm beer and turned on the TV. He wondered what was playing tonight.

Addy felt bad about the conversation with Mike, but she just hadn't been in the mood to cheer up, if that made any sense. She wanted something to go well, to fall into place without her having to bend over backwards. Making the decision to move had been hard enough. She hadn't expected the move itself to be quite so trying. So she just wanted to wallow a little bit. Was that too much to ask?

Addy put her phone on the nightstand and picked up the TV remote. It was too early to go to sleep, and she was in no condition to be sociable. Hugging a pillow to her chest, she found a made-for-TV movie and zoned out. Maybe tomorrow would be better.

Chapter 10

Addy woke up in a slightly better mood, but the feeling of anticipation she had felt the day before about visiting apartments had been replaced by a feeling of dread. She had made two appointments for the day and had bookmarked a few possibilities online if these didn't pan out, but she didn't know how many more disappointing apartments she could handle. Dragging herself out of bed, she got ready for the day and headed downstairs for breakfast before making her way outside.

At least the day was nice. It was chilly, but the sun was shining and the wind wasn't blowing, so it was a pleasant walk to the subway station. If she was thinking rationally, the apartments today had sounded more promising than the ones from the previous day. Friendly potential roommates, and nice parts of town. After the hiccup with the second apartment yesterday, Addy had done a bit more research, and these should be better. Maybe there was reason to be hopeful, after all.

Addy approached the first apartment and pressed the button to be let in. She did a doubletake once she did, though. Were there four names crammed onto the name panel above the button? Once she was let in, she soon learned that yes, she would be sharing the apartment with three other people. No wonder the rent had been lower than other apartments she had looked at. Why hadn't she thought to ask? Perhaps she wouldn't have minded so much, but they would also have to share one bathroom, the bedrooms were tiny, and one woman was definitely a slob while another was not exactly friendly. Maybe if she got desperate, but probably not.

She had some time to kill before the next appointment, so she went for a walk. The second apartment wasn't too far from the first, and she might as well save the fare if she could. She tried to take deep breaths as she walked, letting the cool air revive her and calm her nerves. She tried to think rationally again, to remind herself that she had only been searching for two days, and that she had money to tide her over if things took a while. She had backups if the second appointment didn't go well. She would be okay.

After taking a few wrong turns, she found the correct street but still had a little bit of time before her scheduled appointment. Spotting a cafe down the street, Addy opted to grab a cup of coffee and a small snack. It wasn't quite lunch time, but her stomach was starting to rumble. It had gotten used to regular large meals. She didn't even want to think about what her mother would say about that.

As she sipped and nibbled, she ran through what she knew about the next apartment. Another walk-up, but that didn't bother her. This one had sounded better than her first apartment that day, though it was the most expensive she had seen so far. The woman she spoke to had been friendly and outgoing, and they seemed to have a lot in common. She mentally crossed her fingers that it would work out.

An hour or so later, Addy rang the doorbell and was greeted by a blond twenty-something.

"Hi! You must be Addy. I'm Kate." The blond held out her hand, and Addy grasped it in her own.

"Hi, Kate."

"Come on in." She gestured for Addy to enter, and Addy took a step in, looking around as she let her purse slide to the floor. "Let me show you around, and then we can talk."

The apartment was small, but adequate. It had a galley kitchen, a living room just big enough for a sofa, chair, and TV console, and a small dining area with seating for four. Two bedrooms and a bathroom branched from a hallway off the living room.

"We would have to share a bathroom, which is a bummer, but it's definitely doable. My last roommate and I just made a kind of schedule. It worked with our work schedules. What kind of work schedule do you have?"

Addy turned her gaze from the apartment to her potential roommate. "I don't have one yet. I just moved to the city, so I'm working out the details."

Kate looked at her for a moment. "Not to be nosy, though I guess that's kind of the point," she said with a small laugh, "but are you sure you can swing the rent without a job? With just the two of us, especially, it's not exactly cheap."

"Yeah, Boston is a lot pricier than I expected. But no problem. I sold my old apartment so I have plenty in the bank to tide me over for a while."

"Oh, okay, great. Where did you move from?"

"D.C."

"Cool. I've always wanted to go there."

Addy took a look around, taking in the view and the limited space. It was definitely smaller than the apartment in D.C. that she had shared with her mother, then taken over once her mother died. But did that matter? She was looking for a fresh start, not a penthouse.

"I would be looking for a year commitment, but we could do a trial run before we put your name on the lease, if you want. That way we could see if we click. But I know it can be a hassle to move everything, so if you want to sign the lease right away, we can do that, too."

"I don't have that much stuff, so it wouldn't be a problem either way."

"Okay. Why don't we have a seat and chat a bit? We can go over the boring numbers stuff and get to know each other a little bit."

They spent nearly an hour chatting, and Addy was surprised to realize how quickly the time had passed. It was obvious she and Kate had good roommate chemistry, and she said as much to Kate.

"So does that mean you want the room?"

Addy thought for a moment. "Yeah, I think so."

"Sweet. I would just ask for two months rent upfront, and I have an agreement to sign."

Ten minutes later Addy was walking back down the stairs. She took a deep breath once she stepped outside and looked around. Her new neighborhood. She could definitely work with this.

Mike was happy for Addy. Really, he was. But as hard as it had been to hear the discouragement in her voice the night before, that little part of him kept hoping she would realize the city wasn't as great as she thought it would be. That's all.

Still, it was good to hear the inkling of excitement in her voice. They chatted easily again, and the time slipped by.

When they hung up a couple of hours later, with tentative plans to touch base the next evening, Mike found himself at loose ends. Despite their obvious connection, despite his growing attraction to Addy, he wondered if it was even worth it. She had found a place to live. She just had to find a job, and she would be well on her way to forgetting about him. He was getting attached to a woman who was going to break his heart. And why?

He opened the window near his bed and flopped on his stomach, letting the cool night air sweep over him as he stared into the darkness. After a few minutes of spacing out, Mike grew antsy and got up to make a cup of coffee. Maybe there was a game on. Any game. Just something to take his mind off the growing knot of loneliness deep in his belly.

Chapter 11

Since Addy had brought so little with her, her new room looked pretty pathetic, even after she had completely unpacked. Her bed for the time being was an air mattress on the floor. Her nightstand was an empty box with her clock radio on top. The closet was about half full, and a small stack of books sat on the floor, for lack of a bookcase. Until she found steady employment, furniture would have to wait. But for once she was trying to look at the glass half full. She had a roof over her head, a potential new friend in the next room, and a world of possibilities ahead of her.

Unpacking complete, Addy figured the next step was to pick up a few groceries. She wasn't much of a cook, but she at least needed coffee for the morning. She couldn't afford to keep buying it at Starbucks.

With coffee in mind, she realized she was going to need a coffeemaker, too. She had already learned Kate was a tea drinker. That meant another stop, and another expense. Where would she even go shopping? She didn't know where anything was yet. It looked like she was going to need some information, a list, and a budget. With all of the things she was sure to need, she would also need to find a job sooner rather than later. The expenses would be adding up fast. Since she was no closer to figuring out what she wanted to do, this meant a temporary menial job to tide her over. Yay.

Since she hadn't heard back from any of the jobs she had applied to, it looked like she would have to hit the pavement. Which was probably for the best anyway. Since she didn't yet know her way around, she didn't know if any of the jobs she applied to would even be nearby. An unreliable car meant she would be relying on public transportation instead, and that was yet another expense. It looked like her best bet was to find something within walking distance.

Taking a deep breath to build her resolve, she slung her purse over her shoulder, bid farewell to Kate, and headed out to familiarize herself with her new neighborhood. Groceries, coffeemaker, job. Those were the priorities. She had settled in a decent part of the city – not in the heart, but not quite on the outskirts. It was busy enough to satisfy her without being overwhelming. She hoped there would be enough nearby to satisfy her wallet, too. Would she need to open a new bank account? She hadn't seen any branches of her existing bank anywhere. What else would she need to do?

Momentarily overwhelmed by figuring everything out, Addy sat down on the front staircase of a nearby apartment building and took a deep breath. She felt close to tears. She had been so focused on the escape, the fresh start, the possibilities, that she hadn't really thought about the day-to-day realities. The weight of her to do list was suddenly unbearable.

Addy closed her eyes and took a few more deep breaths, letting the cool air revive her. She could do this. She just had to take one step at a time, check off one item at a time. And she had to start with a cup of coffee. She opened her eyes and went in search of the cafe she had seen yesterday.

Addy tried her best to focus on her surroundings rather than her anxieties. The air was cool but not cold, warmed slightly by the pavement and passing traffic. Buildings were a mix of apartments and retail shops, with the occasional restaurant or coffee shop mixed in. Doctors' offices, nail salons, and some kind of painting place where people could come in and paint their own mug or plate. As she passed, Addy peered into the front windows of the painting place, curious about what they offered. She could see a couple of families painting together, a group of young women near the back, laughing. A middle-aged woman stood behind what appeared to be a reception desk. She smiled when she noticed Addy in the window.

Addy caught her eye, then stepped back as the woman approached her. It was embarrassing, being caught snooping. The other woman's smile, however, never faltered. She stepped onto the sidewalk and greeted Addy.

"Well, hello there," she said. "Would you like to come in?"

"Uh," Addy stumbled. "No, I'm okay. I was just checking things out."

The woman glanced down to pull a brochure from the pocket of an apron she had around her waist. "Here," she said, handing the brochure to Addy. "This has some information about what we offer. You can just come in and decorate something, or you can get a group of friends together and learn to paint something special." The woman smiled again as Addy took the pamphlet.

"Thanks," Addy said, mustering a smile of her own. "I'll take a peek."

The woman went back inside, and Addy watched her go before opening the brochure. Maybe once she had a little cash coming in she could stop by. It sounded fun. With a last glance toward the shop, Addy continued down the sidewalk. Coffee first. Then groceries, coffeemaker, job.

⸺ℓℓℓ ⸻

To Maggie's surprise, business didn't drop off after the article. If anything, people seemed more curious and eager to chat. It appeared that her wanting more out of life made her more interesting, more worthy of a conversation. She had gotten a wide assortment of suggestions, from going back to school to backpacking through Europe. While she appreciated no longer being the subject of pity, she wasn't used to so many conversations revolving around her personal life. It was exhausting.

Maggie felt just about ready to collapse when the bell on the door jangled yet again. With a sigh, Maggie plastered her best attempt at a smile on her face. Richard, a local resident whom Maggie had spoken to numerous times, stepped inside. Maggie felt herself relax. While they weren't close, Maggie felt a kind of kinship to Richard. He had owned a restaurant of his own several years back, before his family decided to move to Pine Valley. He knew the unique exhaustion that came with it.

Richard smiled at her, and Maggie gave a genuine smile back. "How are you holding up, Maggie?"

Maggie let herself sink onto one of the counter stools. "I'm doing alright, I suppose," she replied.

"I've seen the crowds of people. You've really shaken this town up."

"That was not my intention."

"I know. Not much else going on, I suppose." They sat in companionable silence for a moment before Richard asked "have you got any pie left, by any chance?"

Maggie laughed. It felt good. "I might be able to scrounge up a slice." After the day she'd had, she decided to treat herself to a piece, too. She plated up the last two pieces of key lime pie and placed one in front of Richard. He smiled in appreciation.

"My favorite."

"I know."

They sat and enjoyed their pie, and Maggie felt herself relax. With the crowds that weekend, she had barely had time to rest, let alone sleep. She could feel herself drifting.

"You look dead on your feet," Richard commented a minute later. "When's the last time you took a break?"

Maggie thought back. "I snuck in a power nap before the dinner rush."

"It's nearly nine, and you're exhausted. I'll tell you what. Why don't you go get some rest, and I'll cover the diner for a bit."

"Oh, Richard, I couldn't ask you to do that."

"You didn't ask. I offered. I may be a little rusty, but it's quiet, and I think I can handle whoever comes in. Besides, I'm pretty sure I caught a glimpse of Kyle in the back. He's a good kid, and he'll keep me in line."

"Are you sure?" She bit her lip in hesitation. A break sounded heavenly.

"I'm sure. If anything we can't handle comes up, I know where to find you."

Maggie hesitated a moment before standing up. "Thank you, Richard."

"Of course."

Maggie went to her little apartment at the back of the diner. For once it didn't take long for her eyes to shut.

Some time later she blinked her eyes open to sunlight pouring through her bedroom window. After a moment she bolted upright. How could she have slept all night? Poor Richard! She hoped he had locked up and gone home. Did he even know where the keys were?

Maggie quickly dressed and brushed her teeth, then left her apartment to find Richard whistling to himself as he cooked an omelet.

"Morning, sleepyhead," he greeted her with a smile. "Sleep well?"

"Oh, Richard. I am so sorry! I can't believe I slept so long."

"I can. I could tell you were exhausted. When's the last time you had a good night's sleep?"

Maggie chuckled softly. "It's been many years."

Richard shook his head. "That is not a good habit."

"I know." Maggie took a peek at what Richard was making. "That looks good. For a customer?"

"Yup." Richard skillfully plated the omelet and gave Maggie a grin before heading into the dining room. Maggie could hear him place the plate on the counter, then chat for a minute before a short laugh. A moment later he was back in the kitchen. "Did you want me to stay a bit longer?"

Maggie shook her head forcefully. "Absolutely not. You have been a blessing, and I cannot thank you enough, but now you need to go and get some rest of your own. Jessica will be in shortly to help me out with breakfast."

"I had fun. And I'm happy to help whenever needed. Let me know when you need another break."

Maggie followed him into the dining room and watched him go with a wave. Then she greeted the diners at the counter and took a quick stock of other customers in the restaurant. Everyone seemed content. The counter tops were spotless. Fresh coffee was gurgling in the coffeemaker. Straws, napkins, and shakers were well stocked. Everything seemed in order. Maggie shook her head. A blessing, indeed. And her mind began to whir.

Chapter 12

Addy's life began to settle into a routine. Unfortunately, it was not one she could continue forever. After making herself a cup of coffee with her brand new machine, she would search for jobs online. Then she would take a walk, heading in different directions, checking for help wanted signs. Then she would walk back home, discouraged, have some lunch, and binge watch Netflix until dinner time. After dinner she and Mike would talk on the phone until way too late, at which point she would go to sleep and start the whole cycle over again.

She found plenty of jobs advertised. The problem was: none of them interested her. And she knew she was going to have to bite the bullet and just get a job, any job, to tide her over. Her savings were dwindling rapidly, especially with the two months rent she had had to give Kate. Other bills would soon be trickling in, and she was going to get in a pickle.

She also worried about how much time she and Mike were spending getting to know each other. She hated to break off that human contact, especially since she had very few outlets at the moment. But she was feeling way too comfortable with him. She was longing to see him. And, if she was honest with herself, she was longing to do more than just see him. She wanted to be in his arms, and to feel his lips on hers. And that would just make things way too complicated. As if they weren't already.

Okay. Addy closed her eyes and rubbed her temples. She had signed a one year lease. She had to give this a shot for at least one year. It wouldn't be so bad if she just sucked it up and got a job. Addy's eyes flew open. What was she thinking? Based on the train of thought she had just begun, it seemed as if she didn't have a lease she would be considering leaving. And that was ridiculous. This had been her destination, her goal. Where would she go if not here? She didn't dare think about Mike's warm eyes and soft laugh. Pine Valley was not an option. Boston was her home now. Boston, Boston, Boston.

Addy felt tears well up in her eyes. This was not the plan. Taking a deep breath, she built her resolve. Today was the day. She would find a job. She was just feeling depressed because she was in limbo. That was it. Once she put down roots she would feel better. A job. Money coming in. The start of a social life. Getting out and enjoying the city and all it had to offer. She could do this. And she would enjoy it if it killed her.

Maggie's life was settling into a routine, as well. Business was steady, busier than it had been before the "for sale" sign, but not quite as busy as that first weekend. Between customers Maggie would think, play out scenarios in her mind. She thought about places she would like to go, things she would like to experience. And she started making a list. A bucket list, as many would call it. It wasn't a long-term solution, but it gave her something to look forward to.

She and Richard had also settled into a routine. Maggie had subtly asked him if he would be interested in making his participation a regular thing, helping out at the diner so she could catch up on sleep or paperwork or whatever she needed. He seemed eager to take her up on the offer, and each day between the lunch and dinner rush he would come in and cover the diner.

After a few days of this new routine, Maggie entered the dining room at the start of the dinner rush. Richard was wiping down the counters and turned to face her with a smile. Maggie took a deep breath and approached. She had a plan to propose.

"You seem to be enjoying yourself, Richard."

"I am. I've missed this, interacting with customers and whipping up delicious food. I did it for a long time before we moved. To be honest, I hadn't been ready to retire, but I had to do what was right for my daughter and granddaughter. And they needed a fresh start. So we came here, and I never looked back."

"That's good to hear. Because I have a proposal for you."

"A proposal? We're not even dating." He gave her a wink and a sly smile.

Maggie laughed. "Smart aleck."

Richard returned the laugh. "I actually have a proposal for you, too."

"Really?" Maggie was intrigued.

"Why don't you start, and then I'll go."

"Okay. What would you think about taking a more substantial role at the diner? Maybe longer hours, eventually a management role?"

"I'll do you one better."

"Oh yeah?"

"Let's be partners."

Maggie sucked in a breath.

"I've been giving it a lot of thought, Maggie. You want a break. You need a break, deserve one. But you're unsure what to do with yourself. I get that. I was at loose ends when I sold my restaurant. And I haven't found anything that felt right since. You have dreams, and you want to travel, and all that. But you need a source of income."

He wasn't saying anything that Maggie didn't already know. The editorial had put it all out in the open, and she had turned it over in her head many times.

"At the same time, I could use a change. I need something more in my life. My daughter is settled now, and my granddaughter is getting older. They don't need me as much. I am not at all ready to just sit on my laurels and do nothing. I need a project, a purpose. And I haven't been as happy as I have been working in this diner. Not for a long time."

Maggie considered his words, took some time to process.

"You don't need to decide now. But give it some thought. It could be a solution for both of us. You would get time off, knowing you had someone covering the restaurant. And I would have something productive to do, something that brought me fulfillment. You would have money coming in – plus, of course, what I gave you to buy in to the business. You would have options, Maggie. You wouldn't be as tied to this place as you have been. But you wouldn't be set loose, either."

Maggie's mind was buzzing. Would it be enough? Was it the solution Richard seemed to think it was? It didn't solve everything, but still. She looked up to meet Richard's eyes.

"Like I said, think about it. No rush at all. And no pressure. I'll see you tomorrow." He smiled at her again, put down the cloth he had been using, and grabbed his coat. Without another word, he left the restaurant, the bell above the door jangling after him.

Maggie fell onto a stool at the counter. It was food for thought for sure. But customers were coming in, and with a start she realized she had to get to work. Her future would have to wait a bit longer.

Chapter 13

As Addy took her walk that morning, she tried to think about her options with a clear head and positive thoughts. Even if she didn't love the job she ended up taking, it didn't have to be forever. She could just try some things out, cushion her bank account, and ponder the bigger questions as she went. This was just temporary.

The deli down the street was hiring. She could make sandwiches, slice up some meat and cheese. She could feel her mouth scrunch up at the thought. Okay, maybe that wasn't for her. The convenience store needed a cashier. That sounded simple enough. Pay would probably be pitiful, but it was just a start. She entered the store, causing the bell above the door to jingle, and approached the counter.

When he saw she wasn't carrying anything, the cashier gestured toward the lottery machine and the cigarettes stashed behind the counter. "What'll it be?"

Addy flashed him a smile. "Neither, thank you. I was inquiring about the "help wanted" sign."

The man gave her a wary look. "You want to work here?"

Honesty or desperation? It was a tough choice. Addy took a deep breath. "Sure. I'm looking for a job, and this seems as good as any."

"Pay won't be much."

"I figured."

He named an hourly wage that was barely more than her typical coffee order. Good thing she had gotten a coffeemaker.

"Okay."

"Okay?"

Addy nodded.

"Alright. Fill out this application," he said with eyebrows raised as he slid a piece of paper out from under the counter.

"Thank you. Do you have a pen?"

It didn't take long for Addy to fill out the double-sided sheet, and when she was done, she handed it back to the man, who promised the manager would be in touch.

"Thank you."

Addy left the store and headed back toward her apartment. It was a start, even if it was a pitiful one.

Addy soon learned that having a job you didn't like was even worse than sitting around an apartment, bored. The job wasn't difficult, but it wasn't exactly fulfilling. Was it worth the pitiful paycheck? Probably not. But at least it helped fill her days, and it was better to be bringing in a paltry paycheck than nothing. She just didn't know how long she'd be able to tolerate it.

On her fourth day of work, Addy was slowly walking to the store when something caught her eye. The painting place had a new sign in their window: "party planner wanted." Hmm.

Checking for traffic, Addy crossed the street to approach the shop. The woman she had met the week before was putting some holiday decorations in the window. She smiled and waved to Addy.

"Good morning," she greeted as Addy entered the space.

"Hi," Addy replied, suddenly nervous.

"I wondered if I would see you again."

Addy was startled. "You remember me?"

The woman laughed. "I do. You had a hopeful look in your eyes, curious. I love that look. It sticks with me. I always long to hear the story behind it." She put down the tape and garland she had been using. "So what can I do for you? Interested in painting something?"

"Um, actually," Addy began, "I wanted to ask about the job."

"Oh!" The woman looked pleased. "I just put that sign up yesterday. Have you done that kind of thing before?"

"Well, I don't know. What kinds of parties do you hold?"

"We're all about painting, so painting parties, of course." She gave a warm chuckle. "We invite groups of people to get together to learn how to paint something. We also hold birthday parties, usually for kids, during which the guests learn to paint a project together, and then do the typical party stuff, like cake and all that. We have one teacher who will go to people's homes, too, to do a party on the go."

"Does the person you're looking for teach the people how to paint?"

"That is part of it. But you would also be responsible for scheduling the events, getting all the supplies together, setting up and breaking down the parties. We would love to book more parties, so we're looking for someone who could take on the advertising bit, too. And when there isn't a party going on, you would be called on to help out in the store as needed, especially with the holidays almost here."

"Oh."

"Not your cup of tea?"

"I don't really know. I'm not sure I would be qualified to do all that."

"Why don't we sit down and have a chat? I'm Linda, by the way."

"Addy."

"Pleasure to meet you, Addy. Things don't usually pick up until later in the day, so we should have a little time now. Why don't we have a seat at one of these tables, and you can tell me a little about yourself?"

Mike couldn't help grinning at the excitement in Addy's voice.

"I got a job!" He could hear her smile.

"I thought you had a job?"

"Oh, yeah. I quit that one. Well, when I was a half hour later to work because I was applying for another job, they were about ready to fire me. But I found something else. Something better, I hope."

"That's great. What will you be doing?"

As Addy filled Mike in on the details of being a party planner for some place called Paintastic, however, Mike's grin faded. He was glad she had found a job she could get excited about. At least, part of him was. The part that just wanted her to be happy. But the selfish part had been hoping the job would be something else menial and dull, so she wouldn't want to stick around in Boston. Not something that brought her such obvious joy.

"Sounds great," he responded when she had finished. "When do you start?"

"Tomorrow. There isn't a party booked until the weekend, but Linda wants to walk me through everything and make sure I know what to do. She'll be shadowing me during the first party on Saturday, too. I'm nervous but excited."

"I can tell."

"I'm actually surprised I even got the job. I've never done anything like this before."

Silence fell.

"So what made you decide to go for it?" Mike asked after a moment.

"Not sure. It sounded interesting. And I like the creative element. I've never taught anything before, so that makes me a little nervous, but I think I'll be okay. Linda seems to have faith in me."

"That's good."

"Yeah. Not sure if the pay will cover my rent, but I figure it's probably only temporary anyway, a stepping stone or whatever."

"A first step on the way to bigger and better things."

"Exactly."

They both got quiet again. For once they both seemed to be at a loss as to what to say next.

"So what's new in Pine Valley?" Addy finally asked.

"Not much. Been pretty quiet lately. Decorations are going up for Christmas, but that's about it."

They took turns trying to jump-start the conversation, but after a few feeble attempts decided to call it a night. It was barely nine o'clock. Mike sighed as he dropped the phone beside him on the bed. This was it: the inevitable end. He had known it was going to happen, but that didn't help matters. He felt like he'd been punched in the gut. He wasn't ready to lose her, to lose the connection. But, really, what good did it do to prolong the inevitable?

Placing her phone on the pseudo-nightstand, Addy felt some of her earlier enthusiasm fade. Mike was pulling away from her. Not that she could blame him. She was putting down roots in Boston, and he already had roots – a hundred miles away. It made sense to go their separate ways. But the thought alone saddened her. She hadn't felt this close to someone in a long time, maybe ever.

Since the night was young, Addy wandered into the living room. She found Kate putting on a coat, ready to go out.

"Hey," Kate greeted her with a smile. "Didn't expect to see you."

"Hi. Yeah. Just wanted to say hi, see what you were up to."

"I was just heading to the cafe down the block. A friend of mine is reading some poetry tonight, part of a slam thing they have going on. You're welcome to join if you don't have any plans."

Addy grinned. "Sounds great. Let me just grab my coat." This was what she had been hoping for: making new friends and getting a social life. New beginnings, not dwelling on the hollow feeling that had started reappearing in the pit of her stomach.

Chapter 14

As the dinner crowd began to dissipate, Maggie finally had time to breathe. And think. Mostly think.

Richard's proposal had certainly given her much to think about. She had never considered having a partner before. Would it be the best of both worlds, as Richard seemed to think? Would it be enough?

Maggie decided to make a list of pros and cons. As she shuffled beneath the register for a piece of paper, she noticed a stack of mail, placed there earlier in the day. After a moment's hesitation, she decided to tackle the mail first.

Bills. Junk. Typical stuff. She was about to bring them back to the office when an item she had placed in the junk pile caught her eye. It was from a realtor, and it looked official. Curious, Maggie ripped open the envelope.

"Dear Ms. Devin," the letter began. "My name is Rachel Connors, and I represent a party interested in discussing the purchase of your restaurant and the building in which it resides. We would like to arrange a meeting so my client can inspect the property and discuss the matter further. Please call or email me at your earliest convenience using the contact information below. I look forward to hearing from you."

Maggie sank onto a counter stool. As if she didn't have enough to think about, now she had someone possibly interested in buying the diner. And the letter was so professional, too. This wouldn't be a handshake deal. This would involve contracts and paperwork, records and receipts. Come to think of it, Richard would probably want some of that, too. She didn't even know how much to ask for – from either of them. What had she gotten herself into?

The poetry slam was fun, and Addy enjoyed chatting with Kate and Kate's friends. The friend who read, Shawn, was a little depressing for Addy's taste, but there was no denying his talent.

It was nearly eleven by the time Kate and Addy headed back to their apartment – early compared to the times she would party back in D.C., but Addy was exhausted. It had been a good night, and, despite the conversation she had had with Mike, she was feeling optimistic. It had to be healthier to make new friends in her new home than wallow over a non-existent relationship. Right?

Addy got ready for bed, sank onto her air mattress, and reached to turn off the lamp on her makeshift nightstand. As her hand reached for the switch, it paused over her cell phone. A second later she typed a quick "good night" to Mike, turned off her lamp, and went to sleep.

Mike was dozing in his recliner when his phone dinged. Reaching for the phone, he felt a slight flutter in his gut. "Good night," the text read. Simple. Not a conversation starter. But it gave Mike enough hope that he turned off the TV and went to bed with a smile on his face.

Addy's alarm startled her awake. At first she didn't realize what it was; then she remembered she had to get up for work. She had a job. And this one she was excited about. She grabbed some clothes and left her room to shower and get ready. Kate was eating breakfast in the kitchen.

"Hey," Kate greeted.

"Good morning," Addy replied. "Hey, thanks again for inviting me out last night. I enjoyed it."

"Absolutely. I'm glad you had fun. The slam continues tonight if you were interested."

"Maybe. I'll have to see how I'm feeling. First day at a new job today."

"What happened to the other one?"

"It was a total dud, so I quit. Found something better."

"Congrats! Where you working?"

Addy filled Kate in with a quick summary.

"I know that place. My work did a group thing there once. It was fun. I hope you like it."

"Me, too. I'm looking forward to it."

"Well, good luck. I have to head to work now. Fill me in later, okay?"

"Sure. Have a good day."

"You, too."

Less than a half hour later, Addy was outside. She decided to treat herself to Starbucks on her way to work, and there just happened to be one on the way.

When she walked into Paintastic, Addy had a coffee in her hand and a smile on her face. Linda, however, looked frazzled. And wet. Addy's smile faded. "What happened?"

"Pipe," Linda gasped, "burst. Back room is drenched."

Addy put down her coffee and followed Linda to the back room, where they both spent the next two hours pulling out supplies, salvaging what they could. When they paused to take a break, Addy was exhausted. It was a good kind of exhausted, though, the result of hard work. It had been a long time since she had felt that way. Actually, had she ever felt that way?

"Well," Linda said after a moment. "I bet that wasn't how you expected to start work today."

Addy laughed. "No, I can honestly say it wasn't. I didn't mind, though. Happy to help."

"I was glad to have the help."

Addy took a sip of her now cold coffee and grimaced. "So now what?"

Linda sighed. "Well, I'm not in any condition to open up shop." She looked Addy over. "And, no offense, you don't look much better." Addy looked down at her damp, grimy clothes. "So I'm going to assess the damage, call the landlord again, and head home to shower. Why don't you head home and get cleaned up, and I'll give you a call this afternoon."

"Okay," Addy replied. "Will we still be able to do the party this weekend?"

"I really hope so. But until I really take stock of the damage – and find out if it's even okay for us to be open – I won't know for sure. I'm hoping to have more info this afternoon."

Addy headed back to her apartment somewhat less hopeful than she had left it that morning. She hoped this wasn't a sign of worse things to come.

Mike picked up his phone, half eager to hear Addy's voice and half anxious. Could his heart handle hearing her go on and on about how great things were turning out? Could he deny himself the simple pleasure of talking to her? With a sigh, Mike pushed the call button and closed his eyes.

"Hey." It was Addy's voice, but she didn't sound excited. She sounded almost depressed. Mike's eyes flew open.

"Hey," he replied. "You okay?"

Addy sighed. "Yeah, I'm okay. Just disappointed."

"Job turn out to be a bust?"

"No, the job isn't what busted." Addy filled him in on the burst pipe fiasco. "Landlord wants to get someone in to check everything out, make sure there's no structural damage, so we have to close for a few days. Saturday's party had to get pushed, and once again I'm in limbo."

As bad as he felt about it, Mike couldn't keep the grin off his face, and he punched the air in excitement.

Chapter 15

When Richard entered the diner the next day, he found Maggie up to her elbows in paperwork. He chuckled. "What's all this?"

Maggie looked up at him. Her eyes burned. She had been crunching numbers all morning, trying to figure out how much the business was worth, while at the same time trying to determine what she wanted to do. She had called the realtor and left a message. Waiting for that call back wasn't helping her nerves, either.

"The restaurant in a nutshell," she said, rubbing her eyes. "Trying to figure things out." She met his gaze again and handed him the letter from the realtor. "I got this yesterday after you left."

Richard skimmed the letter, then handed it back to Maggie. "You decide to sell after all?"

Maggie shrugged. "I haven't decided anything. But I realized that regardless of if I sell half to you or the whole thing to someone else, I need to know how much this place is worth." She gestured to the piles of paper around her. "Hence the mess." She sighed. "I should probably put it all in the computer."

"Might make things easier. For now, though, looks like you could use a breather. Have you had lunch?" Maggie shook her head. "Okay. Be back in a jiffy. Clear off space for a plate."

He came back a little while later with a bacon cheeseburger and a pile of fries.

Maggie flashed him a grateful smile. "Thanks, Richard."

"Any time." He returned the smile, then turned to greet a couple who had walked in.

Maggie watched him go, then picked up the burger. It tasted heavenly, cooked perfectly with a delicious combination of flavors. Richard had added a sauce of some kind. While she couldn't place it, the flavor complemented the smokiness of the bacon and the sharpness of the cheese in wonderful ways. He certainly knew his way around a kitchen.

It didn't take her long to clear the plate, and when she was done, Maggie leaned back in her chair, resting her hands on her very full belly. If that meal had been intended to sway her decision, it had done its job. But Richard wasn't like that. Truth was, she had been thinking about his offer nearly non-stop since he had made it. She had no doubt she could trust Richard, that he would be a fair and reliable partner. Her real decision was whether she wanted to break completely free of the diner or cling to it like a life raft. Was it too late for a fresh start, a new beginning?

Maggie's thoughts shifted to the young woman who had drifted through town, turning Mike's head. Addy. She was starting over. Of course she was much younger, but she had the courage to try something new. Could Maggie be that brave?

Maggie sighed. Numbers and burgers aside, she had a lot to think about before making her decision.

Addy felt like she was back to square one. Maybe worse. With the store being closed, Addy couldn't go to work, but she also had less of a reason to go out, since she didn't need to hunt for a job anymore.

Her conversation with Mike the previous evening had been a little awkward. Mike seemed animated, but she just hadn't been in the mood. She tried going to the poetry slam with Kate and her friends, but that hadn't been much better. So she moped, unsure how to fill her time.

After scrolling unsuccessfully through the offerings on Netflix, she decided what she needed was to *do* something. So Addy opened her laptop and started researching. Maybe she could prepare herself for her job even if she couldn't be at her job.

Addy first headed to Paintastic's website, to get a feel for the types of projects. She learned that Linda's store was actually a franchise. Maybe if they stayed closed for much longer she could travel to another location and learn there. Then again, the closest location was Pennsylvania. Road trip? Probably not in her dud of a car.

With that dead end, Addy moved on to YouTube. She hadn't done much painting in the past. She could certainly learn a thing or two.

After a half hour of watching other people paint, Addy was itching to give it a try. And that seemed like the perfect activity to fill her time. It was productive, creative, and would hopefully make her more confident when she could actually go back to work.

A couple of hours later, Addy felt like a regular Boston native, clutching a handle on the T with one hand, her other hand grasping a paper shopping bag. She couldn't afford to go too crazy, but she had picked up a couple of plain mugs, a plate, and just for fun, a pack of canvases, along with a starter set of paints and brushes. At the very least they would help her pass the time.

When she stepped back onto the sidewalk in her adopted neighborhood, she felt hopeful again. The air was crisp, more holiday decorations were sprouting up in nearby businesses, and she had a creative project to fill what remained of her day. Things were looking up again.

Mike was at loose ends. He was antsy at the shop, and he was driving the techs crazy with his incessant finger tapping. His mind was filled with Addy's voice sounding forlorn the night before. He felt powerless but at the same time was kicking himself for even caring. What difference did it make if she was happy or sad? She shouldn't even be in his life.

Mike was lost in thought when he felt Ben's hand slap on top of his.

"Man, you have got to stop the tapping," Ben said, releasing his hand to grab the ringing phone.

Mike sighed. He was no use to anyone today. Ben finished the call after making an appointment, then turned to his friend. "Go home, man. I don't know what's bugging you today, but just go home."

"But there's so much to do."

"As if you've even noticed. It's actually a light day."

"Okay, okay. I'll go." He grabbed his coat and slapped Ben on the back. "Thanks."

Mike climbed into his truck and started the engine. Now what? It wasn't as if he would be any better at home. With sudden inspiration, he turned off his truck and re-entered the shop. Ben looked up in surprise.

"Miss us already?"

"Actually, I was wondering if you could cover the shop tomorrow, too."

Usually when Richard helped out, Maggie would take the time to rest. That day, however, she felt rooted to her chair. She could hear the chatter of customers, the grill sizzling and fryer popping. This was her diner, and the sounds were just the soundtrack of her life. Would it be this way forever? If she stayed, even part-time, it would be. Maybe she needed that jolt that a new beginning would bring.

The phone ringing startled her from her reverie, and she answered casually but politely. The phone rang so infrequently she suspected she already knew who was on the other end.

"Hello, is this Ms. Devin?"

She was right. "Yes, this is Maggie."

"Hello, Ms. Devin. This is Rachel Connors returning your call."

"Yes, hello." Maggie's heart was pounding, and it was all she could do to carry on a slightly stilted conversation and schedule an appointment for the following week. When she hung up the phone less than ten minutes later, she was shaking. Was she really doing this? Would she – could she – leave behind everything she knew?

Though not quite a natural, Addy was pleased with her first mug. She was feeling festive, so she had opted for stars and snowflakes. She had started rinsing her brushes when she heard her cell phone ding. Drying her hands, she picked it up.

"Up for some company?" the text read.

Wait – what? Company? She didn't know anyone in Boston yet. Then it registered that the text was from Mike. Butterflies began flapping furiously in her belly. What exactly did he mean? He couldn't be in Boston, could he?

"Company?" she texted back. She began gnawing on a thumb nail as she waited for a response.

"Yeah. I happen to have a free weekend."

"And..."

"I thought I'd take a little road trip."

Addy swallowed. Was she reading too much into this? What was he looking for? Just to be safe: "My apartment's not that big. And I share it."

"Oh, geez. No. I would never... I planned on getting a hotel room. For me."

Addy's nerves settled slightly.

"But I thought it would be nice to see you. Only if you wanted, of course."

Did she want that? She liked Mike. A lot. But there was no future there. Would seeing him make it harder when they had to say good-bye? Dammit, though, she *wanted* to see him. What would her mother say? *If you hadn't started this ridiculous relationship, you wouldn't be in this position.*

Stupid, stupid, stupid. Mike kicked himself. What was he thinking? He had driven off, stopping home only to throw a few things in a duffel bag, then hopped on the highway. He had assumed she would be happy to hear from him, to see him. They talked every night, for crying out loud. But he should have known better.

After about an hour of driving, it had occurred to him that he didn't know where she lived. And Boston wasn't exactly small. He couldn't just surprise her as he had envisioned in his mind. So he had pulled into a rest area and sent that stupid text. From her reaction, he could only guess what she must think of him. Had she thought it was a booty call? Stupid.

Now he sat there, hands gripping his steering wheel as he waited for Addy's response. Did she want to see him?

"OK."

He whooped so loudly he startled the gulls near his truck in the parking lot. Forcing himself to calm down, he tapped out another message. "Great. Should be there in an hour or so. Where should I meet you?"

The cafe down the street was the closest thing Addy had to a hangout. It wasn't an ideal meeting place that night, what with the poetry slam still going on along with the regular Friday night crowd, but she didn't want to attempt to find another location and hope that it would be more suitable. So she sat at a table in the corner, where she hoped it wouldn't be too noisy, and kept her eye on the door.

It felt surreal to be sitting there. The place was starting to feel familiar, but she still felt like an outsider, a newcomer. She was starting to come out of her shell, starting to figure out what she wanted, but so much was still up in the air, uncertain and shaky. She felt such a connection with Mike, but they had met, what? Three times? He probably knew more about her than anyone else did, and yet she wasn't even sure she would recognize him. Maybe this had been a mistake.

When Mike arrived, Addy wasn't even looking up. She was watching the makeshift stage with unseeing eyes, lost in thought. Her phone dinged, and she looked down to find a text from Mike: "I'm here." She turned to the door, and their eyes met. He gave a little half wave, and Addy stood up. When he reached the table, there was an awkward shuffling of arms before they both gave a self-conscious laugh and hugged. For a moment they stood there, wrapped up in each other. Addy closed her eyes, breathing in Mike's scent – a distinct blend of aftershave and motor oil. When he released her, she felt chilled.

"How was the drive?" she asked after clearing her throat.

"Not too bad. A little busy as I approached Boston, but not as bad as I thought it would be."

"That's good." They fell into a somewhat awkward silence. "So," Addy began, trying to fill the air. "What brings you to Boston?"

He stared at her, and she couldn't move her eyes away. "There were some things I needed to say, and they couldn't be said over the phone."

Addy swallowed. What on earth could she say to that? "Oh yeah?"

"Yeah." And he kissed her.

Okay, he hadn't meant to do that. He wanted to. He had thought of little else the entire drive up. But he hadn't meant to do it like that. He just wanted Addy to know how he felt. He wanted to get rid of the doubts. She might be feeling in limbo about her job and settling in, but *he* shouldn't be something she felt unsure about. The whole "should we pursue this" thing that he had been wrestling with was ridiculous. He liked her. He was pretty sure she liked him. So why were they fighting it? But he had meant to say all that with words, not a kiss. But, man, what a kiss.

He was reluctant to pull away, and he could see she was a little dazed when he leaned back and gazed at her. "I have been wanting to do that since almost the first moment I met you," he said with a little smile. "And I know this is crazy. I know you're starting a new life here. But I think we should give this a chance. We should give *us* a chance."

"Mike, I --" Addy's voice trailed off, and she looked away.

The hollow feeling in the pit of Mike's stomach returned. After all this, was she saying no? Had he ruined it? Maybe it was a mistake to come after all. He didn't know what to say. So he sat there in silence, waiting for her to finish.

It took a minute, but eventually she turned to look at him. "The timing is horrible. You realize that, right?"

"I know. But I had no control over that."

Addy sighed and looked back toward the poetry slam. "Long distance relationships don't work."

From her tone it was hard to figure out if she was trying to convince him or herself. At least it wasn't a flat-out no. "Let's take the weekend," he said. "Spend time together, see what happens. If by Sunday we realize there's no future, I'll go and that will be that. But if we think it's worth it..."

Addy took a deep breath and turned to face him. "Okay," she said with a small smile. "We'll give it the weekend."

Chapter 16

After the dinner rush, Maggie tidied up her paperwork and decided to take it easy. It had been a long, stressful week, and she needed a break. It was Friday night, so she was bound to get her fair share of customers as people straggled in for pie or just a place to hang out, but it should be relatively low key. Long ago she had considered bringing in live music on occasion, or having some kind of activity to offer as entertainment to the town. But business had been decent, and it hadn't seemed worth the trouble. Now she kind of wished she had. It may have helped fill some of the lonely hours. Maggie sighed. No use dwelling on what might have been.

It was about eleven at night when Maggie decided to balance the drawer and settle in for the quiet hours. The ding of the register coincided with the bells on the door, and Maggie looked up to smile at a young man she had never seen before.

"Hello," she greeted. "Have a seat wherever you'd like. I'll be with you in a moment. Menus are behind the napkins." She smiled again, then looked down to remove the cash drawer.

The young man didn't move, and Maggie looked up again. He looked nervous, sweaty, despite the chill in the air outside. It took her a moment to register the knife in his hand. Oh, geez. Honestly, of all the nights.

"Give – give me your money," the young man stuttered.

"Sweetie, you don't want to do that. Besides, I've got bigger, sharper knives in my kitchen. How about you have a seat, and I'll make you something to eat, on the house."

The young man's eyes darted around. He seemed unsure how to react. This wasn't Maggie's first attempted robbery, though with a jolt she realized it might be her last. What a strange thing to feel nostalgic about.

After a moment, the young man straightened his back and tried to assert himself. "I – I said to give me your money."

Maggie sighed. "Honey, my giving you money won't solve your problems. Now why don't you have a seat, and we'll see if we can find a real solution."

The young man looked very much like the boy he still was. "I –. I –."

"Are you a burger man or a fried chicken man?"

He regained his composure enough to say softly, "burger, please, ma'am."

"There now. I'll go whip that up for you. Fries?"

The boy nodded.

"Be right back."

There was a peep-through window between the kitchen and counter, and Maggie watched the young man as she prepared his food. He had finally put the knife away, and Maggie took a deep breath. She wondered where he had come from. He was obviously troubled, but someone had taught him manners somewhere along the way, if that "ma'am" was any indication. What had driven him to try and rob her?

A few minutes later, she placed the steaming plate in front of him. "There we go."

"Thank you, ma'am."

Maggie turned to let him eat, but she glanced back when she heard him clear his throat.

"I – I'm sorry about before."

Maggie pulled up a stool and sat across from him at the counter. "Oh, that's all right. Not my first rodeo. I do wonder what drove you to it, though. What's your name, young man?"

"Jordan, ma'am. Jordan Williams."

"Well, it's nice to meet you, Jordan. I'm Maggie, so you can drop that whole 'ma'am' business. Makes me feel about ninety."

Jordan gave a small smile, then stuffed a few fries in his mouth.

"I'll let you eat, then we can chat." She filled a glass with water and placed it down beside his plate. "Can I get you a slice of apple pie for dessert? I've got one slice left."

Jordan's eyes widened, and he nodded eagerly.

Maggie smiled. "Okay, then. I'll be back." She retrieved the pie plate, dished up the last slice, and placed it by Jordan's plate. The burger and fries were nearly gone. "My, you must have been hungry."

"Yes, ma'am – Maggie." He took a long sip of water. "Thank you."

Maggie smiled and nodded, then picked up a rag and began wiping down the counters. She had cleaned up earlier, but she wanted to be nearby for Jordan, without hovering.

A few minutes passed in silence. When Maggie stopped hearing a fork clattering against a plate, she finally approached Jordan again.

"Alright, then," she said, clearing his plates. "Now that your belly is full and your nerves have settled a bit, why don't you tell me what brought you in today. I don't think I've seen you around town before."

Jordan shook his head. "No, I'm just passing through."

"Where you coming from?"

"Bridgeport area."

"That's a bit of a hike."

Jordan shrugged. "I've been going a little bit at a time."

"What brought you to Pine Valley?"

"Didn't have a particular destination in mind. Just started walking."

Maggie paused and examined Jordan for a moment. "Shouldn't you be in school?"

"Graduated in June. Turned eighteen in June, too. That's when I was let loose."

"Let loose?"

"I'm an orphan, Miss Maggie. I was in foster care. I'm eighteen now. Aged out."

Ah. The pieces were starting to come together now.

"The state gave me some money to get started, find a place and all that, but I didn't know what I was doing. Once the checks stopped coming, my last set of foster parents stopped caring about me. They weren't that great before that, either."

Maggie shook her head. This boy seemed like he could have turned out alright if given the chance.

"I found a place to live, but it was a rough neighborhood. Couldn't find a job nearby, so the money went fast. Landlord wasn't exactly sympathetic. So I started walking. Hoped I'd find something better, but not many options when you're broke and living on the streets."

"Well, Jordan, it may not have been your destination, but I'm glad you ended up here."

Jordan looked skeptical.

"Truly. Because now that you're here, we can get you where you're meant to be. I don't mean that literally, of course, more like where you should be in life, that is." Geesh. She was blubbering on, making no sense. This is what she got for trying to be philosophical. "Now, are you a hard worker?"

Jordan stood up, surprised hope showing on his face. "Yes, ma'am."

"Okay. Then I think we can work something out."

Chapter 17

Though the air grew colder as the sun dipped below the horizon, Addy and Mike had decided to take a walk. Addy had introduced Mike to her new neighborhood, shown him where she worked, and which apartment building was hers. They had eaten dinner at an Italian restaurant a block over, and Mike had enjoyed spending time with her, being able to see and touch her, not just hear her voice.

They had plans to sightsee the following day, and as Mike paced in his hotel room, he knew he should be getting some sleep. But he felt wound up, unable to let his body relax. Though he had spent the last few hours with Addy, the real Addy, he felt like something was missing. With a start he realized he missed "phone Addy." He was so used to talking or texting with her every night that the absence of that contact felt strange. Mike laughed at the absurdity. But that didn't stop him from grabbing his phone to text Addy.

They spent a few minutes chatting via text before Mike felt settled enough to sleep. Wishing her good night, he climbed into bed, calling himself an idiot but with a smile on his face.

The next morning dawned clear and cold. Addy was tempted to stay curled up in her covers. But then she remembered what the day would bring, and a smile spread across her face. She hadn't felt this way about someone in so long, maybe ever. Mike was so different from the men she socialized with in D.C., so real. But, as happy as she was to be spending the weekend with him, she knew it would be that much harder to say good-bye on Sunday. Was that why she felt so attracted to him, though? Because when it came down to it, he wasn't really a long-term option?

Addy's smile faded, but she forced herself to stay positive. At the very least they could have a nice weekend. *A nice weekend does not a relationship make, Adelaide. Stop wasting your time.*

Addy pulled herself out of bed and made her way to the bathroom. She stood for a minute, staring at her reflection in the mirror over the sink. Why did she look so lost? And what was she going to do about it?

A few hours later, Mike and Addy were strolling through Quincy Market hand in hand when Addy fell quiet. Their morning had passed quickly but pleasantly, filled with light banter and easy companionship. But sometime over the last hour or so Mike had noticed a shift. Addy was pulling away again. He just wished he knew why.

"Addy, is everything okay?"

She looked up at him, her piercing eyes meeting his gaze. "Of course. Why?"

"No reason." Mike was reluctant to destroy their fragile relationship. After a few more minutes, though, he couldn't help it. "This isn't working, is it?"

Addy remained silent for a minute, then sighed. "I'm sorry, Mike."

"It's okay."

"It's just –. I left D.C. for a reason, you know?" Mike nodded. "I wanted a fresh start, to discover who I am and what I want. I have a real shot here."

"I know."

"Part of it *was* finding someone who wanted to know the real me, but when I thought about it, I realized that *I* didn't even know the real me. And – well, if I let myself get...sidetracked...then I'm not in any better shape. Do you understand?"

It was Mike's turn to sigh. "I get it, Addy, I do. It's always been bad timing with us. I'm sorry. I shouldn't have pushed the issue. I seem to keep doing that."

"I'm sorry, Mike. I know it sounds cliche, but it's really not you."

"I know."

They strolled on in silence for a bit, but they were no longer holding hands.

"I appreciate you showing me around, Addy. And I really wish you the best. I hope you find what you're looking for."

When Addy got back to her apartment, she headed straight to her bedroom. She had barely closed the door when she burst into tears. What was she doing?

Addy collapsed onto her mattress and lay down, rolling onto her belly. Part of her was calling herself an idiot, kicking herself for letting a good man go. The other, more rational, part was telling her she had done the right thing. She needed to stop identifying herself in terms of who she was to other people. She needed to be Addy. Just Addy. And she needed to figure out who that was.

She rolled onto her back and stared at the ceiling, wiping her eyes and sniffling. She was in a rut. And she needed to break out.

Taking a deep breath, Addy sat up and then scrounged for a piece of paper. It was time to come up with some concrete goals. She needed a real plan here, not a day-by-day series of events. How could she tell if she was really making progress if she didn't know what she was supposedly progressing toward? And how could she tell if supposed setbacks were really setbacks?

What did she really want?

Looking around, Addy realized she needed some real furniture. As long as she was sleeping on an air mattress, using a cardboard box as a nightstand, life would feel temporary, in limbo.

She needed to actually start her job and give it a chance. She had been excited before the pipe bursting incident. There was real potential there, especially since she had learned she enjoyed painting.

She needed to socialize more – and not just with Kate. While she appreciated Kate's willingness to include her, Addy needed her own friends, too. That meant breaking out of the shell she had built and going out to meet people. While she was at it, maybe she could pick up some hobbies. Local classes would be a great way to meet people and try out some different activities.

Putting her pen down, Addy took a look at her list. This was good. She would be putting down roots and discovering herself at the same time. This was what leaving D.C. had been all about.

Mike kicked himself the entire drive back to Pine Valley. He had pushed too hard – again – and now he had lost her.

By the time he crossed the border back into Connecticut, however, Mike had acknowledged – if not quite accepted – that he and Addy just weren't meant to be. She was starting a new life, while he had an established life in Pine Valley – a life he loved. The only downside to working and living in the same small town you grew up in was the limited dating pool. Maybe that was why he had fallen so hard for Addy. She was really the first new woman he had met in a while who even came close to what he was looking for. But that didn't mean she was the woman for him.

As he neared home, Mike found himself grateful for one thing, at least. Meeting Addy had shed light on what was missing in his life. He wanted someone to love. He wanted companionship and that feeling of closeness that came with being in a relationship. And if Addy wasn't the one, and he wasn't going to naturally meet someone in his daily life, then he needed to broaden his horizons.

Pulling into his driveway, Mike took a deep breath and then gulped. It was time to enter the world of online dating.

Chapter 18

Maggie wondered what the day would bring. The night before had certainly not gone as expected, but she was satisfied with the plan she and Jordan had agreed to. Now she had to see if he would hold up his end of the bargain.

After a quick call to Ed and Sylvie, she had arranged to pay for a week's stay for Jordan at the motel, with the understanding that he would spend time each day working in the diner. He would gain some valuable work experience, she would get a feel for his work ethic, and then they would see what they could work out for him on a more permanent basis. With the future of the diner unclear, she couldn't promise him a job moving forward, but surely they could find something else in town for him. And the motel was inexpensive enough that Jordan could stay there for at least a little while as he got on his feet.

It had seemed like a perfect plan the night before, but she wondered if Jordan would have second thoughts in the morning light.

They had agreed on a ten o'clock start time. The diner would still be busy, but the big rush would have mostly ended by then, and she would have more time to show him the ropes before lunch. As the hours ticked by, however, Maggie found herself growing anxious. What if he didn't show up?

When Jordan walked through the door, looking nervous, he was ten minutes early. Maggie smiled at him and took a deep breath. Off to a good start. She finished taking the order at her current table, then moved to greet him. He was standing by the register.

"Good morning, Jordan. Did you sleep well?"

"Yes, Miss Maggie. Shower felt nice, too."

"I'm glad to hear it." Maggie took in his appearance. His hair was neat and freshly washed. His clothes were relatively clean but wrinkled. They would have to get him sorted with the laundromat. But he would be okay for today. "Let's bring your coat to the backroom, and I'll give you the grand tour." Maggie delivered her table's order to the kitchen, then showed Jordan around. An hour later he was busy clearing and wiping tables. Maggie was pleased with how eagerly he had jumped into the work. She only hoped it would last.

By the time the afternoon rolled around, Maggie was pleased that her instincts about Jordan had been correct. He had proven himself to be a fast learner and hard worker. He was even great with the customers, friendly and polite.

They hadn't set a time for his first shift to end, but when Maggie asked him, Jordan seemed happy to stay however long she needed or wanted him there. As he pointed out, he didn't really have anything better to do. So they spent the quieter mid-afternoon hours training and talking. Though Maggie was used to high school and college students – having employed many over the years – she found Jordan to be different, seemingly older now that the unpleasantness of the night before was behind them. He was determined, focused. He seemed to appreciate the opportunity that this was, to turn his life around. And she found herself energized, taking him under her wing and teaching him how to be a good employee.

Life worked in mysterious ways, Maggie mused. If Jordan had walked into a different business, he could be sitting in jail right now. If his mother hadn't died, he could be preparing for college. And if he hadn't walked in last night, what would Maggie be doing?

With a jolt, Maggie remembered the meeting scheduled for Tuesday. She was supposed to be preparing, getting paperwork in order, trying to decide what she wanted to do.

What *did* she want to do?

While she wanted to get Jordan headed in the right direction, nothing else had really changed. She still longed to see the world beyond Pine Valley, see what else she was capable of. And to do that, she couldn't remain chained to the diner. Could she?

Addy was feeling positive as she walked to work Monday morning. The pipe was still getting repaired, but Linda had told Addy that while the plumbers were working on it, Addy could be learning the ropes. And there was still the mess with the inventory to take care of. It was sure to be an interesting, productive day. Addy was looking forward to it.

The work crew was not exactly neat, but for the most part they stayed to themselves in the back of the shop. That left the front of the store available for Linda and Addy. And, since the construction meant no customers, they had plenty of space and plenty of time.

The morning passed by quickly. Going through the inventory meant Addy was getting plenty of experience handling the merchandise and supplies and learning what was what. Linda had decided to take the opportunity to clean and organize the stock, and she seemed pleased with Addy's suggestions.

After lunch, they went over the party planning materials. Linda showed Addy the format, the existing contracts, and the paperwork that detailed the clients' options. Then Linda decided that Addy needed some hands-on experience, so they broke out the paints and each selected a figurine to paint. Addy figured her chosen owl's wisdom would help guide her on her path.

They spent the next hour chatting and painting before setting their items aside to dry. Tomorrow Addy would learn how to use the kiln, to complete her owl and make him shine.

Addy had enjoyed her day – even the paperwork bits – and she found herself smiling on the way home. That night she was going to scope out furniture stores in the area and look into some classes. Things were looking up.

Mike wasn't feeling so optimistic. Finding a decent site to try had seemed easy enough, but so far he hadn't felt drawn to any of the women he had seen online. Some were obviously only looking for sex. Some just weren't his type. And some were definitely high maintenance, which was not his style. He had reached out to a few to test the waters, but he didn't have high hopes.

He was pleasantly surprised when he turned on his computer Monday evening to find three messages waiting for him. After popping a TV dinner into the microwave, he settled into his desk chair to read through them.

All three women seemed nice enough. Two had been responding to his initial contact, and he continued the conversation with brief responses. The third message was from a newcomer named Sarah, and Mike took a few minutes to check out her profile before replying. Lived in a small town, ready to settle down. So far, so good. She was attractive. Not a knock-out, but pleasant. She looked sweet, friendly. Mike responded to her message, retrieved his dinner, then returned to the desk, surprised to have already heard back. Apparently Sarah was online.

All right, thought Mike. *Let's see how this goes.*

The site had a chat feature, so they moved to that rather than exchange email-style messages. Once the initial awkwardness passed, Mike found that the conversation flowed naturally. He was surprised when he glanced at the clock and found an hour had passed. And he hadn't even thought of Addy at all. Okay, maybe once. But overall he was enjoying the time chatting with Sarah.

Mike moved his laptop over to the sofa, grabbed a beer from the fridge, then settled in to keep chatting. Maybe this online dating thing wouldn't be so bad after all.

Richard had brought his family to the diner for dinner Sunday night and had seemed surprised to see a new face among the staff. Maggie had assured him she would fill him in on all the details when he came in on Monday.

He was scheduled to help with the dinner rush, and when he strolled in a half hour early, he found Maggie and Jordan reviewing the menu. Maggie looked up to meet his gaze, then turned to Jordan.

"Jordan, why don't you go roll up some more silverware sets? We'll need them for tonight."

"Sure thing, Miss Maggie."

Richard and Jordan exchanged nods in greeting, then Jordan moved into the back room, and Maggie gestured for Richard to have a seat on the stool next to her.

"Surprised to see you hire someone new with everything up in the air."

Maggie sighed. "Oh, Richard, you don't know the half of it." Maggie wasn't sure how he would take it, but she filled him in on the activities of Friday night. At first, she was taken aback at Richard's strong reaction to a new hire. He acted as if he already owned the place. But he was a kind man, and open-minded. And as she told her story, his eyes widened, then softened in sympathy. She decided he was likely just looking out for her.

"So what's the plan?" he asked when she was done.

"I don't know. We've been taking it day by day. He's paid up at the motel until the end of the week."

"Does he know about the business?"

"No. Heck, I don't even know what's going on with the business."

"Meeting tomorrow?"

"Yeah, and I'm not nearly ready. I had planned on tackling paperwork this weekend when I had extra coverage, and that didn't work out."

Richard sighed. "Okay. I'll work with Jordan a bit, keep an eye on him and keep the place running, and you go do what you need to do."

Maggie smiled. "Thanks, Richard. You're a good man."

Maggie entered the kitchen and was just passing Jordan to head to her office when Jordan stopped her.

"Uh, Miss Maggie?"

She turned to face him. "Yes, Jordan?"

"I didn't mean to eavesdrop or anything, but I couldn't help hearing what you and Mr. Richard were talking about."

"Oh, Jordan, I'm sorry. He's a manager here, and I thought he should know what was going on. I hope I didn't invade your privacy."

"Oh, no, Miss Maggie, that part's fine. I got nothing to hide. I was just wondering about what he said, about the business."

"Oh." Maggie took a deep breath. How could she explain when she didn't even know what was going to happen?"

"I'm sorry. It's none of my business." He turned his attention to the silverware rolls he had been working on.

"No, Jordan, it's okay. It's just – well, to be honest, I don't know what's going to happen."

"Okay."

Maggie rested a hand on one of Jordan's arms. When he looked up at her, she sighed. "You are a young man, full of potential. But I am not a young woman. And I have been running this place for a long, long time. It hit me that I am not getting any younger, and I want to see what else is out there, what the world has to offer. So I'm exploring my possibilities, as they say."

"Are you closing the diner?"

"I don't think it would come to that. I have someone interested in buying it, and Richard has offered to be my partner. So I'm looking into those options right now."

"Okay. So I should be extra nice to Mr. Richard in case he becomes my new boss?" He flashed her a grin, and Maggie laughed.

"Yeah, that wouldn't hurt. But be your charming self, and I'm sure you'll be fine."

As Maggie closed the door to her back office, she couldn't help but wonder what would happen to Jordan if she sold the diner. Would the new owners keep him on? Would they keep any of her staff on? It was something to add to her list of questions for the meeting tomorrow. Maggie took a deep breath. She was not looking forward to it.

Chapter 19

Tuesday dawned clear and cold, and Mike's eyes burned. He had stayed up way too late talking to Sarah. That was a good sign, he thought. At least for the relationship. How he was going to make it through the day was another story. He stifled a yawn and opened the door of his shop.

The pungent scent of rubber greeted him, and Mike groaned. He had planned on setting up a snow tire display today, and he had had the guys bring some of the inventory into the lobby. He did not have the energy to move tires today, but he couldn't really leave them as they were, either. It was going to be a long day.

Two of his techs arrived as he hung up his coat and put his lunch in the fridge. They went over the schedule for the day, then the techs went into the garage to get started while Mike turned the phone to day mode and organized some paperwork.

Snippets of his conversation with Sarah came to mind, and, tired as he was, Mike couldn't hold back a smile. They had made tentative plans to meet on Friday, but they were set to chat again that night. He just had to make sure they said good night a bit earlier.

With a sigh Mike looked back at the stack of tires. He might as well just get it over with.

Addy practically skipped to work. The cold air bit at her face, but she was oblivious. Her mind was preoccupied with everything she had found online the night before. She had bounced back and forth between furniture shopping and looking for extracurricular classes, and the options had seemed endless. She had bookmarked her favorites. Her task that night would be to figure out how far away each one was, so she could determine her best options. For now, though, she pushed herself to focus on the day ahead.

There was a good chance the repair work would be done and they could actually open to customers. Addy was a little nervous, but she was excited, too. This would be a new experience, but she used to be a people person. Surely she had it in her to work with the public.

Linda greeted her with a smile. "Looks like we can open the doors today."

"That's great!" Addy replied.

"Let me show you how to open up and get the drawer ready. The cold will probably keep most people away, but you never know."

Linda showed Addy how to prepare the cash drawer and set up the tables for customers. It wasn't long before they flipped the open sign. Addy took a deep breath.

"Okay, all set. When will we fire up the kiln to finish our figurines?"

"Probably tonight," Linda said. "Let's see what comes in today first. The kiln will hold a lot, and it uses a ton of energy, so I try to get it as full as possible before running it."

"Okay. So what do we do while we wait for customers?" Addy was feeling far too anxious to just sit around waiting.

"Well, I wanted to go over some more stuff with you. I'd like to get fresh eyes on a few marketing ideas I had, and see if we can brainstorm a few more. I also have to place an inventory order to replace items that were damaged with the pipe bursting, and some other items that were low. During the days, when it's quiet, I try to take care of the day-to-day business matters so in the late afternoon and evening, when it's busier, I can focus on the customers."

"Makes sense."

They spent the next hour working on ideas to drum up business. They didn't see a single customer.

"Is it always this slow?" Addy asked.

"Sometimes. I'd like to find ways to bring in more business during the day, but that remains the most challenging time period. I've tried a few things, but so far nothing has panned out."

Addy thought for a moment. "What about something for businesses? Like team building? My roommate mentioned that she had done something like that here with her work. Could we do more of that?"

"We could probably expand on that, maybe travel to different locations." Linda grabbed a pad of paper and jotted down some notes.

"That could work. Not sure how reliable my car is, though."

Linda brushed aside her concerns with a wave of her hand. "Logistics come later. Best to get a bunch of ideas down first, then look into the feasibility of each."

"Okay." Addy paused for a moment, thinking. "Well, if we're going mobile, you could do schools and stuff, too. Like a traveling field trip."

"Kids would love it, I'm sure, but schools would likely want some kind of education component. Not sure how we'd handle that."

"Hmm. What can we teach them that ties in to what we do?"

Linda laughed. "I am no teacher, but I'll jot down the idea. We could probably incorporate color and creative expression and all that."

"I'll do some research tonight," Addy said with a grin.

"I love the enthusiasm."

They continued to brainstorm, even through lunch. Addy found herself enjoying coming up with ideas, tapping into a creative side of herself she hadn't known existed. And Linda seemed happy with many of her suggestions, even getting excited about a couple of them.

A few customers trickled in during the afternoon, and Addy found she enjoyed helping them, too. Finding just the right piece to paint wasn't easy, especially when it was going to be a gift, as was the case with two of the day's patrons. Addy enjoyed digging a bit to pinpoint a special detail or memory. At one point Addy caught Linda's eye, and they shared a smile.

During an afternoon lull, Linda met up with Addy as Addy was tidying up a paint station. "You have a real knack for this," she said, helping Addy put brushes and paints away.

"Thanks. I'm enjoying it."

"You sure you've never done anything like this before?"

Addy laughed. "The closest I've probably been was fingerpainting in kindergarten."

"I meant working with others, customer service, that sort of thing."

"Not really. Some receptionist work."

"Let me guess: too boring."

Addy nodded. "Yeah. I only stuck with it as long as I did to please my mother. She was convinced it would help me land a lawyer as a husband." Addy rolled her eyes, and Linda laughed.

"Okay, then!"

Tables clear, they sat together again at the back counter. "Now," said Linda, "let's see what we can do to increase party numbers."

Addy rubbed her hands together, eager to let the creative juices flow again.

Maggie glanced at the clock for the fifteenth time in the last twenty minutes. The potential buyer was scheduled to arrive soon, and Maggie had butterflies in her stomach. She reached for a cleaning cloth, but Richard grabbed it before she could.

"You have wiped the counters about fifty times already. You're going to wear down the surface." He took Maggie by the shoulders and turned her to face him. "Look, I know you're nervous. It's perfectly understandable. But try to remember that you are in control here. You don't have to sell if you don't want to, but if you like the offer, you can take it. The choice is yours."

Maggie looked up to meet his gaze. "But what if I make the wrong choice?" she asked softly.

"That's life, Maggie. It's always a chance. But that's how we learn and grow. And we're not talking life or death here. You sell and regret it, you find something else. You don't take the offer, there will be other opportunities."

Maggie took a deep breath and attempted a smile. "You make it sound so easy."

Richard chuckled. "I know it's not easy. But no matter what you decide, you will survive. And the experience will make you stronger."

The bells over the door jingled, and Maggie closed her eyes, taking a deep breath. It was time.

Chapter 20

"**G**ood morning," the well-groomed woman greeted with a smile. She stuck out her hand. "You must be Ms. Devin. I'm Rachel Connors."

"Yes. Good morning, Ms. Connors," Maggie replied, clasping the woman's hand. "Welcome." She turned toward Richard. "This is Richard Kelley, a friend and manager here." Richard and the woman shook hands.

"A pleasure to meet you both."

"Please, come into my office." Maggie led the woman through the kitchen into the back office. The room felt tiny with the other woman there. Maggie's eyes flitted over the stacks of paperwork, the well-worn desk, and peeling wallpaper. She had thought long and hard about her asking price, and in a flash she was convinced she was asking too much. She gestured toward the vacant chair in front of the desk and took a seat in her sagging office chair.

"I'd like to cut to the chase," Ms. Connors said. "While I would love to tour the facilities and get all the details and numbers, I am prepared to make an offer today."

Maggie was taken aback. She swallowed hard.

"Pine Valley looks like a charming town, with a great location in the state. My bosses are eager to make it happen."

Maggie cleared her throat. "And who are your bosses? You were a little unclear in your letter and on the phone."

The woman smiled. "I work for a chain of restaurants that have a diner feel, like this one. They are looking to expand into New England, and this location looks like a great place to start."

"A chain?" Maggie wasn't sure how Pine Valley would react to that. Residents tended to love their small-town charm.

The woman nodded and smiled again. "Rest assured the company is used to small towns. They love that sense of community."

Maggie took a deep breath.

"I understand this is a lot to process. Why don't you give me a tour of the property, and we can go from there?"

Maggie felt inadequate. Richard had said she was in control, but she didn't feel like it. She felt like she'd been hit by a train. But she smiled and stood up. "Of course."

They walked around the building, inside and out. Rachel Connors kept making notes on a legal pad she had brought with her. Maggie tried to see the building through an outsider's eyes. She had tried to maintain the property, but there were always things that needed to be done. She tried to sneak a peek at the other woman's notes but couldn't get close enough.

After reviewing the restaurant and grounds, Maggie headed toward her apartment at the back. "I'm not sure what you could do with this. It's an apartment. Maybe a perk for the manager?"

They walked over the threshold, and the other woman's eyes lit up. "Oh, I love this space. It's so open!" She took a look around. "It would make a great party room." Another note on her pad.

Maggie was startled. Party room? The community could definitely use more social space, but that had never even crossed her mind. But where would she live? After a moment Maggie remembered that she wouldn't be here.

Following the tour, the two women returned to the office.

"Would you like to see the numbers?" Maggie asked. She had worked hard on this part, plugging everything into a spreadsheet. If nothing else it had shown how little she had taken from the business. A little tucked into savings for a rainy day, but otherwise everything had gone back into the diner.

The woman accepted the folder and perused the printouts. "All as I expected," she said after a moment. "Some profit, potential for growth." After another minute she closed the folder and smiled. "As I said, I am prepared to make an offer today." She opened her briefcase and removed a sheet of paper, then handed it to Maggie.

Maggie looked over the paper, her eyes widening at the offered amount. It was much higher than she had ever dreamed. The woman noticed and smiled again.

"My bosses are very excited about the property."

"I guess so." Maggie cleared her throat. The offer was amazing. But this was all moving a bit too quickly for her comfort. "I – I'll need some time to decide, though."

"No problem," Ms. Connors said, then she stood. "Give it some thought and let me know. Shall we say the end of the week?"

Maggie could only nod, staring at the paper. After a moment she blinked and stood up, placing the paper on her desk. "Yes, that should be fine. Thank you so much for coming in today."

"My pleasure."

As Maggie walked the woman to the front of the diner, her gaze locked with Richard's. She gave him a wide-eyed look that told him they had much to discuss. She had a big decision to make.

When Rachel Connors left, Maggie showed Richard the offer. His eyes widened, as she had expected.

"I can't match even half of this, Maggie," he said, a note of regret in his voice.

"I wouldn't ask you to," Maggie replied.

Before they could discuss the matter further, lunch customers started arriving, and they were swept into greeting and serving.

When the lunch crowd dissipated, Maggie asked Jordan and another teen to watch the dining room, then asked Richard to join her in the office. They both sat down, and Maggie sighed.

"You don't seem happy for someone who just got the opportunity to pursue her dreams," Richard said as he settled into his seat.

Maggie met his gaze. "Is it my dream, though, Richard? I look around this old diner and can't help but wonder if I'll be walking around with a big hole in my life if I let it go."

There was a small window behind Maggie's desk, and Richard's gaze drifted to look outside. "I think any change will be a big adjustment. Have you given any more thought to what you would do?"

Maggie sighed again. "I feel like all I do is think, but I'm not getting any closer to deciding."

"I see. Well, if you do decide to sell, will you sell to Ms. Connors? It's an amazing offer."

"It is. But I have my concerns."

"Like what?"

"It's a chain, Richard."

"A chain?"

"Ms. Connors represents a chain of restaurants that wants to expand. I'm not sure how Pine Valley would react."

"That would definitely shake things up."

"And I don't know. It was really just a gut feeling, but I feel like there was something she wasn't telling me."

"Like what?"

"I don't know. She seemed to like the place, but maybe they just want to knock the whole thing down or something."

"I doubt that. I suppose you never know, though."

"She did say one thing that was interesting though. She envisioned my apartment as a party room."

"Really? Hmm. Not a bad idea."

"That's what I thought. But where would I live?"

They sat in silence for a bit.

"Do you think," Richard said after a minute, "that that is part of the problem?"

"What is? That I live in the apartment?"

"Hear me out for a minute. Most of the time, when someone owns a business, they have the business, and they have home." Richard gestured to indicate two separate sections on the desk. "They have set business hours, and when those hours have passed, they go home."

"But I'm here twenty-four seven."

"Exactly. Maybe the problem isn't that you've owned this diner for so long. Maybe the problem is that it's been your whole life for so long."

Maggie took a deep breath. She knew there was truth in Richard's words. It was also likely the reason that selling made her panic whenever she thought about it too long. "You're probably right."

"Want my two cents?"

"Please."

"Hold off on selling. This opportunity doesn't feel right to you, regardless of the money. Then, move out. Find a place to live that isn't the back of your diner. Give yourself an actual schedule instead of living on cat naps. If you're still feeling stifled, or you figure out that you just don't have the passion for it anymore, then put it up for sale again. But wean yourself off, instead of quitting cold turkey."

Maggie processed Richard's words. He had become such an asset to her, and such a very good friend. "Thank you, Richard," she said after a moment. "You've given me a lot to think about." After another moment she added, "if I do step back, are you willing to work more hours? Even if I don't sell you half the business?"

Richard grinned. "I'd be happy to."

Chapter 21

Addy wasn't used to long work days, but she found that by the time she was on her way home she was still invigorated, filled with ideas she wanted to look into further. She decided to swing by the cafe to grab dinner before heading home. She was glad she had; by the time she entered her apartment her adrenaline had evaporated, and she was ready to crash. It was all she could do to eat her container of soup before getting ready for bed. It was barely eight o'clock.

Despite her exhaustion, Addy had trouble falling asleep. Her brain was whirring with ideas and random thoughts. It was when her mind veered back to her car and its unreliability for mobile events that she thought of Mike.

She hadn't thought of him all day. And since she had decided to focus on her goals, he actually hadn't crossed her mind more than a handful of times. She knew that she had made the right decision. She only hoped he was okay, that he was moving forward as she was. She had never wanted to hurt him.

Glancing at her nightstand, Addy toyed with the idea of sending him a text. Just to check in. With a sigh, though, she realized that was probably a bad idea. No sense in stirring up the waters. So she reached for a pad of paper, instead, and jotted down the ideas that had been floating around in her mind. Maybe then she could get some sleep.

As she wrote down her thoughts, she remembered that she was going to look more into furniture and classes tonight, too. Addy sighed. Should she get up and turn on the computer? Nah. She wouldn't be in the right frame of mind to make good decisions. Best to leave it for the morning. She didn't have to be at work until the afternoon, so she would have plenty of time.

Addy smiled. Her plan was working. Instead of wandering aimlessly through the days, she had a to do list. She was busy! And best of all, she felt she was being productive, moving forward in her goals and being valued for her ideas. With a sigh Addy turned off her lamp and settled into her blankets to sleep.

Mike yawned as he opened his front door after work. He was amazed he had survived the day. He couldn't believe he used to live – and thrive – on a handful of hours of sleep a night. Between the late night and the busy day, he was ready to pass out. He kicked the door closed and tossed his keys on the table in his entryway, then entered his kitchen to heat up a can of soup.

A few minutes later he had the bowl cradled in his hands as he sat on the couch, his laptop on the coffee table in front of him. Sarah wasn't online yet, but it was just as well. It would give him time to eat first.

A half hour later he was sound asleep.

Around midnight, Mike woke up, groggy. It took him a moment to orient himself, and when he did, he groaned. Sarah.

He woke up his laptop to see if she had left him a message. What he found woke him up fast.

It started with a simple "Hey! How was your day?" But when he didn't reply, the friendliness quickly dissipated. By the time he finished reading some thirty or so messages later she had gotten downright hostile. "Geesh," he thought aloud as he closed his laptop. "I think I dodged a bullet with that one." And he went to bed.

The next morning, he reread the messages just to make sure he hadn't been dreaming or jumping to conclusions in his half-asleep state. Nope. She was still crazy. This morning, though, he could laugh about it.

When he got to the shop he decided to share the story with his friend Ryan, who was also one of the techs at the shop. After a low whistle, Ryan switched gears. "Man, I didn't know you were online dating. You looking to hook up or settle down? 'Cause I might have a girl for you."

"Oh, no, no, no. I am not going with another one of your setups. Remember the last time?"

"Oh, yeah. Trish was crazy." Ryan laughed. "This one's different, though. Sweet. She's my cousin. Just graduated law school, and she needs a social life. Her nose has been buried in books for too long."

"I don't think so, Ry. Thanks anyway."

"Well if you change your mind, you know where to find me. I'm sure she'd love to meet you."

Feeling more awake that day wasn't necessarily a good thing. While he was able to laugh about the experience with Sarah, Mike began to worry about his ability to judge people. He had truly thought Sarah had potential, that she had been sweet and sincere. It didn't give him much hope for his next online encounter. Was he really desperate enough for another one of Ryan's blind dates, though?

Operating mostly on instinct and routine, Mike spent the day turning his options around in his mind as he went about his business. By the time he closed up the shop for the night, he had decided to give the online thing one more chance. He couldn't let one bad experience ruin what might be his best opportunity to find someone.

Decision made, he decided to reward himself with takeout from the diner.

He was greeted by a young man he didn't recognize. When Mike said he wanted to place an order to go, the young man's face registered brief confusion, then he held up one hand.

"Hold on one moment, please. I've never done that before." He flashed Mike a grin, then went to the counter to get Maggie. Must be a new hire, though with the current "for sale" status, Mike was surprised. Maybe the increased traffic he'd noticed had meant Maggie needed more staff. Good. He was glad for her.

Maggie looked up, greeted Mike with a smile and a wave, and beckoned him over.

"Hi, there, Mike. Have you met Jordan?"

"Not yet, no." Mike smiled at the young man and held out a hand to shake. Jordan took it with a firm grasp and smiled back. "Nice to meet you."

"Jordan's still learning the ropes, so I'm just gonna walk him through a takeout order."

"No problem."

Ten minutes later, Mike was on his way home, the scent of his open-faced turkey sandwich making his mouth water. He was going to settle on his sofa, log on to the dating site, and see where the evening took him. And if the dating ended up being a dud, at least he would go to bed with a full stomach knowing he had tried.

By the time he decided to call it a night, Mike had replied to a few messages and sent a couple of his own. Tomorrow was another day, and he had a good feeling about it.

If nothing else, preparing the diner to sell had encouraged Maggie to organize her paperwork and take a good long look at her finances. And she had learned that while the diner was making a profit and she had been able to pay her employees and her bills without a problem, she herself was getting the short end of the stick. If she followed Richard's advice and found another place to live, how would she afford it? She had never taken a real salary, and she wasn't sure she could afford to do so now, especially with Richard and Jordan added to the payroll. But if she had been able to add them with very little difficulty, surely that meant she could afford to pay herself. Didn't it? Or had she used up any extra income on her new hires?

With her thoughts taking over her mind, and a very quiet evening ahead thanks to a cold front that had moved in, Maggie decided to pull out the finance binder she had prepared for Ms. Connors. There had to be something she could do.

Though she had never loved math, her years in business had honed the skills she possessed, and Maggie was able to see areas where she could make some adjustments, tighten her belt, and scrounge up a bit to pay herself. It was a start, anyway. And if she moved out and turned her apartment into a party space, that could bring in extra, too, though she would need somewhere to live while she worked on getting that off the ground.

You could always sell half to Richard, Maggie told herself. *That would give you plenty to tide yourself over.* But if she did that, there would be no turning back. And moving out was supposed to be a baby step, to see what more permanent change she wanted to make.

So what did she want to do?

Well, between what she had set aside in her personal account and what she had just determined she could afford to pay herself, she would likely be able to cover the cost of an apartment for at least a few months. Would that be enough time to decide what she wanted? Maybe. It would probably be enough time to at least convert her apartment into a party space. And that would provide more income, which meant more time to decide.

As Maggie thought this all through, her heart began to race. Was she really going to do this? She closed her eyes and took a deep breath. She wanted a change. She wanted to break the cycle. Yes, she was going to do this.

Before she lost her nerve, Maggie grabbed her coat and bundled up. She hadn't seen anyone in over an hour. She wasn't likely to see anyone in the next thirty minutes. Locking the diner door behind her, she stepped out into the cold night. Maggie breathed in the frigid air. When was the last time she had locked that door? Living in the attached apartment meant she had opened on holidays, in bad weather, and every day of the year in between. Already she was shaking things up.

She felt like a newborn, seeing the world for the first time. As she soaked in the sights of the town she had loved for so long, she sniffed. Even if she decided to sell, she didn't think she could move out of town. This was her home, had been her entire life. Which meant that no matter what she decided to do about the diner, moving out was the right choice.

Turning to walk past the playground, school, and library, Maggie explored the buildings around the town center. She knew that many of the shops and offices had apartments on the second floor. Would any be available to rent?

The cold air froze her cheeks, but Maggie felt invigorated. Baby step or not, she felt like a whole new woman.

Chapter 22

Addy woke to sunshine on her face. Rolling over, she glanced at her clock. It was just shy of nine. She had to be at work for noon. Factor in an hour or so to get ready for the day, and she still had time to tackle some online research. Addy stretched, then headed to the bathroom before starting the coffee maker and booting up her computer. Kate was likely already at work, so Addy had the place to herself. She got settled at the kitchen table and grabbed an apple from the fruit bowl. Hmm. Last one. She would have to find time to go grocery shopping, too.

Settling into her seat, Addy opened her internet browser. Which should she start with – furniture or classes? Glancing over her shoulder at her pitiful bedroom, Addy decided to start with furniture. She pulled up the first of the stores she had bookmarked, but as she started browsing, she groaned. She had set aside some of her savings for furniture and other necessities, and it looked like buying a bed would eat up most of her budget. She tried another site but found it was much the same. Eat into the rest of her savings or wait until she had more saved up? It was a tough choice. Maybe a futon from Walmart would be in her budget. That had to be better than an air mattress, right?

Rather than get discouraged and depressed over the furniture, Addy decided to look into extracurricular classes. One good thing about living in a city was the number of options available. What did she want to try? It wasn't hard to find cooking classes, art lessons, language courses, and so much more. But it was almost as bad as looking for a job! The options were endless. Figuring she could start with classes in art or marketing, to help her budding career, she searched for options that met the criteria. Even that was overwhelming. Where should she start?

With a sigh, Addy shut her laptop and took a sip of coffee. The excitement she had felt last night for having positive, productive things to do was waning. Overwhelm was seeping in. *What did you expect?* Her mother's voice was back. *You never should have left D.C. There was no reason to start all over when you had plenty of options back home.*

Addy pushed back her chair and went back into her room. Maybe she would feel better after she showered and got dressed. She couldn't let these minor setbacks distract her. Having to wait a little while for furniture wasn't the end of the world. And having too many options for classes was not necessarily a bad thing. It just meant she needed to do more soul searching, that's all. And there was very little pressure. If she took a class and didn't like it, she didn't have to go. If she had to sleep on the floor, no big deal.

By the time she had dressed and gotten ready for work, Addy was feeling better. Much like when she had first moved in, she just had to take things one step at a time. As eager as she was to be settled in her new life, some things took time. She had to be patient.

Addy sighed. She was not good at being patient. What could she do while she waited? As she packed a bag for work, Addy thought about everything she wanted to do, to have. Maybe what she needed was a wish list. That way she could dream and plan and explore, and then fulfill her wishes when she could. Like on Amazon.

Satisfied with that idea, Addy decided to spend the last half hour before work making wishes.

As Addy walked to work a bit later, she felt a definite chill in the air. Though it was not a far walk, she was already not looking forward to making it in the snow and ice she was sure winter would bring. In the little research she had done on

Boston, she had learned that winters would be much colder than D.C. Blizzards also weren't uncommon. She got cold just thinking about it. She would have to add snow boots to her wish list. And a heavier coat.

Fortunately the painting shop was warm, and Addy shed her jacket and bag as she entered. She greeted Linda with a wave, as Linda was chatting on the phone. Linda beckoned her over. Addy caught snippets of the conversation as she approached. It sounded like someone wanted to book a party. Addy gulped, and butterflies began flapping in her belly. This would be the first new booking since she had started.

Linda met her gaze and pointed at the paperwork in front of her. She had started filling in details, and as Addy stood there, Linda asked the client questions to fill in the rest. Addy tried to take in all the procedures, questions, and information. Soon she would have to know how to do this on her own.

It looked like the event was a child's birthday party. That shouldn't be too bad. From what Addy had learned, each child would be able to choose from a selection of figures to paint, and it would be her job to show them the paints and get any supplies they needed. Adult groups were trickier, since those had the option of learning different techniques or designs – and she would be the one to teach them. That was the part of the job that made her the most nervous. She had just started to learn those things herself. Fortunately the first adult party wasn't until mid-December.

When Linda hung up the phone, she went over the party details with Addy. The party was a month away, so Addy had plenty of time to get comfortable before then. And the afternoon was spent doing just that, helping customers and filling in gaps in her knowledge base. With each hour that passed, Addy felt more and more confident. This job had been the right choice.

By the time Richard entered the diner that afternoon, Maggie had called the local real estate office and made an appointment to discuss what she was looking for. She gave Richard a quick update, then headed out the door for her meeting.

It occurred to Maggie as the door shut behind her that she had probably spent more time outside in the last two weeks than she had in the last six months. The fresh air revitalized her senses, and she had a bounce in her step as she walked down the street.

When she opened the realtor's office door and stepped inside, she was faced with images of beautiful houses. What would it be like to own her own house? She had never even considered it. But if she sold the diner, the income would surely cover the cost of a small house. The possibility set her heart to racing again. At this rate she was going to give herself a heart attack with all of the excitement and stress.

A husband-and-wife team ran the real estate office, and Maggie's appointment was with the wife, Megan. She was a cheery thirty-something brunette whose rounded belly gave away her pregnant state. Megan greeted Maggie with a warm smile and extended hand. Maggie shook the hand, suddenly nervous. Megan led Maggie to her desk, and they both sat down.

"So, Maggie, I understand from our quick chat on the phone that you're looking for a place to live. You've been living in an apartment at the diner, correct?" She pulled out a pad of paper and held a pen in one hand, ready to take notes.

Maggie nodded.

"How's the sale of the diner going?"

Maggie took a deep breath. "I've gotten one offer, but I don't think I'm going to take it. Just doesn't seem like a good fit."

Megan nodded. "I get it. Well, if we can help at all with that, let me know. I'd be happy to put the diner online, draw up paperwork, whatever you need."

"Thanks. I'm not sure what I want to do. I've had an offer for a business partner, too, so I'm weighing my options."

"Smart move. No need to rush. From what I read in the paper, there's nothing pressing pushing you to sell."

"No, just my own anxiety," Maggie said with a nervous laugh.

Megan smiled. "Okay, then at this point it will just be finding a residence. You had mentioned apartments, and we do have a few available near the center of town. What were you hoping to spend?"

"Whatever I can afford, I suppose." Maggie pulled out the notes she had made regarding her potential salary, plus her latest bank statement, and gave them to Megan.

"Okay. So most landlords will require at least a month's rent upfront, often first and last, with possibly an additional security deposit. You definitely have enough to cover that." Megan pulled out the apartment listings she had printed out. "You would likely also need to sign a lease. I don't know of any that are offering month to month right now." She slid the listings across the desk to face Maggie.

As Maggie perused the printouts, Megan woke up her computer and typed in some search parameters. After some scrolling Megan tapped her lip with one finger. "You know..." She clicked a couple of links and sent a few things to print.

Maggie looked up expectantly. The apartments looked sufficient, certainly nicer than her existing arrangement, and she hoped to take a look at them soon.

"Have you considered a house?"

Maggie raised her eyebrows. "Not really. I just started looking for apartments last night. I wouldn't think I could afford a house yet, at least not until the diner sold."

Megan grabbed the pages she had printed. "Well, we actually have two houses on the market right now that are quite affordable. Nothing big, usually considered starter homes, with two bedrooms. But if you used the savings you have as a down payment, then you could probably swing mortgage payments, either with your salary or, if you sell, your profit." She handed the printouts to Maggie.

Maggie looked at the cute little houses. True, they were small, but it was just her. How much space did she need? And they were definitely bigger than her studio apartment.

"If you're interested, we can schedule viewings. They probably won't last long."

"I – I don't know." One more thing to think about.

"How about this? I'll line up appointments to see both – the apartments and the houses. In the meantime, think about your options, how much you want to spend and all that. You could also meet with the bank to see if you even get approved for the mortgage. Then you can make an informed decision."

Maggie nodded. "Okay. That sounds reasonable."

"You can take all those printouts with you, and if anything new comes up, I'll let you know."

"Okay."

They discussed Maggie's availability for showings, and a few minutes later Maggie was back on the sidewalk, heading back to the diner with a packet of papers hugged to her chest. Looked like she knew what she would be doing that night.

Mike's day passed by uneventfully, but he was in a great mood, so it went quickly. The sun was shining, warming the cold air at least slightly, and business was steady but not overwhelming. By the time he closed up shop, Mike was feeling so optimistic he decided he was going to do something he hadn't really done in a long time – cook.

Mike usually resorted to quick meals – sandwiches at lunch, a frozen or canned meal for dinner. There just didn't seem to be much point in cooking for one person. But he actually enjoyed it and decided to swing by the grocery store before heading home.

He ended up with way too many ingredients, but he found himself having fun as he chopped, mashed, sauteed, and roasted. The leftovers would last at least a couple of days, and he could cook again later in the week, too.

Mike plated up his dinner, packed up the leftovers, and settled at his kitchen table to eat. After a minute the silence got to him, and he picked up his plate and moved to the living room. Cooking for one was hard enough. Eating by himself in silence was nearly intolerable. He placed his dinner on the coffee table and turned on the TV. Flicking through the channels in search of a game, he paused as he saw a weather forecast. Looked like snow was on the way. And from the looks of it, it could be a big one.

Chapter 23

The blizzard hit Friday afternoon.

Maggie had been able to see two of the apartments the previous day, and they were going to try and see one of the houses that afternoon, but the buyers canceled the appointment just as Maggie was heading out the door. She took the opportunity to reach out to Ms. Connors instead.

Maggie dreaded making the call. She had considered sending an email instead, but she had a feeling Ms. Connors would just end up calling her back anyway. Maggie was not looking forward to the conversation. She got the impression that Ms. Connors didn't hear "no" very often. Would she try to convince Maggie to change her mind? Would she succeed?

Out of excuses, with extra time on her hands and a nearly empty diner thanks to the snow, Maggie decided to bite the bullet. Maybe she would get voicemail.

"Rachel Connors." The abrupt greeting destroyed any hope of voicemail.

"Uh, yes, Ms. Connors. This is Maggie Devin, from Pine Valley."

"Ah, yes, Ms. Devin. So good to hear from you. I hope you have good news for me."

"Well, uh, actually, I've decided to pass on your offer. While it was incredibly generous, I don't think it will be the right move for the diner or the town."

"I see. I am very sorry to hear that, and I'm sure my bosses will be very disappointed. I would love the opportunity to change your mind, show you the potential and ideas we have in mind for the space."

"I'm sure, but I don't think there's anything that will change my mind at this point. I've decided to go in another direction."

"I see. Well, thank you for meeting with me. I wish you the best."

"Thank you."

Maggie disconnected the call and put the phone down. Her hands were shaking. She hated confrontation, and she hated disappointing people. But she knew in her gut that this was the right choice. Regardless of what else happened to the diner, it would not be turned over to a company that didn't understand her town. Still, she had to be grateful to Ms. Connors for one thing: the idea about her apartment. That had potential, and it could be the deciding factor on where Maggie was able to live. Because the more she thought about it, the more she really wanted a house of her own.

The bank had closed early due to the storm, but they had an online mortgage application available, so when the last of the customers headed home, Maggie decided to spend the evening tackling it. The only downside with such an impersonal system was the inability to express her unique situation. But at least it was a start. She would head to the bank in person on Monday and defend her position. She only hoped it worked.

After sitting hunched over her desk for an hour, Maggie saved her progress, then stood up and stretched. She loved moments like this, when it was so quiet and still. She had told her scheduled staff to stay home, and the snow was keeping the customers away, so it was just her and her thoughts. She wondered if, when she moved out, she would continue to enjoy these moments of silence, or if she would long for the background noise.

Moving into the dining room, Maggie looked out the plate glass windows. The snow was falling thick and steady. The town was blanketed in white. Weather forecasters were telling everyone to stay inside, and she didn't see a single person or vehicle go by. Was it even worth it for her to be open? Probably not. But it was such a habit, and she always got anxious for the unlikely event that someone needed shelter, or food, or that human contact. It occurred to her that when she moved out, it wouldn't be as simple to just stay open. She would want to stay home and hunker down. As things stood, she could just head to her apartment and keep the door open in case she was needed. So much was going to change.

Maggie walked around the dining room, rubbing her hand along chair backs and table edges, adjusting menus and salt shakers. She was getting wistful. Would she be able to say goodbye to this place, her home and sanctuary for so long?

She felt torn, caught between wanting a new life and longing for the comfort of the familiar. *You don't have to sell*, a little voice told her. *No one is forcing you to.* Tears welled in Maggie's eyes, and she sank into a booth. No, she didn't have to sell. But possibilities beckoned her. And she didn't want to be an old woman who regretted being a coward.

From her place by the window she could see one of the apartments she had visited. Would she want to be able to see the diner from her apartment? Would she want to see someone else change, possibly destroy, her beloved diner? If she stayed in Pine Valley, no matter where she settled, that would be a distinct possibility. But how could she leave?

Maggie rubbed her temples. The thoughts moved through her mind like dominoes in a never-ending circle, one thought leading to the next. She would have to decide eventually, but she felt like she was getting nowhere. Maybe she just needed to write down her options, close her eyes, and point. Let God or fate or whoever controlled things decide for her. Or maybe she needed a list of pros and cons, something to stop the vicious cycle.

Actually, what she needed was a good night's sleep. The long nights and stressful days with too little sleep were catching up with her. Maggie decided to make herself some dinner, then, assuming no one came in, she was going to go to her little apartment and relax. No more life choices for today. She would turn on some old reruns then fall asleep to the sound of silence.

Mike usually hated being cooped up at home for too long. When he felt trapped, the loneliness gnawed at him until he wanted to scream. But for once he didn't mind. He had been chatting with two women online, and the possibility of human contact, even virtually, was cause for optimism. Since he had closed up shop early, he had plenty of time to cook himself a good dinner and settle down with his computer.

He had decided to take his time getting to know the women he spoke with. True, he didn't want to jump in head-first like he had been about to with Sarah, but more importantly he had acknowledged that he wasn't in any hurry. He was looking for a life partner, not someone to mess around with or waste time with. It made more sense to really get to know them, to ask the important questions, make sure they were on the same page – and on the same timeline. He had to admit that the situation with Addy was part of his change of heart, too. She had been a decent person, and they had had a connection, but they were at different points in their lives. He needed to make sure that his next love interest was ready to settle down, like he was. And that she didn't live two hours away. So far he hadn't messaged anyone who lived more than thirty minutes away, and more often than not they lived within fifteen or twenty.

Meal made, comfortable position acquired, Mike logged on to the dating site. The two women he had been chatting with most were Leslie and Sam. Leslie was a single mother, with a three-year-old son. Mike had always wanted to be a father, and, though he knew it would be an adjustment, he had no problem inviting someone else's child into his life. Leslie worked as a receptionist, primarily for the steady paycheck and benefits, but she didn't really like the work. Sam was a bit more of a free spirit, but she was open and honest and refreshing. Part of her reminded Mike of Addy, but, unlike Addy, Sam was comfortable in her own skin and knew what she wanted out of life. That included her job as a photographer. While she took family photos to pay the bills, her real passion was nature, and she was just starting to build a name for herself.

Comparing the two, Mike had to acknowledge they were very different. But what appealed to Mike was both of their compassion, honesty, intelligence, and desire to start the next chapter in their lives. He just had to decide which one he saw a more likely future with, as the more he chatted with both of them the more he felt like he was cheating on them both. And he was not that kind of guy. How could he choose, though? They both brought so much to the table. He would give it a few more days and see how it went. Maybe he would start to feel more of a connection to one over the other. In the meantime he would enjoy the conversations.

By the time he closed his computer a few hours later, he was no closer to deciding. But he had given himself a deadline. He would make a decision by the end of the weekend. That gave him two more days to figure out which of these women, if either, could be the love of his life.

Linda had told Addy not to come in until Monday due to the forecast, and Addy was disappointed that she would once again have so much free time on her hands, this time with even more restrictions as the snow kept her stuck inside for the most part. This time, though, she had research to do, decisions to make, and some remaining paint supplies if she felt creative.

Kate's employer let her work from home on Friday, so, while she spent much of the time in her own room, Kate would wander into the common areas on occasion, too, and they ended up eating lunch together. With the likelihood that they would be stuck in the apartment for a while, Addy anticipated they would get to know each other better, and get closer as roommates and friends. She hoped so, anyway.

Addy spent the day looking at less expensive furniture options. She browsed both Walmart and Target, plus Amazon and IKEA, to see if she could find anything decent. She had to decide if she wanted something inexpensive and likely temporary, or if she wanted to save her money and wait until she could afford something nicer. For her mental health, she was leaning toward the inexpensive.

Her current situation was starting to bother her. She didn't like feeling like a squatter. She wanted to have an actual living space.

After shopping online for a bit, Addy started doing general searches for inexpensive bedrooms, and what she found actually got her excited. Why hadn't she thought of it before? Maybe it was because she was just starting to tap into her creative side. Online she found an abundance of options for do-it-yourself headboards and home décor. She could take simple – and inexpensive – supplies and create something beautiful and unique. Of course if she wasn't careful those "simple supplies" could add up, too, but it was something else to consider. Maybe she could get an inexpensive mattress and bed frame and design a headboard to make it less bland and unappealing. And she could get a nondescript, basic nightstand and modify or paint it to make a work of art.

She needed something to store her clothes in, too. Currently the closet space was sufficient for most of her clothes, but she needed something for her undergarments, and she was sure she would want to get some new clothes at some point. While she had brought a decent selection to get her started, she was used to getting new outfits on a regular basis, and wearing the same things over and over would not appeal to her for long. Would it?

As they finished up their lunch, Kate suggested checking online for people who might be giving things away or selling them cheap. Not for a mattress, but at least for any of the wood items.

"If you're really thinking of getting creative with them, anyway, it won't matter what they look like as long as they're sturdy. And if you mess up, you won't feel bad having spent a bunch of money." Kate grinned.

"I hadn't even considered that. I'm so used to just buying something if I want it."

"What happened to all the stuff you had in D.C.?"

Addy shrugged. "I sold most of it. Gave some away. I didn't really want to be lugging a bunch of stuff around. It wouldn't all fit in my car, of course, and I didn't know when or where I would be stopping, so I didn't want it to just sit there waiting for me. And I really didn't want to have to figure out how to get it to me once I did stop. I figured I could just buy new stuff. I had sold my apartment, which brought in enough money to last a while – or so I thought. Boston is more expensive than I expected."

Kate leaned back, munching on a chip she had had with her sandwich. "Yeah, it's really expensive. I don't think we ever really discussed what made you want to move in the first place."

Addy sighed. "No, I suppose we haven't. To be honest, it's hard to put into words."

"Did something happen?"

"Well, kind of. A lot of somethings, probably. But I guess it was one thing that really set me off. So... there was this guy."

Kate laughed. "There's always a guy."

Addy grinned back. "His name was Jack. We had been dating for almost three years. And we were at this party, a very boring office party for some guy he worked with. Anyway, I was playing my role, being the dutiful girlfriend, hanging on to his arm, adoring gaze, the whole bit." Addy took a sip of water and paused a moment. "Well, we were in a group, and as usual the conversation was all about business, so I was just doing the whole smile and nod thing when the conversation shifted. And it was a topic I actually knew something about, because my mom had worked for the guy. So I tried to participate in the conversation, and Jack just gives me this look, like 'how dare you actually speak.' So I shut up. But as I was standing there tuning things out again, I started thinking. And it started to really bother me. I had been going out with this guy for three years, and he didn't care one bit about anything I had to say. And it occurred to me that that was never going to change, not with Jack or all the other Jacks in the world. But that was how I had been raised, you know? To be a pretty face without a brain. My mother had drilled it into me that I was just supposed to find a rich, handsome husband."

"Doesn't sound like much fun. Geesh, that's rough."

Addy nodded. "So with this new realization, I decided to bring it up with my friends." Addy curved her fingers into air quotation marks when she said the word friends. "And they all looked at me like I had two heads. They didn't think there was anything wrong with it. And I thought about all our conversations, all of our outings and time spent together. Everything we did was about looking good and being seen. Even my supposed friends didn't care what I thought beyond fashion, men, and the latest party. They were the same as my mother."

"Wow. I can't imagine living like that."

"It really bothered me for a while, but then I realized I was just as much to blame. I had let myself be led down this pointless, meaningless path. But it wasn't good enough anymore. I wanted to be me, not bimbo Barbie. But when I tried to make changes, I got discouraged. Everyone I knew started turning away from me. My social circles held no appeal. My mother had died a while back, and it occurred to me that I had nothing tying me to D.C. I was clinging to a life that I no longer wanted, and there was nothing keeping me there. So I cleared out my apartment and said good-bye to my old life."

"Wow. That takes guts."

Addy laughed. "I don't know about that. I think it takes desperation."

"No, seriously. A lot of people would just stay where they were, even if it made them miserable. That whole comfort zone thing."

Addy shrugged. "I have my moments, I guess."

Kate evaluated Addy. "Do you do that a lot?"

"Do what?"

"Sell yourself short."

Addy thought a moment, then shrugged. "Maybe. I dunno. I still have my mother's voice in my head, telling me what I should and shouldn't do, telling me what's wrong with me and all the mistakes I've made. It's been a hard thing to shake."

"Hmm. Well, I don't know you very well yet, but I can say that from what I've seen so far you are smart, brave, creative, and resourceful. Yeah, you're pretty, but you have a lot going for you beyond that. I'm glad you decided to break the cycle."

Addy wasn't sure how to respond, but she could feel her cheeks getting warm. "Thanks."

"I'm serious. I think you're just tapping the tip of the iceberg with what you're capable of." Kate stood up and brought her plate to the sink. "I have to get back to work. But seriously, I think you could do awesome things if you apply yourself."

Addy watched Kate retreat to her room, then looked down at her own plate. What *was* she capable of?

Chapter 24

Maggie lay staring at the ceiling for a moment, letting the stillness of the morning wash over her. She heard a plow in the distance, which meant even if the snow hadn't stopped completely, there would be some people who would be venturing out. And some of those people would likely be hungry.

Sliding out of bed, Maggie was grateful she had been able to get a good night sleep. The wistfulness of the night before wasn't completely gone, but it had been joined by logic and practicality this morning, so she had a clearer head with which to make decisions.

And she was pretty sure she had made a big one.

After getting ready for the day, she entered the kitchen, then dining room, where she started a fresh pot of coffee. She had been brave enough to lock the front door the night before, finally convincing herself that the town would survive without her for one night, especially since they were likely all snug in their own homes. It had given her the freedom to sleep without worry of interruption, and she had needed it. But now the sun was shining, and an occasional car passed by, even as the snowflakes kept falling. Roads were relatively clear, and a few brave souls were out, clearing off sidewalks and opening businesses. It was time for her to do the same.

With the forecast, she had tucked a shovel and bag of ice melt in the foyer of the diner, and, after unlocking the door, she grabbed the shovel and headed outside.

The cold air stung her cheeks, but she breathed deeply, loving the clean, fresh scent of new snow. It was early in the season, which meant she hadn't yet tired of the stuff and could instead enjoy the beauty and serenity it brought.

They had gotten about eight inches so far, from the look of it, and Maggie started clearing the front path. It was perfect snow, light and fluffy and easy to clear. She waved to her fellow business owners, and they shouted greetings across the road. She hired someone to plow her parking lot, and as she was finishing up the sidewalk she saw the truck pull in, drop the plow, and push the snow to the sides. She watched for a moment, wiped her brow, then headed back inside. Coffee should be ready, and she needed it.

Her first customers of the day walked in just as she was finishing her mug. She greeted them with a smile, brought her mug to the kitchen, then put on her apron and grabbed an order pad. She would be doing double duty until her kitchen staff came in, but that shouldn't be long. Glancing at the clock on the wall she saw it was almost eight, and Kyle should be arriving soon, barring any complications from the snow.

Maggie took the customers' order, chatted with them a minute, then turned to head for the kitchen just as the bell jingled. She turned toward the front door, expecting to greet Kyle, but she saw Richard enter instead.

"Good morning! I wasn't expecting to see you this morning. Here to eat or work?"

"Work. I figured you might be a bit short-staffed with the weather. How did you fare last night?"

"Actually locked the door and got myself a good night sleep."

"Good for you!" Richard grinned at her as he moved toward the back room and removed his coat.

"I'm glad you're here, actually," Maggie said as she followed him. "I wanted to discuss something with you. Maybe we'll find some time this morning."

"Sounds good. Should I man the kitchen or the front?"

"Kitchen if you don't mind. Kyle should be here soon, but I'm afraid he may be delayed with the snow."

They worked well together, but Maggie already knew that. The questions she had for Richard revolved around his vision for the diner, what he expected their partnership to look like, and how they would help the diner thrive. One of the concerns she had had with the potential buyer, which had resurfaced during her moments of solitude the previous evening, was what would become of her diner if she sold it. How would it be changed? And would she approve of the changes? Even if she took on a partner, would they be on the same page when it came to how to run and improve the diner?

Something about how Richard had reacted to seeing Jordan at the diner still bothered her, too. He had acted, if only for a moment, as if he had a say in her hiring decisions. If they became partners, would he try to take control? Or would he respect her opinions, experience, and ideas?

The questions swirled around her mind as they helped the customers who came in. Business was relatively quiet, but busier than she had expected. Kyle eventually came in, apologizing for his tardiness, and Jordan arrived an hour later to help in the dining room. With it being Saturday, business didn't slow to a trickle until mid-afternoon.

With the quieter traffic, and addition of another line cook, Jessica, who would cover the dinner rush, Maggie and Richard were finally able to retreat to the office.

"Busier than I thought it would be," Maggie began. "Thank you for coming in."

"Any time," Richard replied with a smile. He leaned back in the chair across from Maggie.

Maggie felt nervous, for perhaps the first time ever with Richard. How professional and uptight should she be? Could she afford to stay easygoing and upbeat? This was Richard, but it was also her precious diner. And she really wanted to get it right.

"Last night, when it was so quiet in here, I had the opportunity to really think, without distractions."

"Okay," Richard said with a nod. "Must have been peaceful."

"It was. And it made me nostalgic and sentimental and sad and hopeful and all kinds of things, all mixed together."

Richard nodded again, but he remained silent, giving her a chance to speak her mind.

"I think I've made a decision, but I want to make sure it's the right one, for me and the diner." Maggie took a deep breath. "So I was hoping we could discuss some things, so I could get a feel for what you had in mind when you said you wanted to be partners."

"Of course. Can I just say something before we really dive in?"

"Sure."

"First, I know that this diner is your baby. You've been running it for a while now, and you're obviously doing something right, if the crowds of repeat business and the love this town gave you when they thought you were closing are any indication. I certainly don't want to step on your toes or butt in where I'm not needed. My proposal had more to do with giving you freedom while also giving myself the chance to feel useful, like I was part of something again. Yes, I have lots of ideas to make this place even better, but it is first and foremost your diner, and if you would prefer to split the ownership sixty-forty or seventy-thirty, or whatever, so you would have more control legally, that would be fine with me. Ultimately, I would want this to be a mutually beneficial situation, and one that you were comfortable with."

Maggie took another deep breath. He had addressed most of her concerns in one fell swoop, and it had certainly set her mind at ease. But she was still curious about what he had in mind for the forward progression of the diner. What were his ideas?

"Thank you for that, Richard. You have been so helpful to me, but it can be hard to determine where things stand, or where they would stand if the situation changed."

"I get it. I admit I have felt protective over the diner, and you, since I started working here. I apologize if I've crossed the line at any point. I just feel so at home here, like I did when I had my own restaurant. It's been nice to feel that way again. But feel free to put me in my place if I ever go too far." He grinned.

Maggie smiled back and allowed herself to relax a bit in her seat. "So, what are your ideas for improvement?"

Richard rubbed his hands together and grinned again. Maggie laughed. "Alrighty then. Where should I start?"

They spent the next half hour discussing party room ideas, schedule changes, live entertainment, and more. By the time they determined they should get back to work, Maggie felt exhilarated. For the most part, she and Richard were on the same page. He genuinely seemed to care about the diner and its place in the town, and his enthusiasm was renewing her own. What could they accomplish together?

Maggie told Richard she would make her final decision and let him know the following day. There were some details she had to figure out. But for once her heart and mind were in sync. A partnership with Richard was the right choice.

He had hoped to get one of the women out of the running, not both! Groaning, Mike rubbed his face as he leaned back on the couch. It had been a late night, but he had slept in a bit to compensate. With the snow, he had figured he would close the shop today and had told the guys to stay home. So he had hopped online, hoping to pick up where he had left off the night before. The conversations had not gone as planned.

He had learned a valuable lesson in the last twenty-four hours: trying to cover all his bases when it came to compatibility questions led to big conversations – and quite possibly a tainted view of the other person. While he had legitimate opinions on certain issues, there was something to be said for getting to know people gradually, for easing into those opinions and issues. And now he was no longer interested in Leslie or Sam, and he was back to square one. He was torn between being grateful he hadn't gotten too attached to one and kicking himself for messing up a potentially good thing. Maybe he was single not because of a lack of options, but because he was too darn picky.

Disgusted with himself, Mike closed his laptop and stood up. He should be out shoveling anyway. The snow had just about stopped, and as it was he would have to push some aside to open his front door. With another groan he realized he had never gotten his shovel out of the shed. He had been so focused on finding a girlfriend that he had blocked everything else out. What was wrong with him?

Mike got dressed, put on his boots, and trekked through the snow to his shed. He had to kick aside some snow to open the door, but at least it was light and fluffy. If it had been the thick, wet, slushy stuff like they had gotten last year, he would have been even more miserable.

An hour later the driveway was shoveled, as was the path to his front door. He should probably invest in a snow blower at some point, but he usually didn't mind the exercise. It helped keep him in shape and gave him time to think. Today, however, he didn't want to think. He just kept kicking himself.

Leaving the shovel and boots in his mudroom, Mike returned to the warmth of his house. Without work and without online chatting, how was he going to spend the rest of his day? The hours stood in front of him like a long, dark hallway. Maybe he should open the shop after all. But he couldn't man the front counter and work in the garage at the same time. And it probably wasn't a good idea to work in the garage by himself anyway, just in case of accidents. Maybe one of the other guys would want to come in. Even if they didn't actually open the shop, they had a couple of cars that still needed work, and the snow had set them behind. He was sure the owners would like them back sooner rather than later.

After calling around to his techs, Mike was able to connect with Ryan, who had nothing going on and could use the hours. Feeling at least a little bit less pitiful, Mike got ready for work.

They hired a company to plow out the parking lot, so Mike was able to pull in no problem. The cars that they had to work on had already been pulled into the bays in anticipation of the snow, so the parking lot was empty except for his tow truck parked at one end. It looked quiet, peaceful. He opened the front door, then the door to the bays, where he flicked on the heaters they used when they were working on the cars. He would give it some time to warm up the space before attempting any work. Numb fingers weren't of any use to anyone.

He started the coffeemaker in the back room, then returned to the waiting area to look out the windows and wait for Ryan. Light snowflakes were still falling, but they weren't adding much to the foot or so that had already accumulated. It looked pretty, and Mike found some of his tension easing. So this last round of online dating had been a bust. Better to weed out the unsuitable matches now, right? A little voice told him that maybe he would have been more successful if he hadn't pushed so hard, but Mike tried to ignore it. Did he push too hard? He had with Addy, and it seemed he may have here, too. Maybe that was his problem. But why did he push? Did he care too much, or was he trying too hard, or was he looking for reasons to fail? With a sigh, Mike returned to the office to pour himself a cup of coffee.

Ryan entered the shop as he was pouring, and he shouted an offer to Ryan. After pouring a second cup, he brought them both to the front.

"Hey, man. Thanks for coming in. I just couldn't stand the thought of sitting at home all day with nothing to do." He handed a mug to Ryan.

"No problem. My day was looking much the same." He grinned at Mike.

They sipped their coffee and made small talk, then went into the bays. It was at least a little warmer than it had been, and they each picked a car to start work on. Soon the only sounds were metal tools clanging, jacks moving, and a rock station playing oldies in the background. So much better than the silence of an empty house.

When they decided to call it quits for the day, their work was just about complete, and they washed up, turned off the heater, and locked up the garage. As they were heading out the door, Mike took a deep breath. Might as well bite the bullet. "Hey, Ryan?"

Ryan turned back to face him. "Yeah?"

"What did you say your cousin's name was?"

Chapter 25

With Kate's words running through her mind, and Linda's repeated support and encouragement joining them, Addy found herself deep in thought much of Friday afternoon. Was she as capable as they seemed to believe? She would like to think so, but growing up in an environment that encouraged her to keep her thoughts and opinions to herself made it difficult for her to really take it in. Were these the beginnings of discovering who she was? Or was she just really good at faking it?

Addy and Kate spent Friday evening playing cards and watching chick flicks. It was nice to hang out with someone again, and Addy found she enjoyed the relaxing, peaceful night in. Before heading to bed, she looked out her window at the snow falling. There was hardly anyone on the road, and everything was blanketed in white. She had never seen so much snow. Opening her window, she breathed in the cold air. It was so quiet outside, the snow muffling any noise. She sat watching the snow for a bit before she cold air chilled her, then she closed the window. She wondered what Pine Valley looked like in the snow. It must be beautiful, especially on the town green, where nothing broke the scenery but a picturesque gazebo and pine trees in the background.

When Addy woke in the morning, the sun reflecting off the snow was blinding. She put on slippers and padded into the living area, where she greeted Kate, who was sitting at the kitchen table with a mug of tea.

"I have never seen so much snow. It's beautiful."

Kate grinned. "Yeah, I love it. This is nothing, though. Where I grew up in Maine, we'd get way more than this. Still early in the season, though. I'm sure we'll get more."

"What made you move to Boston?"

Kate shrugged. "Work. Got a good job, and they wanted me local. I enjoy the work, so I don't mind. I miss my family sometimes, though. I'm heading back for Thanksgiving."

"Oh, wow, it is about that time, isn't it?"

"You have any Thanksgiving plans?"

This time Addy shrugged. "Not really. Just another day for me. My family's a dud, remember?" She grinned.

"Oh yeah. Sorry."

"It's okay. I'm used to it. Sometimes I'd get invited to a friend's house, but usually the day just passed uneventfully."

"That's a shame. I'd invite you up to Maine, but the house gets kind of tight with my brothers and their families."

"Oh, no, it's okay. I wasn't looking for sympathy or anything. Just saying how it is."

Silence fell, and Addy excused herself to use the bathroom and get ready for the day. She wasn't sure how she would pass the time, but she would come up with something. Maybe today she would finally sign up for a class or two.

When she returned to the living area, Kate was on the sofa, reading a book on her Kindle. Addy paused behind the sofa, and Kate looked up.

"Yesterday I started looking into people giving stuff away or selling them cheap, and I found some possibilities. But I don't know how I would get them here. Any ideas?"

"Hmm. That could pose a problem. I have a friend who may have access to a truck. Or you could always rent a truck or something, or hire someone to pick it up and deliver it maybe."

"Maybe. Not sure how much that would cost, though. I might be better off just getting something new in that case."

"True. Let me think about it. I know others who have gotten stuff that way, so it must be possible."

"Thanks." Addy got her laptop and settled in the upholstered chair beside the sofa. She was going to tackle classes today, and as she had been getting dressed she had been thinking about what to take. Right now she was thinking an art class to work on her creativity and a business class to work on her marketing skills. That would give her the best of both worlds: fun and serious. She could learn new skills and meet new people.

The morning passed in companionable silence. Since the snow had let up, they decided to order takeout for lunch. It felt strange to Addy, to be with someone else but still be able to relax. She was used to putting on a mask and feigning interest. She hadn't realized how tense she had been until she found herself relaxing. This was how it should be, wasn't it. She should be able to be herself, without worrying about saying or doing the wrong thing all the time. She and Kate were able to chat and eat, and Addy didn't have to worry about being judged or criticized. It was liberating.

She decided to take a walk that afternoon, grateful her new coat and boots had arrived before the storm. The city had woken up from its snowy nap, and the snow wasn't as pristine as it had been the night before. But Addy still enjoyed seeing it glisten on rooftops and tree branches. She smiled at fellow pedestrians. Some even smiled back.

Addy was happy with where she had settled. The neighborhood was nice, filled with shops and restaurants and residential buildings. Not much by way of nightlife that she could tell, but it wouldn't be hard to get to the heart of the city. Whenever she'd thought about doing so, though, she found it didn't hold the appeal it once did. Yes, she still liked to be around people, but the club scene no longer interested her. That was part of the old Addy, the Addy who just wanted – or felt the need – to see and be seen. Now she just wanted to be. And that being didn't seem to include bars or sporting events or big concerts. She was enjoying a more mellow existence.

Though she didn't have a particular destination in mind, Addy found herself heading toward Paintastic. She really did enjoy her job, and she felt it had a lot of potential. She was curious how it would feel to learn more about the business aspect of it, and to really tap into her creativity. All the worry about the cost of furniture, and even classes, though, had reminded her that as much as she may like it, this job would not pay her bills. It was just part time, and it would take almost the whole month just to pay her half of the rent, not including utilities or extras, like food. Should she ask Linda for more hours, even though she had really just started? Should she look for a second job? Or should she just bide her time, whittling away at the money in her bank account and hoping something worked out? Maybe the money she had set aside would be her mother's way of paying her back for the years of misery. After all, it had been her mother's apartment that she sold.

Addy sighed. She didn't want to think about problems on a beautiful day like this. She wanted to enjoy the sun that had started to shine, think about everything she had going for her, and be grateful. She had come this far. Everything else would work out, too.

In the quiet overnight hours, Maggie removed the For Sale sign from the window. She wondered if its absence would cause as much ruckus as its arrival had. Now that she had decided to go into partnership with Richard, she just had to work out the details. Would the town be happy with her choice?

Richard had presented an interesting idea that she hadn't considered. Did she want to have a majority say in the partnership? Or would she be content splitting the business fifty-fifty? Would it ease her mind to know she really did have the final word on big decisions? That was what she had to figure out, and what would likely fill her thoughts for the next few hours. Once that was decided, she could sit down with Richard and a lawyer and draw up the paperwork.

Maggie felt butterflies in her stomach. She knew that, all things considered, this choice really was the best of both worlds, but that didn't mean she wasn't nervous about it. It was a big change. But, she thought, having that money now would also make finding her next home a bit easier. She could afford a house if she wanted one, and, even if she had to take out a small mortgage, she would still be bringing in income. That would make the bank happy.

How much should she ask Richard to pay? She supposed it would depend on how much of the business he ended up getting. Which brought her back to her initial thought. Maggie sighed. It was going to be a long, frustrating night. But she knew once the decision was made, it would be the right one. For once, she was learning to trust her intuition. This would work out for the best.

Mike was not good with phone calls. He had gotten the name and number of Ryan's cousin, and Ryan had said he would put in a good word for him, but Mike did not want to make the call. He just felt so awkward. But would it be weird to send a text as the first contact since he had never even met her? Maybe he should just have Ryan set up a meeting.

Mike felt like screaming. Why did dating have to be so hard? All he wanted was to meet someone, hit it off, settle down, and start a family. Was that too much to ask? It would appear so.

Okay. Mike took a deep breath. He could do this. How hard was it, really, to make a phone call? Maybe he would get voicemail.

She answered after the second ring. "Hello?"

"Uh, hi. Is this Jennifer?"

"Yes, this is she. May I ask who's calling?"

Her formal tone threw Mike off. "Oh, uh, hi. This, um, is Mike? Ryan's friend?" He sounded like an idiot. He thumped the heel of one hand against his forehead.

"Oh, hello, Mike. Yes, Ryan said you might be calling. How are you?" Her voice sounded friendlier now, and Mike released a breath. Thank God. He couldn't handle a prim and proper woman. He was much too laid-back for that.

"I'm good. How are you?"

"I'm fine."

There was a beat of silence before Mike cleared his throat. "So Ryan seems to think we would hit it off, and I was wondering if you might want to get a drink with me sometime. Or a cup of coffee, if you prefer."

"Coffee would be great."

They set a day and time and said good-bye. When Mike hung up, he collapsed back on the couch. That had been painful. But at least he had a date. Jennifer lived in a neighboring town, and he would be meeting her at a cafe there next Friday night. That gave him all week to either calm himself down or freak out about it.

It was going to be a long week.

Maggie decided that in order to feel comfortable enough to travel and not hover too much, she and Richard needed to be equal partners. If she were away, or, heaven forbid, something happened to her, she wanted to know the diner was taken care of. And she wanted Richard to feel like she trusted him, and that he could feel confident making decisions. She would just make sure to put in the contract that any big decisions would need to be made by both of them.

Richard wasn't scheduled to work on Sunday, but Maggie called him and suggested he stop by in the evening, when business had quieted down.

The day was a typical busy Sunday, and Maggie alternated between feeling anxious about meeting with Richard and relieved that the decision was finally made. By the time traffic had slowed and Richard had arrived, she just wanted it all to be done.

Maggie gestured to a booth and grabbed the coffee pot to pour them each a cup. Though Jordan and Jessica were still on the clock, Maggie wanted to be on hand in case business picked up again. Sundays could be unpredictable.

Once they were both settled, Maggie pulled a notebook from her pocket and they got to work, hashing out details and working on items to put in the contract. By the time they were done, quiet had fallen over the diner. Jordan and Jessica had both left for the night, and all the customers had gone home. Maggie and Richard sipped from fresh cups of coffee.

"Is it always this quiet at this time of night?" Richard asked.

Maggie shrugged. "Depends on the day. Fridays and Saturdays people tend to come in and stay later. The other days it's usually quiet. Sometimes in the summer there will be more people. Or if there was a big sporting event."

Richard nodded and took another sip. "You know I have lots of ideas, and one of them was to adjust the hours of operation, but I won't push for making any quick changes or anything. We can ease into things and see what feels natural."

Maggie took a deep breath. "Sounds good." It would definitely be an adjustment to have someone else making plans and decisions. Her practical side knew it would be a good thing. Her emotional side was going to have trouble relinquishing some control. And she wasn't sure how she would feel about the actual changes.

Richard patted Maggie's hand and smiled. "You'll be okay. I know it will be an adjustment, and not an easy one. But we'll be equals. And that means I won't force you to do anything you're not on board with. I won't be able to, anyway, according to the contract." He grinned.

Maggie tried to smile back. "I know." Then she cleared her throat and looked at her notepad again. "Speaking of contracts, we need to find a time to meet with a lawyer and draw that up."

They discussed possible times, and Maggie told Richard she would make some calls the following day. By the time Richard left it was almost ten. Maggie sighed and tucked the notepad in her apron pocket. She felt like it was midnight at least. She was exhausted. The tense emotions were taking their toll. She wondered what the next few weeks would bring.

Sunday was a lazy day for Addy. She didn't have to work, and she didn't have anything in particular she had to do around the apartment. She had signed up for classes the day before, and she was waiting for Kate to get more info about how best to pick up furniture that was being given away online. All in all, she was at a bit of a loss as to how to spend her time. So she decided to do a bit more painting and brainstorming ideas for work.

Addy had settled on two classes to try: painting and marketing. She had really been enjoying getting in touch with her creative side, and since her work dealt primarily with painting, she wanted to learn more techniques and project ideas. She figured the marketing class would help her hone her business skills, so she could figure out how best to help Linda bring in more parties and customers. Even if her job was only part time, she had plenty of time to devote to it, and she enjoyed it. So why not? She was just disappointed that she had to wait until January for the classes to start.

In the meantime, she would do her best on her own. Today she decided to try abstract painting. She was just going to put on some music and see where her mind took her. She found herself drawing swirls and lines and triangles, using the beat of the music to inspire her. By the time Kate got home from a lunch date, Addy had completed one painting and moved on to another. Addy looked up as Kate opened the door.

"Hey. How was the date?"

"Pretty good, actually. We made plans for Friday."

"Second date already. That's great." Addy smiled. "Tell me all about him."

Kate filled Addy in, taking a seat at the dining table next to her.

"So how did you two meet, anyway? I never seem to meet quality guys."

"At work, actually. He's in a different department, but we'd seen each other around."

Addy sighed. "Bummer. That's not an option for me. I work with women." Aside from Linda, two other women worked part time at Paintastic. "I'm happy for you, though. He seems great. I hope it works out."

"Me, too. Paintings look good, by the way. I love the colors."

"Thanks. I was just going with the flow, depending on how I felt with the music playing."

"Well they look great. Are you going to hang them up?"

Addy shrugged. "Maybe. They might give my bedroom a little oomph. It looks pretty pathetic as it stands." She laughed.

"Yeah, no furniture will do that." Kate laughed, too. "Oh, that reminds me. I asked my friend Jess about the furniture pick-up thing. She's gotten a couple of things that way. She had just borrowed a friend's truck. He lives outside Boston, but he's in the area all the time."

"Hmm. Would he let a complete stranger borrow his truck, though?"

"Dunno. But she's going to ask. Doesn't hurt."

"I appreciate it. Thanks. In the meantime I could probably pick up a night-stand or small table in my car. It would really just be a dresser that I need help with, maybe a headboard. I definitely wouldn't get a mattress that way."

"Yeah, I wouldn't either. I'll let you know when I hear back."

"Thanks."

Addy finished her second painting and set it aside to dry. Maybe she would hang them up, though she would need to get frames or something to mount them. She smiled to herself. She had finally found something she enjoyed.

Chapter 26

B y the time Friday rolled around, Mike had worked himself into a bundle of nerves. What was wrong with him? It wasn't as if he never dated. Was it because it was a blind date? Ryan had given him some details on his cousin, and Jennifer sounded like a great woman, smart and interesting.

Though Mike had offered to pick her up, Jennifer had preferred to meet at the cafe. Ryan had shown him a picture, so he would at least know what she looked like, but they had also agreed to text each other when they arrived. Whoever got there first could grab a table and direct the other. Maybe it was the whole situation that was making him nervous.

When he pulled into the parking lot, freshly showered, fingers scrubbed, and in a button-down shirt and slacks, he had to take a couple of deep breaths before climbing out of his car. He hadn't gotten a text yet, but he had also intentionally arrived early, so he could get his bearings and hopefully calm himself down. Just as he climbed out of his car, however, his phone pinged. Apparently Jennifer liked being early, too.

He entered the cafe and, using Jennifer's message as a guide, found her seated in a corner booth. She was pretty, and she had a pleasant smile when she greeted him.

"Hi, you must be Mike." She held out her hand to shake.

He took her hand in his own. Soft, smooth skin, but a firm handshake. "A pleasure to meet you." He felt like he had entered a business meeting. "Have you ordered yet?"

"Not yet. I thought we could go up together and decide. They have great pastries here, too."

"Sounds good."

The cafe was busy, but the line moved quickly, and they were back at a table within ten minutes. Mike had ordered a simple coffee and a chocolate croissant. Jennifer's drink had been a bit more complicated, but she had also opted for a chocolate croissant, so at least they had that in common. But by the time they parted ways an hour or so later, Mike decided that may very well be the only thing they had in common.

Jennifer was very pleasant. She was a good conversationalist, and she seemed to be a caring person who was passionate about her chosen profession. Mike learned she had gone into law to fight for the little guy, and that appealed to him. They had very different preferences when it came to books, movies, and music, though. And he couldn't get a good read on what she thought of his career. Experience had taught him that many "professionals" looked down on what would be considered blue collar workers, despite the skill and hard work that went into doing what he did. While Jennifer hadn't snubbed him, she didn't seem all that interested, either.

Mike walked away from the date unsure if it was worth pursuing a relationship. Jennifer had indicated she was looking to settle down, but it seemed to him their lives were moving in different directions. With a mental shrug, he decided he would wait and see how he felt in a day or two. He had told Jennifer he would be in touch. The following week was Thanksgiving, and he was going to be heading to Florida for a few days to see his parents, so it didn't make sense to schedule something now, even if he was interested. Maybe stepping back from his life would give him clarity. He could certainly use some.

Maggie and Richard had been able to make an appointment with a lawyer for Thursday afternoon. Since they had hashed out most of the details ahead of time, the meeting went smoothly and was really just a formality. When they parted ways, Maggie had a cashier's check in her pocket but had lost half of a diner. She found herself getting more emotional than she had expected. When she went to deposit the cashier's check on Friday, however, she was feeling more upbeat. She had an appointment to see a house that afternoon.

All her life, Maggie had heard people talking about how she would know when the right man, the right wedding dress, the right house came along. She would supposedly feel it in her gut. And when she approached the cute house on Tucker Lane, she was all ready to feel that instinctive pull. Unfortunately it didn't happen.

Megan Sullivan, her real estate agent, encouraged her to look around anyway. "It will give you a better sense of what you're looking for. That will help us in our search."

Maggie had told her that she wanted to pursue a house now, rather than an apartment as she had originally intended. Knowing she could afford most, if not all, of the house with what she had just made from the diner helped her feel more confident in her choice. When one door closes, another one opens and all that. Now she just had to find the right house.

They made an appointment to see a different house the following week. And Megan promised to let her know if anything new came on the market. It was a slow time of year for real estate, but there were always houses available. It was just a question of finding the right one, and with Maggie being insistent it had to be in Pine Valley, that could be tricky. Maggie tried not to get discouraged.

Since it looked like moving out could take longer than anticipated, Maggie wasn't sure how to proceed in terms of converting her apartment. She and Richard were in agreement that turning the studio apartment into a party room would be a smart move. The only challenging part would be accessing the room, since as it stood the entrance was off of the office at the back of the diner. Should they try to install an exterior door? Could they knock down a wall to make an entrance from the dining area?

Maggie spent some of the quiet hours Friday night examining the space. They would probably have to call in an architect or something. She would hate for them to start knocking down walls just to learn one was supporting the ceiling. It looked like it would be a bigger project than originally thought.

After looking at the space from different angles and even going outside to see where a new entrance would go, Maggie collapsed onto a counter stool and fought back tears. Everything had seemed so perfect. She had finally made some decisions. Plans and ideas were coming together in her mind, and it looked like everything was going to work out. But now nothing was working out. It could be months before she found the right house. And until she moved out, the apartment couldn't be converted. But even if she moved out next week, she had no idea how they were going to pull it off. Would nothing go smoothly?

Maggie brushed away the tears that had started to trickle down her cheeks. She took a deep breath and stood up. No. She was not going to let this get her down. She had wanted a change, and she was getting a change. It would just take a bit longer than she had thought. But that didn't mean she couldn't do anything. Maybe she should start with something smaller. How about a vacation? Surely that would be a possibility.

With determination in her step, Maggie went to the back office. From there she could hear if any customers came in, but she would also be able to research vacations on her computer. The only question was: where would she like to go?

The days slipped by, and before Addy knew it it was Thanksgiving. The apartment felt empty without Kate. Though their schedules rarely lined up, knowing that Kate had been in and out of the apartment, and that there was a chance of human contact, even in passing, made Addy feel less isolated. And with so much closed for the holiday, Addy wasn't sure how to pass the time. She had used up the last of her canvases on Sunday, so painting was out. She was still waiting to hear from Kate's friend's friend, so looking for furniture didn't make much sense. And she had already signed up for her classes, so there wasn't much she could do there, either. She tried exploring online for creative inspiration for her furniture, whenever she happened to get some, but that quickly grew boring. Addy found herself lying on the sofa staring at the ceiling.

This was ridiculous. There had to be *something* she could do that didn't involve staring at the ceiling or zoning out to a movie or TV show. Maybe she would go for a walk. A little fresh air could do her some good.

As she walked, she thought. Thanksgiving aside, she needed something to fill her time. She was at work maybe twenty hours a week, and that left a whole lot of time that needed filling. She knew her classes would help somewhat, but those were in the evening, so earlier in the day she still needed something to do. She couldn't afford to keep buying art supplies. Once in a while was fine, but enough to fill all of her free time just wasn't feasible. And she didn't want to overdo it with that, anyway, and get bored and lose interest. So what else could she do?

Addy thought about getting a second job. That would certainly help fill the time, and it would help with potential money trouble, too. As she had been thinking after the blizzard, her job did not pay all of her expenses. And dipping into her savings for everything wasn't sustainable, even if there was a good chunk of change in there from the sale of her mother's apartment. She needed a long-term solution. But with all the trouble she had had finding one decent job, what were the chances of finding a second? Was picking up a dull, minimum wage job just to fill the hours any better than zoning out to TV? With a mental shrug, she acknowledged that the extra money would make it a little better. But, as she had learned with her brief stint at the convenience store, the hit on her mental health might negate any benefit there.

As she passed by a church, Addy saw a lot of activity in the attached hall. People were unloading vans, and the open doors showed other people setting up tables and chairs. What was going on? Figuring she had nothing to lose, she approached someone standing near the side with a clipboard in her hand.

"Hi," Addy began. "What's going on here?"

The woman turned and smiled at Addy. "Good morning. We're setting up for Thanksgiving dinner."

"At a church?"

"Yes. Every year we host a Thanksgiving dinner for less fortunate folks in the area, homeless and such."

"Wow. That's great." Addy watched the hubbub for a moment. "Do you need any help?"

The woman beamed at Addy. "Sure! We're always looking for volunteers. What's your name?"

The woman introduced herself as Cathy and had Addy fill out a volunteer application, then directed her to talk to a man named Mark, who was unloading one of the vans. With a deep breath, Addy approached the man, introduced herself, and was handed a box filled with what appeared to be produce. Mark told her to bring it into the hall and to the right, where she would find a kitchen.

The next two hours flew by, with Addy helping unload, set up, and even helping to prepare the meal. By the time the doors opened to guests, she was tired but happy. She took her place in the serving line and began dishing up mashed potatoes, her assigned station. Everyone she met was in a cheerful mood, grateful for the meal and the companionship. When everyone had been served, Addy took her own plate and approached a table with an empty seat.

"Mind if I join you?" she asked as she gestured to the seat.

"Not at all," one of the men seated around the table asked. He greeted her with a smile and introduced himself and some of the others at the table. Addy enjoyed her meal with pleasant conversation.

By the time Addy had helped with clean-up and headed home, she was feeling joyful. That was the only word for it. Not only had the experience lifted her loneliness, but she had felt useful. She had met some wonderful people, learned new skills, and helped others. She couldn't think of a better way to spend Thanksgiving.

Cathy had told her that some of the church members sometimes helped at a soup kitchen a few miles away. She had promised to pass Addy's information along to the soup kitchen's organizers, and if they needed more volunteers they would let her know. Maybe she should look into more volunteer opportunities. There had to be other organizations in town who could use help. Maybe that was something else she could research.

When she walked into Paintastic the following day, Linda was in take charge mode. With it being Black Friday, Linda was expecting a busy day, and in addition to Addy there was another woman she had met on occasion, Sam. They spent the half hour before opening setting up workstations, making sure all supplies were well stocked and easily accessible, and getting the cash drawer ready. And once the doors opened, they were busy until closing time, with barely enough time to eat lunch. Addy was exhausted. And they would have to do it all again the next day. But it had been a good day, busy and productive. Addy didn't mind one bit.

Mike loved his parents. Really, he did. Since they had moved to Florida, he would travel down to see them every year for Thanksgiving. And they would come back up to Pine Valley for Christmas. It had become their tradition, and Mike enjoyed spending time with them for the most part. This year, however, conversation around the Thanksgiving dinner table seemed to revolve around his relationship status, or lack thereof. Why wasn't he settled down yet? They wanted grandchildren, didn't he know?

He had gone back and forth about telling them about Jennifer. One date did not a relationship make, but at least it would be something. Just to get them off his back, he told them he had started seeing someone, but it was too early to tell if it would work out. He knew he would end up regretting it, though. When they came up for Christmas, they would want to meet her. And if they weren't still dating, the pestering would begin again. But at least for now he had relative peace.

As Mike lay staring at the ceiling in the guest bedroom on Thanksgiving night, he thought back to his first date with Jennifer. She was pretty, and smart, and personable. Just because they didn't have much in common didn't mean they couldn't make it as a couple. Opposites attract, don't they? With that, Mike decided to contact her the next day and see if she wanted to go out again. Decision made, he rolled over and went to sleep.

Friday dawned chilly by Florida standards, but warm compared to what Mike was used to. He decided to go out for a run, something he didn't do nearly enough of back home. As he ran, he let the sun warm him inside and out. He had been feeling so lost lately. Ever since Addy had come into his life, he had felt like something was missing. Sure, he had been lonely before, but not like this. It was as if she tore a hole inside him, and when they parted ways it sat there, gaping, reminding him he was lonely and refusing to let him acknowledge everything else he had going for him.

Maybe if he and Jennifer started really dating he could pick up the rest of the pieces of his life. He could get back to hanging out with friends on occasion, start exercising again, keep up the cooking. He supposed he didn't have to be dating someone for all that to happen, but it was as if he couldn't focus on anything else until he had resolved his relationship status. What was wrong with him?

Mike paused on a street corner and rubbed the sweat from his forehead. Okay. He was going to call Jennifer this afternoon. And regardless of how the conversation went, he was going to get back to doing things that he enjoyed. He didn't need a girlfriend or wife or kids to be happy, as much as he wanted them. He could still have a meaningful, full life without them. It was time he started living his life again.

Years before, when the novelty of a place of her own had worn off, and her parents had passed away, Maggie had decided to open the diner on holidays. The thought of being alone didn't appeal to her, and she knew there were others in town who needed a place to go on the days usually reserved for families. Over the years things had evolved from just being open to actively creating a place for people to go. She now offered a traditional turkey dinner on Thanksgiving, served either family style or restaurant style, for anyone who was looking to spend time with others or who just didn't want the hassle of cooking. On Christmas it was a ham dinner with the same options. And on Christmas Eve she hosted an open house so friends and neighbors could socialize and wish each other a happy holiday. She served an ongoing buffet of food choices, free to all who chose to visit.

These special meals were quite the production, but over time Maggie had gotten the preparations down to a science, and popularity had grown so she had a full diner each time. As a result, Maggie spent Thanksgiving day in a constant state of motion.

When the last customers left just after nine that night, Maggie was ready to collapse. This was one of the few times she would close for the overnight hours. She needed sleep. Morning, and the Black Friday shoppers who wanted breakfast first, would be there before she knew it.

The sun hadn't yet risen when Maggie dragged herself out of bed. Friday would be busy but not as bad as the day before. By the time she had gotten dressed and ready and started the coffee maker, the first group of customers was congregating at the front door. They greeted Maggie with smiles and chatter, and she ushered them in. Her morning help would arrive shortly, and she got the cook surfaces warmed up as her customers drank coffee and looked at menus. It occurred to her that the morning would have looked very different if she had moved out already. She would have needed to get up even earlier and made the trek over, bundled up against the cold. There was a lot to be said for living where you worked. But she knew it was time to move on.

The day passed in a blur, as did Saturday and Sunday, as the official start of the holiday season kept more people out and about and looking for a place to eat. Richard spent much of the time at the diner, as well, helping with the crowds and making sure everything ran smoothly. They hadn't officially announced the partnership yet, just informed their staff members, but if anyone asked for an update Maggie told them what was happening. She and Richard had agreed to keep things as they were for the most part until after the new year. The holidays would be crazy enough without worrying about business upheaval, too.

Maybe this time next year they would be able to host holiday parties and Maggie could actually participate in town events. It was a nice thought, and Maggie kept it in mind as she flitted through the day-to-day tasks. While the house she had seen earlier in the week hadn't been right either, Maggie was trying to stay positive. She didn't have an urgent need to move, and it wouldn't hurt to keep the money in the bank for a bit longer. She had options, and she kept reminding herself to be grateful. At the very least, spring would be here before she knew it, and new houses always came on the market in the spring.

Chapter 27

When Addy had moved in to the apartment, Kate had let her know that she would need to move her car every two weeks for street cleaning. It was a bit of a hassle, especially since finding a temporary place to park could be a challenge. But Addy had embraced the challenge, turning it into a game to try and find the best time of day to move her car. She wondered if it was even worth keeping the car, between the hassle, the expense, and the known electrical issue. But something in her gut was telling her to hold onto it. So she did.

As luck would have it, Christmas Eve was the day to move the car. She didn't know if the schedule would be affected by the holiday, but she wasn't taking any chances. With so many people away for Christmas, the streets were a bit lighter, anyway. So Addy bundled up to head outside.

While people and cars were still bustling about, Addy felt disconnected from it all. Except for holiday parties and projects at work, she hadn't really done anything Christmassy this year. She and Kate had put up a tree, but Kate had been out most weekends with her new boyfriend, and this week she was in Maine with her family. Addy hadn't really felt like doing Christmas by herself. The church had activities going on, but Addy wasn't very religious, and she wasn't really a member of the church, so she hadn't gotten too involved. And the soup kitchen was so overloaded with volunteers this time of year that she hadn't been able to help much there, either.

Addy was looking forward to her classes starting in January. Then she could meet more people and hopefully get more involved in area activities. She had hoped to find community events in her neighborhood, too, but so far nothing she saw appealed to her. Was she being too picky? Was she looking for excuses not to take that step? As social as she had been in the past, she found herself getting anxious when she had to put herself out there. The idea of opening herself up and actually letting people in scared her. Though she had opened up somewhat to Kate, she hadn't shared as much as she had with Mike.

Mike. She hadn't thought about him for a while. She wondered what he was up to, how he was doing. Pine Valley probably had a lot going on for Christmas. Houses probably all had lights, and there would be a big tree on the town green. They probably had community events. Maybe carol singing or a festival or something – like she saw on all those Christmas moves that took place in small towns. With a sudden pang, Addy found she wanted that. She wanted a small-town Christmas, where even if you didn't know anyone you were welcomed, embraced, and encouraged to participate. Was that actually real, though, or was it just something from the movies?

She thought back to her time in Pine Valley. She hadn't been there very long, but it had stuck with her. Yes, she had felt welcomed. Everyone had been friendly, even that strange guy in the diner. What would it be like to go back? Would they even remember her? Probably not.

With a start, Addy realized she had been driving aimlessly for ten minutes. She could have passed twenty free parking spaces and not even realized it. But what she had realized was that she wanted to go back. Back to Pine Valley. Just to see it again, for Christmas. With a deep breath, Addy steered her car back toward her apartment. She had to pack. She hoped the motel had a vacancy.

As she pulled into Pine Valley a couple of hours later, the sun was just starting to set. Where should she go first? Probably the motel. She vaguely remembered how to get there, and after a slight wrong turn, pulled into the parking lot. She breathed a sigh of relief when she saw the lit-up vacancy sign.

Ed was at the front desk and greeted her with a smile. "Why, hello there. I remember you. Weren't you that young lady whose car broke down?"

Addy smiled, her heart beating a little faster. He remembered her. "Yes, that's me. I'm Addy."

"That's right. Hello again. What can I do for you, Addy? Looking for a room?"

"If you have one, please."

"You're in luck. Almost booked up. But I have one room left."

It had to be a sign. "Great. I'll take it."

Ed showed her to the room, handed her the key, and left her to get settled. After placing her duffel bag on the floor by the bed, Addy returned to her car. Next stop was the diner.

She pulled into the parking lot but paused after getting out of her car. There it was, across the street: the colorfully-lit Christmas tree. A dusting of snow lay all around it, and a family was taking pictures in front of it. It was perfect.

The diner was lit up with festive decorations, too. Garland hung around the windows, and a wreath greeted visitors from the front door. Addy opened the door, and a bell jingled to announce her presence.

She was surprised to see so many people at the diner. With it being Christmas Eve, she had expected most people to be home with their families. But the place was packed, with everyone talking and laughing. Tables had been pushed together. Food lined the counter. Holiday music filled the air. It was a party. And she was intruding. Her smile faded. Maybe this was a mistake. Should she leave?

Maggie spotted her and made her way over. "Welcome, welcome. Come on in." Maggie paused. "Wait, do I know you? You look familiar."

"Um." Addy swallowed. "Kind of? I was here a couple months back. My car had broken down."

Maggie's face lit up in recognition. "Addy! Of course. Please, come in."

"I don't want to intrude. You obviously have a party going on."

"Well, kind of. But you are more than welcome. This is my annual holiday open house. My way of giving back. Everyone is invited, to visit with neighbors and friends, eat some food, and get in the Christmas spirit. Can I take your coat?" Maggie gestured to a couple of overflowing coat racks near the back of the room.

"Um, sure," Addy said, removing her coat. "Thanks."

Maggie took the coat, then waved a hand in the direction of the counter. "Help yourself to some food, and feel free to mingle."

Addy got herself a glass of punch, then stood awkwardly near the counter, taking in the groups of people around her. They all seemed to be having fun, but, just like in Boston, she felt disconnected from it all. She didn't know anyone here. She shouldn't have come.

"Hi, Addy."

She turned in the direction of the voice and came face to face with Bill, the awkward man who had greeted her back in October.

"Hello, Bill. Good to see you."

"Oh, good, you remember me. I have a good memory, but I know not everyone does, so I didn't know if you would."

"You're hard to forget, Bill."

He seemed unsure how to respond to that, so he shifted the conversation. "Are you moving here?"

"No, just visiting. Pine Valley seemed like a nice place to be at Christmas."

"It is. It's a nice place all the time."

"I'm sure it is. It seemed nice when I was here in the fall."

"Okay. I'm going to say hello to other people now."

"Okay. Have fun."

Addy watched him go, a warm feeling growing in her belly. They remembered her here. She had only been in town for two days, but they remembered her. She wondered if Mike was here.

Before she could really take a look around, Maggie rejoined her. "So what brings you back to town?"

Addy shrugged. "Didn't have any Christmas plans, and it seemed Pine Valley would be a nice place to spend the holiday."

Maggie nodded as she looked around the diner. "It most definitely is, even if you're all on your own, like I am."

"From what I can see, you're not alone at all."

They shared a smile, then Maggie cleared her throat. "Actually, I'm glad you're here."

"Really?" Addy's face registered her surprise. "Why?"

"Because I never got the chance to thank you."

"Thank me? For what?"

"For turning my life around."

"How in the heck did I do that?"

Maggie shook her head. "That is a complicated question, and the answer would take more time than I have at the moment. How long are you staying in town?"

Addy shrugged. "Not sure. At least a couple of days. I don't have to be at work until Saturday."

"Okay. Good. You have plans for tomorrow?"

Addy shook her head. "Coming here was a very spur-of-the-moment decision. I didn't really plan or think anything through."

"Okay. I'm open all day tomorrow, so stop in whenever you want. Might be busy around lunchtime, but we'll find time to talk at some point."

"Okay."

The bell over the door jingled. "That's my cue. We'll talk tomorrow." Maggie met Addy's eyes and put one hand on her shoulder. "It is so good to see you." Then she walked away, leaving Addy feeling curious but happy. Coming to Pine Valley hadn't been a mistake after all.

Mike turned from where he had been laughing with a group of friends. Maggie had gotten a good turnout this year. Maybe all the publicity from the sale controversy had been good for her. He was curious to see what changes were in store.

He was about to turn back toward his group when he caught something from the corner of his eye. Was that *Addy*? Talking to Bill of all people? What on earth was she doing in Pine Valley?

Bill moved on, and Mike was just about to head over when Maggie approached her instead. Suddenly impatient, Mike shifted from one foot to the other, half paying attention to the conversation around him. As soon as Maggie left to greet a few newcomers, Mike excused himself and moved toward Addy.

She was looking away, her eyes following Maggie, but at the last minute she turned, and their gazes met. Mike felt as if he'd been punched in the gut. Addy gave him a small smile.

"Hi, Mike. I wondered if I'd see you here."

"Hi." He paused for a moment, unable to do anything but stare. "What are you doing here?"

"Thought it would be a nice place to spend Christmas."

"Nothing going on in Boston?"

"Lots going on. Just nothing I felt like doing."

They stood in silence for a moment.

"So how have you been?" Addy asked.

Mike nodded. "Good. Good. Business is good; weather hasn't been too bad." Had he really resorted to talking about the weather? "I've started seeing someone."

"Oh. That's good. What's her name?"

"Jennifer. Jen. She's a lawyer. Well, she will be. She just graduated law school." Great, now he was babbling.

"That's great."

"Yeah."

"Is she here?"

"No, she had a family thing. It was still a bit early to do the whole 'meet the parents' thing. So I came here."

"I thought you spent Christmas with your parents."

"I do. Big plans tomorrow. But they're here, too, somewhere around here." Mike looked around the room. "They love Maggie's open house. It gives them a chance to catch up with old friends." He pointed toward the other end of the diner. "They're down there, talking to the Hudsons."

"It's great that Maggie does this."

"Yeah. It started as a way for people who didn't have anywhere to go on Christmas Eve to have fun and socialize. And it just kinda took off. Maggie's always been great at taking care of us lonely hearts." He flashed Addy a grin. "So how's Boston?"

"Good. Great. Job's going well. I'm getting more confident with that. And I'm starting a couple of classes in January."

"Really? In what?"

"Painting and marketing. I figured they would help me meet people, plus help with my job. I'm excited."

"That's great."

"Yeah."

Silence fell.

"Well, I won't take up any more of your time." Mike looked at her a moment. "It was good seeing you, Addy."

"Yeah, you too."

"Merry Christmas."

"Merry Christmas."

Mike could feel Addy's eyes on him as he walked away. Addy was back. But just for Christmas. It didn't mean anything. And he had Jen now anyway.

As he rejoined his group of friends, Ben nodded in Addy's direction. "Was that the girl from Boston?"

"Yeah."

"What's she doing in town?"

Mike shrugged. "Just visiting."

"Huh," Ben said. Then he clapped a hand on Mike's shoulder. "Remember what happened last time she was just passing through. Messed you up for weeks."

"Yeah, I know. Nothing's gonna happen." But he couldn't help a glance at Addy as the conversation shifted. How long would she be in town?

Having spoken to the three people who could possibly even remotely remember her, Addy wasn't sure what to do with herself. She had figured she would stop in, say hello to Maggie, and have some dinner, then spend the rest of the night on her own. Maybe she would walk around the center of town, absorbing all of the holiday decorations and pretending like she belonged here. But the open house had thrown her off. On one hand she felt at peace, realizing she had made an impression, however small, on some people here. On the other hand, she felt awkward, not knowing anyone else, and not really being a part of this community. Should she leave? Should she stay and try to meet people? But what was the point of that?

With a sigh, Addy decided she at least had to eat. Her stomach was grumbling, and the food looked and smelled really good. So she grabbed a plate and added an assortment from the buffet. Once her plate was filled, she looked around for a place to sit. The diner was pretty full, but many of the guests were standing around and chatting, so she saw a couple of empty tables. Choosing a booth that was tucked mostly in a corner, she sat and began eating her dinner.

After a few minutes, a couple approached her table.

"Mind if we join you?" the woman asked with a smile. "Looks like all the tables are taken."

"Oh, um, sure." Addy swallowed the bite she had been chewing and gestured toward the other side of the booth.

"Thank you so much." The couple slid into the booth. "I'm Megan, and this is my husband, John." She gestured to the man next to her, placing a hand on his arm. He held up a hand in greeting.

"Addy."

"Nice to meet you, Addy. Sorry to intrude on you like this. Normally I would just stand, but this little one does not let me stay on my feet too long these days." She rubbed her protruding belly affectionately. "Are you new in town?"

Addy shook her head. "No, I'm just passing through. My car had broken down near here a couple of months ago, as I was on my way to Boston, and it seemed like a nice place to spend Christmas, so I came back to visit."

"That is so nice. Pine Valley is a great place."

They spent a few minutes eating and making small talk. Addy's tension eased a bit as the meal continued. Megan and John were such friendly, welcoming people, it was hard not to relax. Just as they were finishing up, someone caught Megan's eye across the diner.

"Excuse us, Addy. Looks like we need to get back to mingling." Megan smiled as she and John slid out of the booth.

"It was nice meeting you, Addy," John added. "I hope you enjoy your time in Pine Valley."

"Thank you so much. It was nice meeting you, too."

Just as they were passing Addy, Megan paused and placed a hand on Addy's shoulder. "Oh! If you ever decide to come back for good," she said, fishing in her purse, "give me a holler. We run the real estate office here in town. We'd love to have you join our little community." She handed Addy a business card, smiled, and waved as they moved on.

Addy kept the smile on her face as they left, then looked down at the business card. They had seemed like nice people, but maybe they were just trying to drum up more business. Or maybe she was just being cynical again. Tucking the card in her pocket, Addy stood up to bring her plate to the tray set aside for that purpose. Now that she had eaten and socialized a little bit, she figured it was time to move on. She would be back tomorrow.

After collecting her coat, she waved to Maggie and left the diner, her breath catching at the cold night air. It was quiet out here, especially after the hubbub at the open house. Bundling up further, she decided to walk a bit around the center of town.

That was one thing she had discovered during her time in Boston: she enjoyed walking. She liked feeling the fresh air on her face and being able to take in the sights around her. She especially enjoyed times like this, when there weren't many people around, and she could be quiet and still. Funny, she thought. She had wanted to move to a city because she wanted to be around lots of people, and yet she had learned she liked more limited interactions. While she still wasn't too comfortable opening up to people, being in smaller groups made her feel like she was building connections, rather than just adding to a list of acquaintances. And she found she enjoyed that more than being absorbed into a crowd.

Addy took another look at the lighted tree on the town green. It looked peaceful, hopeful, joyful. Checking for traffic, Addy crossed the street to get closer. She had seen at least one movie that involved making a wish on the lighted town Christmas tree. Would that work here, too? What would she wish for?

She closed her eyes, breathing in the cold air and the stillness around her. What *would* she wish for? She was starting to feel settled in Boston. She liked her job, and she was hopeful about her upcoming classes. She was starting to meet people, get a sense of fulfillment from volunteering, however limited. She felt creative and motivated and inspired to move forward. Yet something was missing. She still felt incomplete, but she couldn't pinpoint what she needed. Sure, it would be nice to be in a relationship, but she didn't think that was it. It was something deeper.

"I wish," she whispered, "to feel complete, content, at peace with myself." Then she sighed. A bit vague, and a bit of a tall order. But at least she was moving in the right direction. Wasn't she?

Chapter 28

Maggie watched the sky lighten early Christmas morning. She hadn't closed up the night before. By the time the last guests had trickled out, and she had finished cleaning up and resetting the dining room, there didn't seem to be a point. She had sent the last of her staff home hours ago, and it didn't seem worth it to sleep for just a couple of hours before she would need to open for breakfast again anyway.

Christmas morning was usually pretty quiet. She would get a few early birds, but most families would be home opening presents. There were some families in Pine Valley who didn't celebrate Christmas, of course, but with just about everything in town closed, they had a tendency to stay home, too, enjoying a rare day off. Two of her high school staff members were Jewish, and they usually came in to help her with the midday meal, but they wouldn't be in for some time yet. So Maggie was able to enjoy the quiet sunrise, even as clouds filled the sky. She wondered if it would snow again.

The party had been a success, full of happiness and excitement over the holiday. She loved watching friends and neighbors greet each other, sometimes after long times apart. The joy on their faces brought Maggie joy, too. She was glad she could be a part of it, even as just a spectator. She hoped Richard wouldn't have a problem continuing the tradition. Surely he loved this community as much as she did and would see the value in it. He had stopped by last night, too, and had seemed to enjoy himself. Today he would be working alongside her, once he had spent time with his own family that morning.

Maggie sipped her coffee and thought back to the night before. Of all the people she had seen, the one she had least expected had been Addy. She hoped Addy would come to the diner that day, but how could she explain that Addy had inspired her, without sounding like a crazy person? That, though they barely knew each other, Addy had given her that final push to make changes in her own life? She sighed. She hoped the words would come to her.

When Addy opened her eyes Christmas morning, she had to take a moment to remember where she was. Her impulsive decision the day before had brought her to Pine Valley. The Christmas party. *They remembered her.*

Addy took a deep breath and sat up. It was Christmas day. She had no plans. But she had been invited to eat at the diner and talk with Maggie. Something about changing her life? She had no idea what that was about. But she was curious to find out.

Since she didn't have anything else going on, Addy showered and got ready for the day, then left her motel room. Should she drive or walk? She was tempted to walk, even if it was a little bit of a hike. But it was cold, and the sky looked like snow was on its way, so she opted to drive instead. As she passed through the center of town, she could see all the other businesses were closed. Just as she pulled into the parking lot near the diner, though, she saw that the cafe across the street was open. Since she would be eating at the diner for lunch, maybe she should have breakfast there, instead.

An older couple was seated at a small table by the window, drinks and pastries in front of them, smiles on their faces as they chatted. Otherwise the cafe was empty. Addy approached the counter and smiled at the barista.

"Merry Christmas," the barista said with a returning smile. "What can I get for you?"

"Merry Christmas," Addy replied. "I'll take a black coffee and a cinnamon roll."

"Coming right up."

As the barista retrieved Addy's order, Addy decided to be sociable. "I was surprised to see you open on Christmas. Looks like just about everything else is closed."

"Yeah, I went back and forth on whether or not to close, but when it came down to it I didn't have much else going on, and I figured why not?" The woman smiled again. "We're only open through lunch, anyway, so I'll still have the afternoon and evening to stuff my face and watch Christmas movies on TV." She laughed.

Addy returned the smile and paid for her meal. "I love Christmas movies, too. I'm such a sucker for a happy ending."

"Me, too. I choose to live vicariously, since my love life is non-existent."

"Same here." Addy took a sip of her coffee. "Thanks for the breakfast."

"My pleasure. Enjoy your day."

Addy left the cafe, thinking she would walk while she ate. The biting wind and snowflakes that started falling changed her mind, though, and she headed back to her car instead. She would finish eating then decide what to do. She couldn't spend all day at the diner. But with the weather taking a turn, her options were limited. Sitting in the motel room by herself didn't hold much appeal, either. She turned on her car, found a radio station with holiday music, and took her time with her cinnamon roll. Maybe she would just sit here for a little while and watch the snow fall.

Maggie was just setting up the family-style tables when Addy walked in. A few couples were still enjoying late breakfasts, but the diner was relatively quiet. Maggie turned at the sound of the bell jangling and greeted Addy with a smile and a wave.

Addy approached, looking unsure but not quite as tense as she had appeared last night.

"Good morning," Maggie said. "Merry Christmas."

"Merry Christmas," Addy replied. She looked at the large table Maggie was preparing. "Expecting a large group?"

"In a way. This is one of my family-style tables. Families or couples or individuals can all sit together and enjoy a meal. Helps ease some of the loneliness that pops up on days like today."

"Mike said you took care of the town's lonely hearts."

Maggie chuckled. "Yes, I suppose I do. Or try to, anyway. I understand how they feel, being one myself." She put down the silverware she had been holding and beckoned Addy toward the counter. "Can I get you a cup of coffee?"

Addy shook her head. "No, thanks. I've already had one this morning. I probably shouldn't have come by so early, but I didn't have anything else going on, and our conversation yesterday piqued my curiosity."

Maggie sighed. "Yes, I suppose it did. Have a seat."

Addy sat on a counter stool while Maggie poured herself a cup of coffee.

"I may have been a bit melodramatic last night, but I was serious when I said that you changed my life." She took a sip of her coffee. "How to begin?" She paused. "I have owned this diner for a long time. And don't get me wrong, I have enjoyed it. It has given me a home, financial stability, and a way to help others as part of this community. But the more time that passed, the more I felt like something was missing. I put the needs of the diner, and its customers, ahead of my own. I've never taken vacations, or really explored the possibility of a relationship, for example. So I was feeling a bit down in the dumps, you could say."

Maggie paused, gazing out the front windows at the snow that was still flurrying.

"The problem is: I have never been brave. I have never been one to take risks or try new things. The only reason I even own this diner is because the previous owners wanted to retire and had no one to take it over." She looked at Addy. "And then you came along. Yes, you're much younger than I am, but you had the courage to start over, to just leave your life behind and find a new life. I envied that. But then I realized that there really wasn't anything stopping me from doing that, too. Yes, I had the diner to consider, but I could make changes. I could take control of my own life, do some of the things I've been missing while I still had the chance."

"Is that when you decided to sell the diner?"

Maggie nodded. "Pretty much. I hemmed and hawed a bit, but when it came down to it, that seemed the best option." She met Addy's gaze. "How did you know I was selling?"

"Mike told me."

Mike again, huh? Interesting... "I didn't realize the two of you had kept in touch."

"We...chatted for a bit after I left."

"But not anymore?"

Addy shook her head. "No. Though I saw him here last night."

"Yes, we had a good crowd last night. I was glad his parents were able to come, too."

"So did you sell the diner?"

Maggie shook her head. "Almost did. But it didn't feel right. Not the selling part, but who would be buying it. So I went back and forth about what to do. I had gotten a partnership offer, too, so I could just sell half of it if I wanted to." Maggie sighed. "And, after a lot of thinking on it, I decided that was the way to go."

"So you're not changing things too much, after all."

Maggie shook her head again, more forcefully this time. "Oh, no, I am. I'm moving out of the apartment in the back, and I'm going to cut way back on my working hours, and we're going to make some changes to the diner, too. Open up the apartment to make a party room, and maybe bring in some live entertainment." Maggie sighed again. "If we can figure out how to go about doing it. And if I can find a house in a reasonable amount of time."

Addy cocked her head to one side. "I guess I still don't see how I helped you. Though I'm flattered you think so."

"Don't you see? You were the catalyst. It was all just wishing until you gave me the push to do something about it."

Addy looked down, her fingers playing with the edge of the counter. "You give me a lot of credit, but I don't feel very brave, either."

"Well, maybe that makes you even braver, then. You were able to make big changes even if they scared you."

Addy looked up at Maggie. First Kate, now Maggie. To an extent, even Mike had been that way: thinking so highly of her, when she felt like she was floundering, just struggling to make it through. Was it really brave to just decide she had had enough? That she wanted something more substantial? And for Maggie to look at her as some kind of role model, something to aspire to. It was certainly not what Addy had been expecting.

"Okay, I think I've made you uncomfortable," Maggie said. "How about you help me finish setting the tables, and we can just chat. How's Boston?"

Addy stood up and followed Maggie back to the large table, then followed her lead to spread out the plates and silverware. "It's okay. No, it's great. It's going really well."

Maggie paused in the middle of putting down a plate. "That was not very convincing."

Addy sighed. "No, really, it's going well. I have an apartment in a nice neighborhood, and my roommate is really nice. I found a job that I really enjoy, and I've been tapping into what I really want and who I really am."

"That's a lot of 'reallys'." Maggie tried a grin, but it didn't quite make it to her eyes. "How are things really?"

"All of that is true, actually. And I'm signed up for a couple of classes that start in January, to meet new people and learn more about painting and marketing, which tie in to my job."

"Okay. If all that is true, why do you not sound happy?"

Addy met Maggie's gaze, and tears began welling in her eyes. "I don't know."

The tears began to slide down Addy's face, and she pulled out one of the chairs and sat down. "Oh, sweetie," Maggie said with concern, moving around the table to sit next to Addy, pulling Addy into her arms. "Shh. It's okay. Let it all out."

After a couple of minutes with tears dripping on Maggie's apron, Addy sniffled and looked up. "I do like my apartment and roommate, and I do like my job. I even started volunteering at a soup kitchen once in a while. And I've been enjoying tapping into my creativity. But I just – ." Addy sniffled again and sighed. "I feel lonely. My bedroom is so bare. And I'm starting to worry about money. Boston is so expensive, and my job is only part time, and I don't know what to do about that. And I enjoy my job, and my boss Linda seemed so supportive and excited about so many of my ideas, but now I learn there are limitations because it's a franchise, and so some of the things I was excited about we can't do. And as much as I want to learn and meet people, I'm nervous about taking classes. It has been so long since I've been in school. And what if I fail? What if I hate it? What if the other students hate me?"

"I don't think the other students will hate you. You might make some real friendships there. You know you're starting with a common interest, so that's something."

Addy wiped her cheeks with her hands. "I guess."

"Why don't we take things one step at a time? What was the first problem? You were lonely. Well, it sounds like you have some people in your life, and over time I'm sure you'll build those relationships. And getting out there with the soup kitchen is good, too. You're giving back, but you're also putting yourself out there, both with the people you're helping and the people you're working with. And, like you said, you'll be meeting people in your classes. I imagine that problem will remedy itself in time." Maggie sighed. "I know it's hard to be lonely. I've been lonely, too. Do you have any friends from your former life you could reach out to?"

Addy shook her head. "No. That's one of the reasons I left. All of my supposed friends were just superficial. They didn't actually care about me, and to be honest I didn't really care about them. We were just existing in the same area."

Maggie tutted. "That's unfortunate. Okay, so it sounds like you need some real friends. Well, I imagine you'll get there with all of your reaching out, but in the meantime, you can also feel free to reach out to me at any time. I think we're becoming friends, aren't we?" Maggie smiled at her, and Addy tried to smile back.

"Yeah. But would you want to hear from me? Seriously?"

"Of course! You can fill me in on your exciting life up there, and I can keep you posted about my pitiful life down here." She gave a little chuckle. "Really, though, I would be happy to hear from you, whenever you needed a chat or just wanted to share something or whatever."

"Thanks."

"Of course. Okay, so one problem solved. What was next?" Maggie thought a moment. "Oh, yes, your bedroom is bare and Boston is expensive." Maggie sighed. "I can't do anything about the expensive part, I'm afraid. And I don't really know anything about that. I do know I'm a bit nervous when I think about how much I'm going to be spending on a house. But I imagine that's not the same."

"Not really. I went online to do a little research, and apparently Boston is one of the most expensive cities to live in."

"And you didn't know that before?"

Addy shook her head. "No. I was just so anxious to leave D.C., and I needed to at least feel like I had a destination, so I grabbed onto Boston and started driving. Wish I had looked into a bit more, though I'm not sure it would have changed my mind. I didn't have a job or anything lined up, but I had a bunch of money in the bank from selling my mom's apartment, so I figured I would be set. Once I got a job, the rest would just fall into place."

"But you didn't count on the job being part time. Are you thinking of getting a second job?"

"I've thought about it. But I considered a lot of jobs before I found this one, and none of them appealed to me. Unfortunately I don't think it will go full time at any point. There isn't much room for advancement. Unless, maybe, I'm able to really book more parties. I do painting parties for a paint-your-own pottery place. And help out with other things, but my main job is the party planning."

"And you enjoy it?"

"I do. I have found I like being creative, and I'm pretty good at the business end of it, too."

"That's great. You said it's a franchise. Could you open your own franchise?"

Addy sighed. "Probably if I really wanted to. But franchises can get really expensive. You have to pay to be able to use the name and stuff, on top of all the risks with starting a new business."

"You said you have money in the bank. Would it be enough?"

"I don't know. But I'm also not sure I would want to tie up all the money in buying a franchise, especially with no guarantee that the business will be successful. Honestly, though, I hadn't even considered it."

"Well, it might be worth looking into at least."

"Even if I did want to go that route, though, I couldn't set up shop so close to the current location. There's no way both would be successful. So I would have to move again."

"Hmm. True. Though considering your other concerns, moving now might not be the worse idea, before you got really settled."

Addy sat for a minute, her brain processing all of these new ideas.

"You also wouldn't have to buy a franchise. You could just start a business doing the same kind of thing. Then you wouldn't be limited by what the home office approves. You had said that was one of your concerns, too."

Addy looked up to meet Maggie's gaze. "You have given me so much to think about."

Maggie gave a soft laugh. "Probably too much."

"No, it's good. I was feeling a bit stuck."

"I'm glad I could help. Pay you back a bit for the help you gave me." She smiled. "Now," she said, standing up and putting her hands on the table, "I really do have to finish setting these tables."

Addy helped Maggie with the tables and other set-up, her mind whirring with all of the possibilities she had just discussed with Maggie. Did she really want to even consider starting her own business when she was just getting started in her new life? What if this ended up being a passing phase and she hated it a year or two down the line? And where would she even go? She couldn't compete with Linda, but the thought of figuring out a new location was overwhelming. And even if she wanted to move, she had a lease. She couldn't just up and leave. That wouldn't be fair to Kate, and it would probably be expensive. She gave a mental sigh. Too much to think about.

But it was Christmas. As the customers started arriving, Maggie expertly directed them to individual booths or a family-style table. Soon one family table was full, with Addy seated among the other guests, and bowls and platters were brought out. Determined not to think about her troubles, Addy settled into introductions and light conversation with her table mates. By the time dessert was brought out, she felt like she was friends with these people who had been strangers hours before. She imagined that was Maggie's intention, and it had worked. She could see two other family-style tables settling into similar situations, filled with chatter and smiles and laughter.

What a place Maggie had built here. Whether she had really chosen to go into the diner business or not, she had a knack for it, for making people feel welcome and content. Addy was glad she wasn't giving it up completely. She would hate to think all of this would be lost to someone who just didn't care as much. And she would be interested to see what Maggie and her new business partner did with the place, how they helped it grow. If it was this great now, how amazing would it be then?

Chapter 29

Though Mike hosted Christmas at his house, he didn't do much of the preparation work. His mother always insisted she missed cooking big meals, so he gave her free rein of his kitchen, helping as needed or wanted. In addition to his parents, he had aunts and uncles and cousins coming, and his house would be full by lunchtime. His mom had tried to get him to invite Jen, but so far he had been able to convince her that Jen was spending the day with her own family. Though that was true, he was sure they could have worked something out if they had wanted to. Honestly, he just wasn't ready to have her meet his parents. Especially since he wasn't even sure how he felt about her.

They had been going out for a few weeks now, seeing each other a couple of times a week and chatting on the phone or online in between. Jen had passed the bar exam and found a job, which she would be starting in January. She seemed happy about it, so he was happy for her. She would be working for an organization that helped low- income individuals who couldn't afford lawyers. It was what she wanted to do, and Mike was impressed with her determination and her desire to help others.

Jen was a great woman, and she was interested in settling down, especially now that her career was getting established. Her working at a smaller organization rather than a high-powered firm would help give her better work-life balance, she had said, while also giving her a sense of fulfillment. It was admirable. She had really thought things through. The question was: did she want to settle down with him? And did he want to settle down with her?

He could see them having a happy life. Maybe there weren't fireworks when they were together, but they got along. He respected her and enjoyed talking to her. He imagined deep, fulfilling love would come with time. After all, fireworks didn't last forever. Better to build a solid foundation to grow from. Right?

At the moment he hadn't come to any conclusions. But it was still early, and they had plenty of time to decide what they wanted. He figured he would give it his all and see where it took them. At the very least it helped ease his loneliness, making that gaping hole in his heart smaller. And since they didn't see each other every day, he had been able to get back to the other important things in life: spending time with his friends, re-establishing an exercise routine, finding time for cooking and other hobbies he had enjoyed. As much as he said his life had had a lot going for him, he had gotten into a rut. And now, with Jen's help – whether she knew it or not – he was pulling himself out. So no matter what happened with Jen, his life was improving.

Lunch went well. Mike had a great family, and they chatted and bantered around the table throughout the meal, catching up on lives since the last time they had seen each other, a year ago. After the meal was cleared, they participated in their Secret Santa gift exchange, followed by coffee and dessert, and then board games and relaxing. It was what Christmas was all about, as far as he was concerned, and Mike enjoyed himself.

By the time everyone had left, Mike felt happy, but as the house grew quiet again, the happiness dimmed. What would it be like to say good-bye to everyone and still have a wife and children with him? To hear laughter and playing, to feel an arm around his waist as he waved good-bye to the last stragglers pulling out of the driveway? Yes, he definitely wanted those things. He hoped he was on the right path to get them.

When Addy arrived back at her apartment the day after Christmas, her mind was still working through the ideas Maggie had had. It was interesting how getting someone else's take on a situation could send her in completely different directions than she would have gotten on her own. Owning her own business? That hadn't even occurred to her. And, to be honest, the idea freaked her out. What did she know about running a business? And what if she put in all the hard work and it failed? Then she would feel even worse than she did now. And it wasn't as if painting was a necessity. It was frivolous, just something fun to do.

Addy pushed open her bedroom door to put her things away. The paintings she had hung greeted her, and she smiled. Painting might be frivolous, but it made her happy. And she really did feel like she was tapping into a part of herself she hadn't known existed. She would miss it if she had to give it up.

With a sigh, Addy opened her duffel bag and started putting things away. She was going to have to head to the laundromat at some point, but she wasn't in the mood. She could get through another couple of days. As long as she had clean clothes for Saturday she would be fine. That was going to be her first solo party, and, while she was a little nervous, she was excited. She had learned enough and become confident enough that having someone else hover, watching her, had gotten annoying and made her feel uneasy. This time she would be in control. She just hoped she didn't screw up.

Once she was unpacked, Addy flopped on her air mattress with her laptop, all ready to put on a movie. Just a couple of minutes into the movie her phone rang.

She didn't recognize the number, but it was local. "Hello?"

"Hi. Is this Addy?"

"Yes. Who is this?"

"Hey, my name is Jake. My friend Jess said you needed some help with some furniture?"

"Oh!" Addy sat up. She had just about given up hope on that front. "Probably. I don't have anything ready yet. I was trying to figure out how to get it first."

"What kind of furniture are we talking?"

"Um. Probably a nightstand, maybe a dresser, possibly a headboard?"

"Okay. That's doable."

"I was looking online at buy nothing sites and marketplace, so I don't know what exactly I'll find or when."

"No problem. Let me know when you find something, and I'll help you grab it. I imagine you'll also need some help getting it up to your apartment."

"That would be amazing."

"Okay. So just give me a call when you're ready."

"How much will I owe you?"

"Tank of gas."

"That's it?"

Jake chuckled. "That's it. Though my truck can be a bit of a gas guzzler."

"Wow. Thank you so much."

"No problem. Talk soon."

Addy hung up the phone feeling a bit more positive. She could get real furniture! Turning off the movie, she decided to scour the online offerings instead. She couldn't wait to have a real bed again.

The day after Christmas was relatively quiet at the diner. She had her regulars, but disrupted schedules and vacations meant a lot of other potential customers were simply doing other things. That was fine. Maggie could use a little breathing space. She and Richard were going to take the opportunity to discuss some of the ideas they were thinking of implementing in the new year.

One of the first things they would be changing, though it had been a harder sell to Maggie than the others, was the hours the diner was open. While Maggie was worried about the people in need who would have no place to go, she had to acknowledge that she wasn't a young woman anymore. She needed more rest than her current schedule allowed. And at the same time, it didn't make sense to pay someone to cover the diner in the overnight hours when she hardly saw anyone. So they were going to compromise: she would let go of the twenty-four-hour schedule during the week, but Friday and Saturday nights they would remain open. So from Friday morning at five o'clock to Sunday night at eleven, the diner would be open nonstop. Monday through Thursday they would be open from five in the morning to eleven at night. Those six hours a night might not seem like much, but for Maggie they represented a nearly full night sleep that she rarely got. She just wondered how the community would react.

Next on the agenda was the party room. Maggie hadn't yet been able to find a house, but when she did, they needed a game plan. Were they going to need to bring in experts to knock down a wall or two? Possibly. Richard promised to make some calls and see if he could get someone in to at least give them an educated assessment and price quote.

Deciding that was enough big changes to start with, Maggie and Richard spent the rest of the morning dreaming.

"Christmas was amazing, Maggie. Really impressive. I never realized you put on such a production."

Maggie chuckled. "It didn't start out that way. It has certainly grown over the years, and I'm grateful. The response I've gotten has been very positive."

"I'll bet. Do you do something like that at other times, too?"

"Not to that extent. Christmas seems to be the hardest time of year for people."

"Maybe once the party room is set up we could host our own events, not just rent it out for others."

"What did you have in mind?"

"Well, we could do something for New Year's, for example. Maybe a Valentine's Day event for single people. I've heard speed dating is popular these days."

Maggie laughed. "Oh my. I don't even want to know. But I'm sure we could put some things together, drum up some business and offer social events. You and I both know that entertainment is sorely lacking in this town."

"That it is."

"Years ago I considered bringing in live entertainment. Bands and such."

"Why didn't you?"

Maggie shrugged. "Seemed a lot of work, and I wasn't sure if there would be enough room, or if it would be worth the expense."

"Well," said Richard, thinking. "With the open room, you would have enough space for the performers and most likely chairs and maybe some small tables for spectators. And if the doorway is open, or we keep the doors open, even people eating in the main dining room could hear."

"Do you think we would get enough extra business to make it worth the cost of hiring performers?"

"I think so. People watching would order drinks and appetizers. You could even have a special menu for events. And if you – we – look for local talent rather than big names, the cost would be lower. We could even have open mic nights, which would cost very little to produce. Though we would probably need some equipment." Richard made some notes on a legal pad. "And with open mic nights, we'd get friends and family members of the people performing. Yes, this could be good." He made more notes.

Maggie laughed. She was glad Richard was so eager to try new ideas. It was certainly sparking her own enthusiasm, something that had been sorely lacking over the last several years. She could now see possibility, where she had started to only see burdens. She took a sip of her now-cold coffee and cringed. "Shall I get us more coffee?"

"Wouldn't hurt, I suppose." He was still jotting down notes. Maggie retrieved the coffee pot and, having dumped her stale coffee, poured them each a full cup.

"You know, I know you love giving back to the community – as do I. I wonder if there would be a less labor-intensive way to involve the community in something. Some way to get people in the door, but without having to put on a big event." Richard seemed deep in thought, his pen resting on his lower lip.

"What were you thinking?"

"I'm not sure. I'm trying to think of things that would get people excited to stop by. Maybe to see something, or experience something. You know how the town does the holiday light displays? Something like that, where we could set something up and just have a rotating stream of people."

"Hmm. An interesting thought. I'm not sure what would fit the bill, though."

"Me neither." Richard grinned and turned to look at Maggie. "Just brainstorming I guess. Maybe something will come to me." He took a sip of his coffee and leaned back in his chair. "I'm really excited about this, Maggie."

Maggie laughed again. "I've noticed."

"I'm glad you decided to take me up on my offer. I think we'll work really well together. I know there will be some adjustments, but together we can make the diner even more successful, and keep building on the momentum you've already started."

Maggie smiled and leaned back in her own chair. "It will be nice to share the burden, but I must admit that seeing your excitement has gotten me excited, too. I'm seeing this old place in a whole new light."

Richard lifted his mug to clink with hers. "To exciting changes and new beginnings."

"Indeed." Maggie tapped her mug against his. "It will be interesting to see what all these changes bring."

Chapter 30

January

Jake and Addy placed the dresser down against a wall and stepped back. Addy couldn't keep the smile off her face. It wasn't perfect. It had its share of dings and scratches – a few of which had been added on the trek up the stairs – but it looked great. And it would look even better after she added her personal touches. She took a deep breath and turned toward Jake. "Nightstand?"

Jake nodded once. "Nightstand." He turned to head out the door, and Addy followed. "No need to come with. I can handle that one on my own." He flashed Addy a grin and left the apartment.

He was such a nice guy. Addy wondered if he was single. With her starting to feel more settled, she was beginning to think she might be ready to date again. Addy sighed. What a wishy-washy sentiment. Was she really feeling more settled? Was she really ready to date? She thought back to Christmas and her conversation with Maggie. She had been an emotional mess. Some of it was probably the holiday, but there had definitely been truth in there, too. As much as she was trying, Boston didn't feel like home yet. But maybe she was just being impatient. After all, it had only been three months.

Addy gave herself a mental shake. Today was not the day to ponder big life decisions. It was a day to celebrate little ones – like real furniture. They had picked up a bed the week before, and she had had a mattress delivered a few days ago.

Now, with a dresser and nightstand, she would finally feel moved in. That had to help her mental state. She grinned and did a little happy dance, then went to the bathroom cabinet to get cleaning wipes. They would definitely need a bit of scrubbing before she added her clothes and personal items. Creative alterations would be done piecemeal so she could keep at least most of her items put away. She couldn't take one more minute of living out of cardboard boxes.

When Jake returned to the room, Addy was cleaning out the bottom dresser drawers.

"Left or right side of the bed?"

Addy thought for a moment. "Left. No, right. No, left." She grinned. "Sorry. Left, please." She stayed out of his way as he carried it over. "Thanks."

Jake wiped his hands against each other and brushed his shirt and thighs. "Alright, then. I think we're set. Are you looking to get anything else?"

Addy looked around the room and laughed. "I don't think I could fit anything else in here."

Jake smiled. "Probably not."

"Thank you so much," Addy said as they made their way back to the living room.

"No problem at all."

"So... tank of gas? How much would that run? I feel like that's not enough for all your help."

"What would you say to a cup of coffee instead?"

"I'm thinking that would definitely be not enough. Quite a bargain for me, but a bit unfair to you."

Jake shrugged. "You could join me. That would make it worth it."

Addy blushed. Had she really been out of the game so long that she had missed a pickup line? "Um. Sure."

Jake laughed. "Gee, don't sound so enthusiastic."

"Sorry. I..." Addy took a deep breath. "I'm not really dating right now."

Jake held up one hand. "No worries. And no pressure."

"No, it's okay. Coffee sounds good." She gave him a small smile.

"Yeah?"

"Yeah."

"Great. Did you want to go now, or... " He gestured with one thumb toward the door.

"Sure." Addy grabbed her coat and purse and locked the apartment door on the way out. "There's a cafe down the street. We could walk if you want."

"Sounds good."

The walk passed in companionable small talk. Addy learned that Jake owned a small construction company, hence the access to a truck. As they sat down with their coffees, Addy found herself asking him about owning his own business. Did he like it? Was it hard? How long had he been doing it? After a while, Addy paused and blushed "I'm sorry. It just occurred to me that I've been interrogating you."

Jake grinned and leaned back in his chair. "That's okay. I don't mind. Curious, though. You thinking of starting your own business?"

Addy sighed, resting both her hands around her mug. "I don't know. A friend recently put the idea in my head, and I didn't think I was seriously considering it, but here I am trying to find out more."

"Nothing wrong with that. You need to learn as much as you can to decide if it's the right choice for you."

"You're right. I'm starting classes to learn more for my job. Why should this be any different?"

"Exactly. So what is it you're thinking of doing?"

"You'll probably think it's silly."

"Hey, if it's something you're passionate about, it's not silly."

Addy took a deep breath. "Okay. Well, I work for this place called Paintastic."

"Yeah, I've heard of that. Painting pottery, right?"

"Right. I kind of stumbled into it, but I've found out I really like it. I run the parties there, plus help out in the shop."

"You must be pretty creative."

Addy laughed. "I never used to think so, but apparently I am. I have found I enjoy painting, creating, making something from nothing."

"That's awesome," Jake said, leaning forward. "That's one of my favorite parts of my job, too, actually. Seeing something I built being used and appreciated. So that's what your business would be?"

Addy nodded. "Kind of. I like what Paintastic does, but I have all these ideas for additional things to offer or try. And unfortunately, since Paintastic is a franchise, there are limits on what we can do."

"What do you want to do?"

"Well, I actually found I enjoy the teaching part of things, showing kids in particular what they can create. I'd love to offer classes or something for kids. And I want to find a way to give back to the community. I recently started volunteering at a soup kitchen, and they are always in need of more money and resources." Addy could feel herself getting more animated. "I'd like to go into schools and maybe reach kids who never even realized they're creative, or who never wanted to admit it. And stuff for the grown-ups, too. My friend Maggie does all these things to bring lonely people together, and I'd love to find ways to do that, too."

"Wow. Looks like this is something that really excites you. I would say it's definitely worth pursuing."

"Thanks," Addy said, settling back in her seat. "It's funny. I guess I didn't realize how much I cared about this until I started talking about it."

"That happens."

"Unfortunately, even if I do decide I want to start a business, it probably wouldn't work out."

"Why not?"

"Because Paintastic would be my competition. I would be doing at least some of the things they're doing. So I would be setting myself up for a struggle if I started it around here. I would have to go further out or somewhere else."

"Hmm. Competition isn't necessarily a bad thing. And it sounds like you would be offering enough things to set you apart."

"Maybe."

"Or you could move."

Addy sighed. "Yeah, I could move. Again."

"I guess you'll have to give it some more thought. And decide what's most important to you."

Richard had scheduled a contractor to check out the potential party room on a Tuesday morning in the middle of January. As the local church bells chimed ten o'clock, Maggie, Richard, and the contractor Mick stood staring at the blank wall at one side of the diner. On the other side of the wall was Maggie's apartment. Mick had already been up to the crawl space that served as an attic and had been around both sides of the wall.

"From what I can tell," Mick said. "This wall was added after the diner was built, most likely to create the living space. I pulled the original blueprints from the town records, and it does not show an apartment, and the wall seems to have its own frame, just connected with brackets and plaster."

"So we can take it down?" Maggie asked.

Mick nodded. "You can take it down. There are likely some electrical wires running through it, since there's an outlet on the other side, but that just requires some investigation and planning. Shouldn't be a problem."

Maggie breathed a sigh of relief. Finally some good news.

"So now you would just need to decide what kind of entryway, and how you would want the apartment space to be modified. And, of course, a timeline for it all."

Maggie turned to Richard, and they grinned at each other. That was the fun stuff. Or it would be once Maggie moved out. But there was nothing to stop them from planning it now.

"Thank you so much, Mick," Richard said, shaking the contractor's hand. "And your crew would be able to handle the job?"

Mick nodded. "Most likely. I'll know for sure once you decide what you want. Then we can discuss a quote."

"Sounds good."

Mick shook Maggie's hand, as well, and the three of them walked toward the front door.

"We'll be in touch," Maggie said as Mick left with a wave. She turned again toward Richard. "Looks like we're good to go."

"Looks like it. Shall we celebrate with pie?"

"Pie!" Maggie laughed. "It's ten in the morning."

"No better time for pie. Besides, fruit is good for you." He winked at her.

"Oh, you," Maggie replied, swatting Richard's arm. But she headed over to the case and dished up two thick slabs of apple pie. How could she refuse?

"So," Richard said after swallowing his first bite. "Now that we know we can knock into that wall safely, we have some decisions to make."

They chatted as they ate, discussing options for the party room and debating the pros and cons of an open archway versus closing doors. By the time they put their forks down they had made some decisions and were still considering others.

"I guess now I really do need to find a house," Maggie said with a sigh.

Richard patted the hand that lay by her coffee cup. "You will. The right one will come along. Just have a little faith."

"Easier said than done."

"I know."

They lapsed into a companionable silence. Lunch customers were starting to come in, and they both got up, grabbing their dirty dishes before heading to the kitchen. Jordan was greeting and seating incoming customers, and Jessica was prepping in the kitchen. Maggie and Richard placed their dishes in the sink, then each put on an apron. Richard would be working the kitchen while Maggie headed back to the dining room. They were still working on a permanent schedule, but with Maggie still living at the diner, she wasn't in a hurry to change the hours yet. Soon. It would definitely be an adjustment for everyone, her most of all. But this was progress, and it was good. Progress was good.

With a smile, Maggie greeted an older couple as they came in. Jordan was taking orders, so she chatted for a bit before retrieving beverages. The regular routine would continue – for now at least.

Chapter 31

"M aggie?"

"Yes, this is Maggie."

"It's Megan." The normally cheerful and chatty woman was speaking very curtly. Was she okay?

"Hello, Megan. How are you?"

"Just peachy." The sarcasm practically dripped over the phone line.

"Oh my. What's the matter?"

"Nothing." Megan paused a moment, and Maggie could hear her taking deep breaths. "Well, I'm in labor, but that's a good thing."

"Oh! Maybe you should go to the hospital. Or the medical center?"

"No, no, no. It will be hours yet." Megan took another deep breath. "Okay, I'm better. As I said, it will be a while. So I'm just doing business as usual, willing the time to pass."

"Good luck."

"Thanks." Silence fell. "Oh! I almost forgot the reason for calling. I was looking at all the listings again, seeing if there was anything new to show you. And I don't know why, but I had been hung up on finding houses with at least two bedrooms for you. Force of habit, I guess. But would you be open to a one bedroom?"

Maggie thought for a moment. "Well, it is just me. And I don't have many things. I don't need much space."

"There's this adorable little one-bedroom house that's been on the market for a while. Close to the center of town. Want to take a peek?"

"Of course. When will you be available though? Sounds like you'll have your hands full for a while."

"Are you free now? They say walking is good for moving labor along."

Maggie looked around. Business was quiet, and she had sufficient staffing. And she wouldn't be gone for long. "If you're sure."

"Absolutely. I'll meet you at the diner. It's within walking distance."

Maggie had her concerns, but Megan was insistent, so she acquiesced. She only hoped it was worth it. And that Megan's baby would wait.

When Megan opened the door to the diner, it was after she had paused right outside, taken panting breaths, then straightened. Maggie had a feeling she was going to have to start timing these contractions. She took a quick peek at her watch before greeting Megan and grabbing her coat.

"I should be back soon," she told Jordan.

"No problem, Miss Maggie. Kyle and I can handle the crowd," Jordan replied with a smile. There was only one customer in the diner.

Maggie returned the smile and held up a hand in farewell.

The house was very close to the diner, so close she was surprised she hadn't noticed it before. But there wasn't a for sale sign up.

"The owner was afraid it would ruin the lawn or spread rumors or something," Megan said by way of explanation with a roll of her eyes. "The reason changed every time we asked. But I think it was just because she didn't really want to move. Something must have changed, though, because she just decided to lower the asking price. That's what put it back on my radar."

Megan unlocked the door and pushed it open. The moment Maggie stepped over the threshold she felt it. The spark.

The house was small, but, especially coming from a studio apartment at the back of a diner, it felt spacious. The kitchen was more modern than Maggie had expected based on what Megan had said. And the living room had a fireplace that Maggie fell in love with. The backyard was desolate, as was everyone's in town this time of year, but it was a good size. Maybe Maggie could have a garden. Or set up a hammock to lounge away the summer. Or just sit out here with a book and a cup of tea. She would actually have time for that now.

They moved back inside, and Maggie checked out the bedroom. Pleasant. She would easily be able to fit her queen size bed in there, and she would have a view of the backyard. The nearby bathroom would likely need a little updating, but nothing too drastic. Manageable.

They were about to head down to the basement when Maggie heard Megan panting again. She took a peek at her watch. Twenty minutes had passed since the last contraction.

"Okay, Megan, time to go."

"We haven't finished looking at the house yet," Megan argued, trying to catch her breath.

"We'll come back another time. John can bring me back, if you're not able to. There's no rush."

Megan took a deep breath. "Nope, no rush." She smiled at Maggie. "And I'm feeling better. We have time."

"One quick peek at the basement, and then we're out of here. And you are staying up here."

Megan sighed but gave in. "Fine."

Maggie went down the stairs to the basement. Basements always made her uneasy, but this one was relatively low key. It was partially finished, so she was greeted by painted walls and linoleum flooring. A washing machine and dryer stood against one wall, joined by a sink and an ironing board. It would be nice to not have to go to the laundromat. Behind a closed door Maggie found the typical utilities, including a furnace and water heater. Nothing looked decrepit or terribly outdated. Satisfied, she turned to head back up the stairs.

As she stepped back onto the first floor, she could see Megan sitting on a chair at the kitchen table. She was panting again.

"Alright, Megan. Let's go."

"Okay," Megan said feebly. "I called John. He's on his way to pick me up."

"Good. I don't think you'll make it back to the office in your condition."

Five minutes later, Megan was belted into John's car and on her way to the medical center. Maggie stood outside the house, shaking her head. Still, despite Megan's questionable priorities, Maggie was grateful she had shown her this house. Maggie turned to look back at it. Yes, it would do nicely. And the price was decent, too. She would almost be able to cover the entire cost with what she had in the bank. As long as she was approved for the rest – and a little extra to cover any expenses that came up with moving in – she would be in good shape. Talk to the bank first or make an offer first? Considering the current state of her realtors, it looked like the bank would be the next step. But not today. She had to get back to the diner. She couldn't wait to tell Richard the good news.

Despite their rocky beginning, Addy had enjoyed her date with Jake and agreed to dinner with him the following weekend. As she got ready, their conversation regarding her possible business rolled through her mind. She hadn't realized how much the idea of starting her own business appealed to her, but she still had her doubts and concerns, not least of all was her competence when it came to running a business. She had never even had a long-term job. What did she know about starting and running a business? Nevertheless she had started jotting down ideas, spending some of her free time brainstorming and dreaming. Maybe she should pick up a book or two about starting a business, or see if there were online seminars or something. She was sure there were websites with information. But was it worth doing the research when she was convinced it wouldn't work out?

That's always been your problem, Adelaide. Head in the clouds without any follow-through. Be practical.

It had been a while since she had heard her mother's voice. But it never failed: as soon as her insecurities began to poke their heads to the surface, that voice was right there, making sure she knew how much of a failure she was. She had started getting good at ignoring it, pushing it away, but with her current doubts she knew that would be difficult.

You're never satisfied. You move to a strange place, find a job, and it's still not enough. What do you want, Adelaide?

What *did* she want? Maybe this time her mother was actually right. It was like she had told Maggie: she had a good place to live, a job she enjoyed, and she was starting to get settled. So what was the problem? Maybe the problem was her. Maybe she would never be happy, always looking for some reason to be disgruntled.

Addy sighed and finished brushing her hair. She wasn't going to think about this tonight. She was going to go out, enjoy a nice dinner with a nice man, and have fun. She would keep the conversation light and upbeat, not dwelling on big life decisions. It was too early for that anyway. She had only discussed her business idea with him before because he was a business owner. She had been doing research, that's all.

The buzzer to the front door went off. Addy took one last look in the mirror, flicked off the light to the bathroom, and made her way to the door, grabbing her purse on the way.

She greeted Jake with a smile, and he returned the smile, holding out a curved elbow to take her arm. Addy laughed. "Such a gentleman."

"I try." He grinned again and led her to his car.

"No truck this time?"

"Nah. This is what I drive most of the time. The truck is for work. And helping women in need." He winked, and Addy laughed again.

As she slid into the front seat, Addy evaluated what she had just done. Had his comment really been that funny? Or was she slipping back into her "charm the man" mentality? Maybe her mother's voice was starting to affect her a bit too much again. Or maybe she was overthinking things again. She took a deep breath, buckled her seat belt, and turned to face Jake. "So where are we off to?"

"I was thinking Thai if that's okay with you."

"That would be fine."

"I know a great little restaurant just outside the city."

"Sounds good."

They settled into the rhythm of driving, filling the silence with small talk. He was a nice man, Addy reflected. Maybe he didn't give her butterflies like Mike had, but he was nice. And a decent, hard-working man, too. And easy on the eyes. It might go nowhere, but it was worth a shot. Didn't hurt to try.

The meal passed pleasantly. Conversation flowed smoothly. And when Jake dropped her off, he kissed her and asked to see her again. She agreed, despite not feeling a spark. What was wrong with her?

Addy made her way up to her apartment, opened the door, greeted Kate, and went to her bedroom, where she closed the door and flopped on her bed, kicking her shoes off as she went. Staring up at the ceiling, she felt her eyes fill with tears. Seriously, what was *wrong* with her? Now on top of settling into her chosen home, finding a job she enjoyed, and connecting with who she was, she could add finding a decent man to her list of accomplishments. And she was *crying*?

She heard a knock on her bedroom door and wiped her face with her hands.

"Addy? Are you okay? You looked upset."

Addy stood up and opened the door. "Hey. Yeah, I'm okay. Just having a quarter life crisis." She attempted a smile.

"Well that's no good. Want to talk about it?"

Addy shrugged but held open the door and returned to her bed. Kate followed and propped herself on the edge of the bed after Addy sat back down.

"So what's up?"

"I had a date tonight."

"Must have been a bad one for you to be this upset. What happened?"

Addy shook her head. "No, it wasn't a bad one. He was perfectly pleasant, and we got along just fine. We have another date next weekend."

Kate's face registered her confusion. "Then why the tears?"

Addy met Kate's concerned gaze and felt the tears bubble up again. "I don't know."

"Maybe you should start at the beginning."

"Well, you know the beginning. My disastrous life in D.C. and my flee to Boston."

"Yeah. And I thought things were going well. You seemed to be enjoying your job, and you got furniture, so yay!" She held up her fists and shook them in an expression of joy.

"Yup. On paper everything is going great."

"Then what's the matter?"

Addy shrugged again. "I wish I knew. Like, I enjoy my job, but it's part time and I worry about the money, right? And my date today was fine, great even. But I felt myself slipping into old habits, trying to do and say things to please my date rather than be who I am, you know? And I have all these ideas, and as I'm trying to learn who I really am I'm starting to figure things out, but then I keep getting stuck with obstacles and problems that I just don't know how to get around."

"No one said life would be easy."

Addy sighed. "I know."

"You haven't been here very long. Do you think you need to give it more time? Maybe some things will work themselves out?"

"Maybe. I've tried to tell myself that a hundred times."

"What's your gut telling you?"

"That I'm not happy. But it can't tell me exactly why not."

"Hmm." Kate slumped back a bit, leaning against the footboard.

They sat in silence for a moment, Kate thinking and Addy looking miserable.

"Okay," Kate finally said. "So maybe you're getting hung up on details. Your brain is focusing on all the facts, all the reasons you should logically be happy: job, home, guy, whatever. But your heart and gut are telling you something is off. And I learned a long time ago that those things can't – and shouldn't – be ignored. So let's get back to basics. When you left D.C., what brought you to Boston?"

"Um...a vague idea of what and where it was?"

Kate laughed. "Seriously? There wasn't anything that specifically made you want to move to Boston?"

"I wanted to move to a city. And New York City seemed so cliché. Boston seemed the next best thing."

Kate shook her head. "Okay, then. Why did you want to move to a city?"

"I like being around people. I..." Addy could feel tears welling up again. "I wanted to be able to lose myself in a crowd of people and forget my problems." She sniffed.

Kate's expression turned to one of sympathy. "Oh, Addy." She rested a hand on Addy's shoulder to comfort her new friend. "Did it work?"

Addy shook her head.

"I can guess why." Addy looked up and met Kate's gaze with watery eyes. "You were used to crowds of people. That's what you came from. But you left to discover who you were, not lose yourself. You were already lost. So you ran from one isolating place to another., and your heart has been rebelling."

Addy sniffed but remained silent, letting Kate's words sink in.

"Me? I love Boston. Yes, there are lots of people, but that's not what appeals to me. I love the culture and the history, the access to so many amazing things. I moved here because I was offered a great job that I love, and everything I learned about Boston appealed to me. It was an extension of who I was and what I wanted, not an escape. Does that make sense?"

Addy nodded.

"Now, the good news is that despite the reason for moving here, you have made some progress in what your original goal was. From what I can tell, you have started getting to know yourself. You've started painting. And I've seen you scribbling who-knows-what on a notepad."

"Ideas," Addy said between sniffs. "For a business."

Kate's eyes brightened. "You want to start a business? That's amazing!"

Addy shrugged. "Maybe."

"Are those some of the obstacles you were talking about?"

Addy nodded.

"Personally I think it's great. At the very least you've found something you're passionate enough about to want to do it for a living. If that's not discovering who you are, I don't know what is."

"But what if it's a passing phase? What if I go through all the trouble of starting this business and decide I hate it?"

"That's a real possibility. But even if that happens, it wouldn't be the end of the world. Think about everything you would learn in the process. And if your goal is to learn who you are and what you want, failing can be just as important as succeeding. Maybe more so."

"You sound like a motivational speaker."

Kate laughed. "Good. Maybe it will motivate you." She smiled. "Seriously, though, you need to follow your gut."

Addy took a deep breath. "One of the obstacles is location. And if I follow my gut, as you say, that would likely mean I'd have to move. Again."

"Hmm. Well, I'd hate to lose you, but I'd hate for you to be miserable here even more. Where would you move to?"

"I don't know."

"One more thing to figure out?"

Addy nodded. "Plus I signed a lease."

Kate waved her hand in a dismissive motion. "The lease is whatever. Don't let that be the deciding factor."

"I wouldn't do that to you, though."

"Well, if you really feel that badly about it, take that as a sign. It's January now, so that means you have about nine months or so until it's lease renewal time. Use those nine months to figure things out. Do some research and brainstorming and problem solving and all that. Decide what you really want and learn how best to get there. Weren't you starting some classes soon?"

Addy nodded again. "They start next week."

"There you go. I hope they would be useful for your business, too?"

Another nod.

"Good. Then learn all you can so you can make an educated decision. At the very least, getting more exposure to what you would be doing might make it easier for you to decide if it's the right choice for you or not."

When Addy didn't respond, Kate patted her knee and stood up.

"I'm here if you want to talk more, but I get the impression that you have some thinking to do, so I'll leave you to it."

Kate closed the bedroom door behind her, and Addy flopped down to lie on her back. Kate had certainly given her a lot to think about, and a lot of it aligned with thoughts Addy had already had. Maybe Boston, this apartment, this job, were just stepping stones to help her figure out what she actually wanted. And they had helped her. Despite her current distress, she had made a lot of progress in a short amount of time, finding something that interested her, feeling more like a whole person instead of just a shell. She had learned a lot about who she was and what she did and did not want. But now it was time to figure out the next step.

Chapter 32

Mike found himself whistling on the way to work Tuesday morning. *Whistling.* When was the last time he had whistled? He must be in a good mood. Maybe that's what a successful business, good friends, and a budding relationship could do for you.

As he opened the door to the shop and stepped inside, though, something felt off. It was usually quiet, nearly silent, in the shop before things really got going. That hadn't changed. But there was something in the air. He walked around, evaluating, examining, listening and smelling. As he approached the entrance to the back office, he finally identified it. *Damn,* he thought. *Rotten eggs.* Gas leak.

Mike stepped back outside and pulled out his cell phone to call the gas company and his scheduled workers. Looked like he was closed for the day.

Once a technician had arrived and looked around, he came up to Mike and sighed. "When's the last time you had the furnace serviced?"

Mike cringed. "It's been a while."

"It's gonna have to be replaced. Rust spots in several places. That's what brought on the leak. Nothing on our end that I can tell."

Mike sighed. "I'll call the heating company."

"I turned off the gas. Once the furnace is replaced, the tech can turn it back on. I don't recommend repairing. It's too far gone for that. And with these cold temps, I suggest replacing it sooner rather than later. Don't want burst pipes on top of the furnace problem."

Great. After bidding farewell to the guy from the gas company, Mike dug out the contact information for a local heating company. He hoped they could get this done soon. As he chatted with the company and made an appointment, he walked around the shop, opening doors to let the residual gas escape. No need to add an explosion to his list of problems. So much for his good mood.

With money in her account and her remaining ownership in the diner, the bank had no problem approving Maggie's small mortgage. So, approval in hand, she called the real estate office. A woman's voice she didn't recognize greeted her.

"Good morning, Pine Valley Realty. How may I help you?"

"Oh, hello, this is Maggie, from the diner. I am a client of Megan and John's. I assume Megan is still out with her baby. Is John taking some time as well?"

"Hello, Maggie. Yes, Megan will be out for a few weeks, but John should be back next week. Is there something I can help you with?"

"Well, I don't know. Who are you?"

The woman laughed. "I am so sorry. My name is Priya. I'm a friend of Megan and John. We're part of the same real estate association. I'm a realtor, also. I'm helping out for a bit while they get acclimated to their new little family."

"It's a pleasure to meet you. You may be able to help me, if you're a realtor, too. Megan showed me the cutest little house last week, actually the day she went into labor, which is how I knew she had had the baby, and I wanted to put in an offer."

"That's wonderful. Do you happen to know the address?"

"I'm not sure of the number. It was on Long Drive, and it was a light blue one-bedroom house."

"That should be easy enough to find. Let me see."

The line fell quiet. Maggie could hear tapping keys coming from the other end of the call, and she waited patiently while Priya located the listing.

"Yes, here it is. I can certainly draw up the paperwork and submit that offer for you. Are you able to stop into the office?"

They made arrangements for Maggie to stop in and complete the paperwork, then Maggie hung up. Butterflies were flapping furiously in her belly. If all went well, she would have a house, her own house, very soon.

So as not to panic, Maggie spent the next hour keeping herself as busy as possible. She cleaned counters and kneaded pie dough and started new coffee, until it was time to head to the real estate office. Richard watched her with a bemused expression on his face. "Good luck," he called as she headed out the door.

The office was close, but Maggie's legs felt like jelly by the time she reached the door. She couldn't remember the last time she had been so nervous. The woman seated behind the reception desk greeted her with a smile.

"Hello, you must be Maggie. I'm Priya." She held out a hand, and Maggie wiped her sweaty hand on her thigh before clasping the offered hand and shaking it briefly.

"Sorry, I'm a little nervous."

Priya shook her head. "No apology necessary. It is completely normal. I spoke briefly with John and Megan about your situation, and I understand this will be your first house purchase, correct?"

"Yes. I own the diner, but it's been so long, and that wasn't really a purchase since the previous owners more or less just gave me the diner with a handshake deal. I live there, but I wouldn't really call it a home, so this will be the first time I've really had a home of my own." Maggie realized she was babbling, so she stopped talking and rolled her lips to keep her mouth closed.

"No problem. Let me just go over the process with you, then."

Priya and Maggie sat down and went over the paperwork. Maggie nodded in all the right places, indicated how much she was offering, and signed the paper at the bottom.

"Excellent," Priya said once everything had been filled in. "I will approach the seller with your offer and let you know what she says. It is my understanding that she has moved out of town, so there may be a delay, but hopefully we will hear soon."

They shook hands again, and Maggie left the office. For better or worse, it was done. Now the waiting began.

By the time Addy walked into work on Wednesday, she had started to formulate an inkling of a plan. She canceled her date with Jake, having realized that she was falling back into old habits. He was nice, and attractive, but there was no connection, and they had very little in common. She had been feigning interest and going along with what he wanted because that little voice of her mother had pushed her to do so. But not again.

She had also attended the first session of each of her classes and really enjoyed them. She was excited to see what she would learn, and was finding herself hungry to learn more, too. She had started looking for additional classes to take once these had ended, though that was still three months away. Unfortunately since the organization that offered the classes separated them into semester-like sessions, the new line-up wouldn't be released for a couple of months. But she went through the current session's offerings and jotted down the names of any that appealed to her, so she could look for those when the new list was released. They seemed to offer classes on just about everything, and she was going to try and continue her combination of something creative and something business-oriented.

Addy had liked Kate's idea of using the rest of her lease time to learn as much as she could, so she could make an educated decision. She didn't have to have all of the answers now. It had, after all, been only three months since she had moved to Boston. A lot had happened in that time, yes, but some things took more time, like figuring out what you wanted to do for the rest of your life. And the only pressure to make a quick decision had been the pressure she had put on herself. She was young, and healthy, and had that money in the bank as a backup. There was really no rush.

Now, as she walked into Paintastic to help out and prep for a party on Saturday, she could do so with her head held high, a smile on her face, and an eagerness to learn and have fun. If this was truly what she wanted to do, then she had to soak up all of the knowledge and wisdom she could while she was here, even if she couldn't do everything she wanted. And if she decided it wasn't what she wanted to do, then that was valuable, too, maybe even more valuable. Then she wouldn't have wasted her time and money. If she was honest with herself, part of her wished that was the case. Then she wouldn't have to make big decisions, like whether or not to start a business and whether or not to move again.

"Good morning," Linda greeted her with a smile. "Looks like you're in a good mood."

"Yeah, I'm feeling pretty good. How's business?"

Linda sighed. "Quiet. But it's the time of year, so no surprises there. You do have that party to get ready for on Saturday, though, so you'll have some things to work on today."

"That's the plan."

They settled into a routine, with Linda handling phone calls and paperwork while Addy counted and prepped supplies for the party. It would be a birthday party for a 10-year-old girl, so she was making sure they had enough of the most popular girly items for the seven guests. As she prepared, she let her mind wander, brainstorming ideas that she would love to implement, like having kids make their own pottery, then coming back to paint it. Or letting them paint on canvas or wood, expanding the options. They could have regular events with the feel of a party, but open to the public, maybe with games or other art-related activities. Match the color? Trivia? Speed painting?

While Addy's hands were busy, her mind was racing. She was sure some – maybe most – of the ideas weren't very good. But her fingers itched to get them all down on paper so she wouldn't forget. Would Linda be mad? From their previous conversations, she knew that many of her ideas weren't able to be implemented at Paintastic. But she couldn't tell Linda she was thinking of starting a business and being her competition. Maybe the next several months would be harder than she thought.

Chapter 33

February

Addy felt like she was living a double life, being a dutiful Paintastic employee by day and a scheming future business owner by night. Her classes had only fueled her desire to learn more, plus added pages to her lists of ideas. At this point she had pretty much surrendered to the fact that she was working toward opening her own business. When brainstorming other options, they all felt too limiting, too confining. Even Paintastic, which had been her salvation, the catalyst in her journey of self-discovery, felt restrictive. Her ideas were exploding, and too many of them just didn't fit in there.

Addy had never felt so jittery. Gone were her days of sitting around, bored and aimless. Her free time now was spent researching, brainstorming, or daydreaming. She could now picture her shop, with long tables for classes and community events and small tables for individual projects. She had played with designing fliers and menus of offerings, sketched out visions of her store from the inside and out, and made more lists of ideas than she could have ever thought – business names, staffing needs, marketing ideas, and, of course, lists of programs and projects and classes.

Despite her restlessness, Addy tried to learn all she could from Linda. Linda had been in business for a while, and she knew the ups and downs of traffic, what to order and when, and how to keep efficient records. Trying not to be obvious,

Addy had kept one eye focused on Linda's actions while she did her own work. After a month of doing this, though, Addy felt uneasy. It just felt *wrong*. She didn't want to deceive Linda. After all, Linda had given her a chance, opened up a world of possibilities for her, and helped her through a tough time.

One Wednesday morning in February, when no one was in the shop except Addy and Linda, Addy put down her inventory sheet and sighed. "Linda?"

"Yeah?" Linda was on the other side of the shop, tidying up the paints and figuring out what needed restocking.

"Can I talk to you about something?"

"Of course." Linda turned away from the paints to face Addy. "What's up?"

Addy stood up and rested one hand on a nearby chair. How to begin? "You know how when I first started we discussed ideas for marketing and ways to grow the business?"

"Of course. You had lots of great ideas. We implemented some of them around the holidays, remember? Snagged a couple of parties for January, and I think business is up a little from last year. I'd have to look at the numbers."

"Remember how we haven't been able to try some of the ideas because they didn't align with what home office would approve?"

Linda nodded. "It's always tricky when you're dealing with a big company. Sometimes it's great, like when you can take advantage of their ideas and offerings and name recognition. And sometimes it puts limits on what you can do."

"Well..." Addy took a deep breath. "I've had a lot more ideas since then, and I've been writing them down and brainstorming. And I feel like I'm going to explode with all of the ideas." She gave a small smile.

"That's great! I'd love to take a look at them, see what we can use."

"The thing is... I know we won't be able to use most of them. Based on what you said, the guidelines you got from home office, most don't align with their goals and vision for the company."

"Okay..."

"I think, long term, that I want more than Paintastic can offer."

Linda sighed. "Does this mean you're leaving?"

"Not yet. But, eventually, I think so."

"I'd hate to see you go."

"You have helped me in so many ways, Linda. When I walked through that door, I had no clue what I wanted. And you gave me a chance. More than that, though, you helped me find my purpose. The reason I will eventually leave is because, aside from the limitations that Paintastic has, I want to have a place of my own. I want to be able to try out new ideas, and expand in ways I maybe hadn't originally thought of. I want options."

"There's a lot that goes into running a business. Not just coming up with ideas, but the day-to-day operations, getting people in the door, and making sure things run smoothly."

"I know. I've been doing a lot of research, and I've started taking classes."

"You're serious about this."

Addy nodded. "I am. It came on kind of suddenly. Actually, a friend gave me the idea. But the more I've thought about it and processed it, I think it's the right choice for me."

"I wish you luck. I know you're bright, and you have a lot of potential. I just hope you don't just jump into it. Make sure you do that research and learn everything you can. It won't prepare you completely, but it will get you started in the right direction."

Addy paused for a moment. "I want you to know that I don't plan on competing with you. Even if there's overlap in what I offer, I won't do it around here. I'm not sure where I'll go, but I don't want to compete with you. I respect you and appreciate you too much for that."

"I appreciate that."

"I understand if you want me to leave, though. I don't want to put you in a tough position." Addy sighed and looked down at her hands, resting on the chair back. "I have felt so bad keeping this from you."

Linda approached Addy and placed one hand on her shoulder. "Don't feel bad. I'm glad you've found something you're passionate about. I'm glad I was able to help in some way. I will be sorry to see you go, whenever you decide to leave, but

I don't regret hiring you. And I would be happy to keep you on, help in any way I can, until you decide the time is right."

Addy met Linda's gaze. "Thanks, Linda."

"No problem. And if you happen to come up with any ideas you think I'll be able to use, I would love it if you would share them. You're the best ideas person I think I've ever had."

"Absolutely. And thank you. They kind of just tumble out. I'll go through my lists and see what might work."

Feeling better than she had in a while, Addy resumed her project. Linda wasn't mad, and she didn't have to quit. But now Addy felt she had more brainstorming to do; she had to find a way to thank Linda for everything she had done and would do to help her.

Every time Mike had stepped into the shop for the last month he had closed his eyes, walked around, and breathed deeply, making sure there wasn't anything amiss. He had had to close for an entire week before he was able to get the furnace replaced. An entire week of canceled appointments, free tows for vehicles that had already been parked at his shop, and missed opportunities. Between the lost business and the expense of the new furnace, his bank account had taken quite a hit.

Perhaps more important, however, had been the strain it had placed on his relationship with Jennifer. It caught him by surprise, but she had been really taken aback by the situation. Didn't he know he had to have regular maintenance done? He was lucky that the problem hadn't been worse, that there hadn't been an explosion or someone hadn't gotten hurt from the fumes. If he had stayed on top of things, he wouldn't have had to lose an entire week's business. The judgment went on and on.

He tried explaining to her that when it came to his house, he was on top of everything. Maintenance happened like clockwork. But for the shop, he had a tendency to focus so much on the business, that the other things slid a bit. He vaguely remembered the last time he had had a maintenance technician come out to clean the furnace, and that tech had said something about it needing replacement soon. But he figured he had time, and it had slipped his mind. He was only human, after all.

Jennifer had canceled their last date, and he hadn't heard from her since. He wasn't sure if she just needed time to cool off, or if this was her way of breaking off the relationship completely. Either way, he wasn't sure how he felt about it. On one hand, he thought things had been going well. He had started to feel closer to her, more of a connection. But did he want to be with someone so quick to judge? Who couldn't accept that he made mistakes and poor decisions once in a while? That he wasn't perfect? What would she be like if they lived together? What would she be like with their kids?

He tried not to dwell on it. But he had gone around the building after the furnace was replaced, looking for anything else that might need repair or replacement, or just general maintenance. And he had made a list, scheduled a couple of appointments, and vowed to keep up with a regular schedule. Regardless of what Jennifer said or did, he had to make sure his shop ran at peak efficiency. This was his livelihood. And he was always telling his customers to take care of their vehicles, so they would last longer and run better. It was time he practiced what he preached.

Satisfied that everything was as it should be, Mike turned on the heater in the garage and pulled out the paperwork for the day. At least business was getting back to where it should be. He had worried for a bit that his customers would continue to go elsewhere. But most of them were loyal, many of them saying they had just waited the week to get what they needed done. He was grateful and had offered discounts to those who had had to wait.

Ryan and Ben arrived, and they settled into their regular weekday routine: steady but not too busy, filled mostly with the longer repairs. It was a low-key day, and by the time Mike locked up for the night he was feeling at peace. Quieter days were great for calming and clearing the mind.

He swung by the grocery store, picked up ingredients for dinner, then headed home, ready to make himself a great meal. Just as he placed the bags on the kitchen counter, though, his phone rang. Jennifer. He groaned before accepting the call. He did not feel like doing this today, but better to get it over with, he supposed. He put away groceries as he greeted her and carried on his end of the conversation.

He heard Jennifer sigh. "I know I probably overreacted when you told me about what happened at the shop, and I'm sorry."

Mike wondered if someone had put her up to it. A month for an apology? Did she actually think she had overreacted, or would she do it all over again? And how did he feel about it?

Mike sighed, too. "Okay. Apology accepted."

Silence fell, and it was a bit uneasy. He didn't know what to say, not really knowing how he felt about the situation, or how she really felt.

"So, um." Jennifer seemed unsure, which wasn't like her. Usually she was the confident one, tackling any conversation or situation with ease. "Are we good? Would you like to get together? I have tickets for a play on Friday. I thought maybe you'd like to come."

Mike didn't mind the occasional play. He had been known to enjoy his fair share. But he wasn't sure how he felt about going to see one with Jennifer right now. "I don't know. I'll have to think about it."

"Oh. Okay. Well, um, let me know when you decide then, I guess."

"I will."

"Okay. Have a good night."

"You too."

He disconnected the call and turned toward his meal prep. The peace he had felt earlier that evening was gone. In its place was turmoil. Part of him was saying to give her another chance. Maybe she had been in a bad mood, and she was triggered by his situation. Or maybe she realized she had overreacted and really did want to get back on track. Did he want to give up what they were starting to have over this? But another part of him felt he had just seen part of her character, and it had really bothered him. Was this insight into what their future would be like?

Mike sliced the chicken and chopped some veggies, sauteing them in a frying pan with an Asian sauce. But his mind wasn't on the cooking. It was running through all the possibilities and trying to figure out what in the heck he wanted.

Maggie felt like squealing like a schoolgirl. She had just finished signing the closing papers and walked right over to her new house. She inserted the key in the front door and pushed the door open. Taking a deep breath, she closed her eyes and smiled. A tear trickled down one cheek. She had done it. She had finally gotten a home of her own.

Since she had also finally started a schedule with reduced hours, she would now have time to get it ready to move in. There was cleaning, of course, and she would love to paint at least some of the walls. Would she have the energy for that? Maybe she was better off hiring someone, though her much reduced bank account said otherwise. She would definitely need help bringing over her furniture, however minimal it was. And her clothes and such. She wondered how pitiful her sparse belongings would look in this space. Though the house was small, she was sure it would look vast when she moved her things in. That meant shopping, and she was actually looking forward to it.

Maggie moved into the kitchen, and she laughed when she realized she would need to get everything for the kitchen. Despite owning a diner, she had never had a kitchen of her own. She had never needed one. That meant a table and chairs, pots and pans, dishes and silverware, not to mention food. She was going to need to start making a list. But first she just wanted to enjoy this sense of satisfaction that had settled over her. She had done it.

She peered out of her new window over her new sink in her new kitchen and gazed at her new backyard. She could picture how it would look with trees and flowers blooming. Maybe she would put in a patio, or maybe she would just pick up some lounge chairs to enjoy the fresh air. There was already a fence surrounding the yard, so she would have privacy and feel like she was in a world of her own. She was definitely going to start a garden. She could see it there, tucked against one side of the fence. Tomatoes and cucumbers and peas. Nothing too fancy or complicated. Maybe a birdbath so she could enjoy some visitors.

It had been a long time since Maggie had dreamed like this. She had pretty much given up on this kind of life, surrendered to what had become her reality. True, she had never had the family she once dreamed of having, but maybe it wasn't too late to find someone to share the rest of her life with. That would be something. What would it be like to have someone beside her, sharing in the chores and the joys, someone to curl up with at the end of the day? Maggie sighed. She didn't want to get down today. She wanted to bask in the simple pleasure of her own home.

With a quick nod of determination, Maggie decided to go out and grab some cleaning supplies. She had taken the rest of the day off, not knowing how long the closing would take and knowing she would want to spend some time in her new house. She couldn't just stand here looking at blank walls and bare floors. Time to get to work.

Maggie didn't have a car. She had never needed one. Everything she needed was within walking distance, even if some of that walking ended up being more than a mile or two. And if she ever felt the need to go farther, she figured there were buses and taxis that could get her there just fine. But she had never needed house supplies before. For the diner, she had hired painters and workers, and any cleaning supplies were usually ordered online. But she didn't want to wait for that here. So where could she get them nearby? Hmm. Wasn't there a hardware store on Garden Street? She thought she remembered something like that. But it was a little far to walk on a cold February day, especially once she had to carry everything back. Taxi? Or should she impose on someone to take her? She was weighing her options when she heard a knock on the front door. Her first visitor! She felt like squealing again.

She opened the door to see Richard standing there, a grin on his face. "Richard!"

"Hello, Maggie. I saw you walk out of the real estate office, so I figured the paperwork was done. Thought I would head over and see how it felt. Hopefully you're still happy with your choice?"

"Oh, Richard, come in, come in. It is perfect." She showed him around, practically tugging him from room to room. She gestured to show where she would put things, furniture layout and ideas she had for decorations. He nodded appreciatively at all the right times and took it all in.

"Sounds good, Maggie. I'm happy for you. So how does it feel?"

Maggie met his gaze and grinned. "Amazing. I've never had a place of my own, not really. I don't count the diner because I share that with the entire town." She laughed then took a deep breath, looking around. "This is the first thing that's really mine. Thank you, Richard." She turned back to look at him.

"Me? I didn't buy it for you."

"No, though you certainly helped with that." She laughed again. "I mean thank you for giving me the push I needed to finally move out of the diner. I can't begin to express how much it means."

"Happy to do it. We've helped each other, remember?"

"I do. You've been a good friend." She took one of Richard's hands and squeezed it.

"As have you," Richard said, squeezing back before releasing it. "So," he said then, looking around. "What's next?"

Maggie sighed. "Cleaning. The previous owner hadn't lived her for a while, so there are definitely dust bunnies, and I want to give it all a good scrub. Unfortunately that means I'll have to go out and get some cleaning supplies. I don't suppose you would let me take advantage of your friendship and have you drive me to the hardware store?"

"I would be happy to. I told Kyle and Jordan that I would likely be an hour or so, so that should give us plenty of time. Shall we go?"

They headed to the hardware store, where Richard made suggestions on what she would need to get started. Maggie also picked up several paint swatches so she could decide what she wanted to do in each room.

"I'd be happy to help paint, Maggie, and I'm sure I could recruit a few others. It would be fun. If you wanted help, that is. I know sometimes you may want to do things on your own, so whatever you want. Just know the offer stands."

"Thanks, Richard."

They pulled into her driveway and unloaded all of the supplies.

"I should probably get back to the diner. The dinner customers will be coming in before we know it."

"Thanks, again. I don't know how I would have gotten everything here without you."

"Any time."

Richard put up a hand in farewell, got back in his car, and drove back to the diner. Maggie watched him go, then turned back to the house, now with a pile of cleaning supplies in one corner of the entryway.

"Okay, Maggie," she said aloud. "Let's get cleaning."

Chapter 34

The days flew by for Addy. She was doing her best to find balance, so she didn't get consumed by her new obsession of starting a business. She made sure she still volunteered at the soup kitchen, and she still worked diligently at Paintastic. She completed all of her classwork and created her own paintings, as well. She had finished decorating the furniture she had bought, and she had purchased a new comforter for her bed, to coordinate with the paintings she had hung on her walls. Even if was only temporary, she wanted her bedroom to feel comfortable. She was not looking forward to moving everything out again, whenever and wherever that ended up taking place, but she tried not to dwell on it. She was focusing on the here and now, on what she could learn and do to make sure she was making the right decision.

It occurred to her, as she sat staring out her bedroom one sunny morning, that she had never reached out to Maggie to let her know what was going on. At the very least she had to thank Maggie for the idea that had sent her on this journey. With a little time to kill before she had to be at work, Addy powered up her laptop to send an email. She didn't know what Maggie's work schedule looked like these days, and she would feel awkward trying to carry on a phone conversation, anyway. So she composed a short email to catch Maggie up on the basics: classes were going well, she was learning lots, and she had decided to pursue starting a business. She still had logistics to figure out, but she was spending the time left on her lease to work out details.

That should do it. If Maggie decided to write back, then perhaps Addy would go into more of an explanation. It had actually been nice to have someone to really open up to. Kate was available, too, of course, and had been a sounding board more than once. But somehow having that different perspective, from someone who had seen more of life, had owned her own business, and didn't see Addy on a daily basis, made a bigger impact. Maggie was almost like the mother she would have liked to have had, if that made any sense. Where would Addy be if her mother had been supportive and encouraging instead of judgmental and superficial?

Shaking her head to clear out the philosophical musings, Addy closed her computer and stood up to get ready for her day. She tucked a notepad into the bag she had gotten into the habit of carrying with her. Today Linda had wanted to see her updated list of ideas, to see if there was anything new they would be able to implement. So far they had decided to try an occasional after school program, and to market to scouting troops to try and bring in more groups of people. Not only would the immediate business be good, but it would also be a way to advertise and encourage them to come back in the future. It was a bit of a gray area with home office, but Linda was willing to give it a shot.

Addy was quite pleased with her lists of ideas. She had never considered herself a creative person, but between the painting and the brainstorming, she was learning she had untapped stores of creativity within her. She was thrilled to have finally found her "thing." Would she have found it if she hadn't walked into Paintastic that random day back in October? Probably eventually. Maybe she would have found it years earlier if she had had someone to encourage her to go looking. Regardless, though, she was where she was meant to be, finally on the right track. She hoped.

Despite the sun shining, a bitter wind blew, clawing at Addy's face. By the time she arrived at Paintastic she felt chilled to the bone. Linda was on the phone, so Addy greeted her with a wave before making her way to the back room to shed her outerwear. A moment later she returned to the front room, carrying her notepad of ideas. Linda was just hanging up the phone, and Addy heard a sniff before Linda turned to face her. There were tears in her eyes.

"Linda? Are you okay? What happened?"

Linda sniffed again and wiped her nose. "My mother collapsed. She's being taken to the hospital. I'm sorry, Addy, but I have to go."

"Okay. Do you want me to put up a sign saying we're closed?"

Linda shook her head as she made her way to the back to claim her coat. "No, there's no need. You can open up and run things until I get back."

Addy froze. She knew business was quiet during the day, but could she handle the pressure? "When do you think you'll be back?"

"I have no idea. I can give you a call when I know more." She paused on her way out the door. "You can do this, Addy. You've been learning the ropes for the past month, longer than that if we're honest. You say you want to own your own business. You can handle overseeing the shop for a day."

Addy took a deep breath and swallowed. "Okay. If you're sure."

"I'll be in touch," Linda said, and she nearly ran out the door.

Addy stood for a moment, stunned and unable to process what had just happened. After a minute she gave herself a mental shake and began going through the motions of opening up the shop. With it being so frigid, she didn't expect much traffic this morning. Part of her wondered why Linda stayed open on days like this, or most weekdays in the winter. They rarely saw anyone before mid-afternoon. But she supposed it gave them a chance to take care of the boring stuff, the day-to-day business matters like inventory and bookkeeping, and the marketing to drive traffic the rest of the time.

Much to Addy's surprise, the morning saw a steady stream of customers, families with children mostly. Was there no school today? Either way, Addy was busy helping children pick items to paint and deciding what colors to paint them, making sure everyone had their supplies and was familiar with the fancier options for making special effects on their pottery pieces. She barely had time to think until just after lunch when the phone rang.

"Hello, Paintastic, this is Addy. How can I help you?"

"Addy, it's Linda. How are things going over there?"

"Busy, actually. I'm surprised to see so many kids."

Linda groaned. "I totally forgot. It's President's Day weekend. A lot of schools give them the day before the weekend off. I should have warned you."

Addy laughed softly. "Actually it's probably a good thing you forgot. I would have freaked out and refused to open. How's your mom?"

Linda sighed. "She had a heart attack. We're waiting for the results of some tests now. She may need surgery."

"Oh, Linda, I'm so sorry. Well, don't worry about anything here. I've been doing okay. I don't think I've messed anything up, and no one has left upset, so we should be good. Just take care of your mom."

"Thanks. Cathy should be coming in later this afternoon, so that will help. It will be up to you if you want to stay past your shift or not. Cathy's closed before, so she would be okay by herself if needed."

Addy thought for a moment. It was Friday, so she didn't have a class that evening. There was really nothing she needed to head home for. "I'll see how busy it is and decide later. I don't have anything going on tonight, so I don't mind staying if it's busy."

"Okay. I'll try to call when I have more of an idea on time frame. I appreciate your taking over on such short notice."

"No problem. We'll talk soon."

Addy hung up the phone as another group of customers came in. She greeted them and led them to a table, set them up with supplies, then moved to ring up a mother and daughter who had just finished their pieces. She had this. No problem. At the very least being so busy meant she had no time to dwell on her potential inadequacy to handle the business.

Though not as busy as it had been earlier in the day, traffic was steady all afternoon. The evening brought out the couples, and Addy didn't feel comfortable leaving Cathy by herself. In honesty, Addy was enjoying herself. Though she had slightly panicked when Linda had left that morning, she had handled the day with ease. Well, relative ease. There had been some moments of feeling overwhelmed. But she had handled them, made it through, and even felt invigorated by it all.

By the time Addy returned to her apartment late that night, she was ready to collapse. What a day. And with things up in the air with Linda's mom, Addy wasn't sure what to expect the next day, either. As she was getting ready for bed, she heard her cell phone ding. It was nearly eleven at night. Who would be texting her?

"Sorry it's so late," the text from Linda read. "Meant to call sooner. Mom will need surgery, and it's scheduled for tomorrow. I have to be here. No party tomorrow, so you and Rebecca should be able to handle it. If it's really busy, call Cathy."

Addy replied with her own text, assuring Linda it wouldn't be a problem and saying the day had gone well, with lots of happy customers.

Linda responded with a quick "thx. Good night."

Addy plugged in her phone to charge, finished getting ready, and climbed into bed. If she hadn't been so tired she might have allowed herself to worry about the following day. Saturday. Their busiest day of the week. But as it was she barely remembered to set her alarm before she drifted off to sleep.

The moment of truth had arrived for Maggie. The first night sleeping in her new house. Richard and Jordan had helped her move her furniture in earlier that day, for which she was grateful. What jewels she had found in those two. And now it was time to sleep. Supposedly.

It was quiet. Too quiet. The rare times she actually slept at night she was usually so exhausted she didn't think about it. And when she slept during the day she had background noises to get her to sleep: traffic and birds singing and movement in the kitchen. It was never shockingly quiet, with nothing but the ticking of the clock keeping her company.

Maggie moved around the house, theoretically ready for bed in her nightgown and slippers, teeth brushed and glass of water by her bed. But she felt restless. It was eleven o'clock at night. Morning would come very quickly. Saturday morning, with crowds of people coming in for her heaping breakfast platters and hot coffee. But Richard had said he would cover the morning crowd, give her a chance to really settle in at her new house. She sighed. As excited as she was about moving out of the diner, this place just didn't feel like home yet.

She knew it would take time. Eventually she would get the hang of this, being truly alone for perhaps the first time ever. The house would take on its own personality, just as the diner had. She would learn its quirks, what each sound was and how it looked at different times of day. But right now it felt like a stranger.

She was pleased with the colors she had chosen for the living room and kitchen. Soothing, relaxing sage green for the living room, and a golden yellow for the kitchen. Her bedroom she was less sure of, it being a bit bolder than she had anticipated. But she expected the indigo would grow on her. It had a tendency to give her a jolt every time she saw it, and she could use a little perking up sometimes. Maybe it would inspire her, make her feel like a younger woman not past her prime, a woman who didn't question the recent choices she had made just because change was hard.

Maggie sighed and moved into the kitchen to make herself a cup of tea. The list of things she had had to buy had been hefty, and she was not looking forward to her credit card bill. But for now she was grateful for a new tea kettle, a flavorful assortment of tea bags to choose from, and a cheerfully-colored mug to warm her hands around. Her feet made shuffling noises on the linoleum floor, a strange sound she wasn't used to. The apartment had been carpeted, and she never walked around the diner in slippers.

Tea in hand, she pulled out a chair from the kitchen table, cringing slightly at the scraping noise. She was going to have to get some of those felt pads to put at the bottom of the legs. Silence fell again as she sat, staring out at a dark backyard lit only by a half moon. She should have bought a radio. It hadn't even occurred to her. She had music playing in the background almost constantly at the diner, but it was just part of the atmosphere. She hadn't thought about the never-ending silence in her new house in the middle of the night and how she might need that background music. Maybe she could find something online. All the kids streamed music these days, and radio stations were all on the web. She could find something to listen to.

Leaving her tea at the kitchen table, Maggie went to the living room to claim her laptop. She had forgotten to plug it in. Hopefully it had enough power. She brought it back to the kitchen, lifted the lid, and pressed the power button, taking sips from her mug as she went. She wasn't in a hurry. She had all night to fill. And at the rate she was going, that night was going to be filled with aimless wandering and introspection.

Internet service had been installed the week before, so Maggie entered her wifi password and let the computer connect. She had almost decided not to bother with the internet, figuring she would just use the connection at the diner if she needed it. But Richard had convinced her she would want it at home, too. To plan her vacations, he had said. Maggie chuckled. Vacations, indeed. She just wanted to make it through the night. But she was grateful she had gone along with it.

She wasn't sure what sites the kids used to get their music, but she figured she would start by searching for a radio station she knew she enjoyed. Lo and behold they offered streaming on their website. Maggie connected to the feed, then leaned back and finished her mug of tea. Lite rock filled the kitchen, and Maggie took a deep breath. Finally. Something familiar. She stood up, placed her mug in the sink, and carried her laptop into the bedroom. Maybe if she left the station playing she would be able to get some sleep. She looked around for a place to rest her laptop, and then kicked herself and called herself an idiot as she looked at the nightstand. Of course she had a clock radio beside her bed. Why hadn't she thought to put that on, instead? She turned off the live feed on the station's website and turned on the radio instead, tuning it to the same station. Then she placed her closed laptop on the top of her dresser and crawled into bed. After a bit of tossing and turning she finally drifted off to the sounds of Barry Manilow serenading her.

It took Maggie a minute to realize where she was the next morning, when the sun beaming through the window woke her. She had made it through the night. The radio was still playing, though the talk show that was currently on was not as appealing as the music of the night before. She rolled over to turn it off, then sighed and got out of bed, sliding her feet into the slippers at the side of the bed. She had made it through. And would have to go through it all again Sunday night. At least tonight she would be at the diner for the night shift. That reminded her. She should probably plug in her laptop so she could bring it with her. After she used the facilities.

After plugging in her laptop, she strolled into the kitchen to make some breakfast. This was strange, too. It was her first time cooking in this brand-new space. It was much smaller than the diner, but it was cozy, and it contained everything she would need. She hoped. She had tried to think of everything when she went grocery shopping, but she was sure she forgot something. At least she knew she had eggs and bacon. And a frying pan. She moved about the space, trying to remember where she had put everything. Though the birds were now singing outside, and the bacon was sizzling on the stove, it still felt too quiet. How long would it take her to get used to this? With a sigh she finished cooking her breakfast and brought her plate to the kitchen table. She looked at the clock on the wall. Two hours until she could reasonably go to the diner. She would still be early, but not so early as to appear pathetic. She could do that, couldn't she? Survive two hours on her own? With another sigh, she took a bite, then another, the clock on the wall sounding like a ticking time bomb.

Chapter 35

Four days Linda had been out. Four days Addy had taken charge of the shop, and she had done a pretty good job, if she did say so herself. She had gotten quite adept at opening and closing the store, handling the customers in between, and staying on top of projects that needed to be fired in the kiln. Linda didn't know when she would be back, her top priority being her mother's health, understandably so. She told Addy that the store could be closed at least part of the time, but Addy didn't want to let Linda down. Plus she was learning so much along the way, gaining confidence and even subtly putting some ideas to the test.

If she was honest, the financial end of things was her biggest concern, not only for Paintastic, but for when she opened her own business, too. Math had never been her strong suit. And she was so afraid of messing something up for Linda that she was reluctant to even start.

But over four days the paperwork had accumulated. Some supplies were getting low, and an inventory order would need to be placed soon. And Addy had even booked a party, plus a Girl Scout evening program. She hoped Linda would be back in plenty of time for those events, but she still needed to make sure they were ready for them. That meant that Addy would have to take on at least some of the bookkeeping.

True to her word of helping Addy however she could, Linda has shown her the basics. Addy had seen some of the spreadsheets, and, though she didn't have access to them, she knew how Linda kept track of things. The least she could do was organize the records, make notes, and make it easy for Linda to enter things when she came back. And she knew the suppliers that Linda used to order paints and pottery. She would just need to touch base with Linda to get the okay to actually place an order.

Addy felt like this was the test, like she had been playing at running a business for the last few days, but now it was time to see if she had learned anything. So on Tuesday morning, she arrived at work an hour earlier than she needed to. She dug out the paperwork from the last four days and went through it, making sure numbers added up, that all reports had been run, and that everything was properly filed. She put sticky notes on the top of each day's paperwork, indicating she had gone through all of the receipts and checked numbers. Then she totaled up how many of each pottery piece had sold so she could check it against stock levels. It may not be necessary after just a few days, but she wanted to make sure nothing had gone astray during her time in charge. She was just about to start counting the inventory when Linda walked in.

"Linda!" Addy put down her paperwork and approached her boss. "How are you? How's your mother?"

Linda sighed. "She's doing better. The surgery went well, and they're pleased with how she's recovering. It will be quite a while before she's back to her old self, but so far so good."

"That's great. Welcome back."

"Thanks. Glad to be back. I'm not sure if I'll be putting in a full day today, but I wanted to be sure to come in and see how things were going. How's business been?"

"It's been busy. Holiday weekends are good for business, I guess, especially Friday and Monday for families." She showed Linda the stacks of paperwork, now neatly organized with her notes on top. "I was just going to check inventory. I know we're going to need to place an order in the next couple of days. We're just about out of a few things." She held up the inventory list she had printed.

"Wow. You've been busy. Thank you for stepping in and making sure every-thing ran smoothly. I hope you found time to rest somewhere in there."

Addy shrugged. "I just wanted to make sure it all went well. I didn't want you to come back to a mess. Plus it was good practice. The training you've given me came in handy."

"I guess it worked out all around." Linda took a look around the shop. "I can definitely see gaps. Let's do the inventory together so I can see what's been popular and what we should order more of. Let me just put down my things."

They spent the next hour counting and checking and making a list of what to order. Business was back to its normal weekday quiet, so they had the shop to themselves. Addy breathed a sigh of relief when the numbers all matched what they should be. She gave Linda input on what customers had said they wished to see, and together they looked in the supplier's catalog to see what they could add to their available options that could meet the demand.

"Oh! And I booked a couple of events." Addy pulled out the events binder and showed Linda the new additions. "We may want to order more of the typical girly choices in preparation for the troop. The leader who called said they were big fans of unicorns and rainbows and all that."

"Sounds good. Those are popular anyway, so I have no problem ordering an extra case of each." She added something to their notes. "I usually place the orders online. It's faster that way, and there's less likely to be an error. Let me log in, and then if you want to place the order, I'll walk you through it."

"That would be great." Addy felt a little bubble of excitement. She had passed the test. The business had not only survived, but it seemed to have thrived. Linda was pleased with what she had done. And now she was getting more training and experience. True, it had only been four days, but it had been a busy four days, and a trial under fire that Addy was grateful for. Yes, she could do this. But maybe her next set of classes should include one on bookkeeping.

"You have been down in the dumps all week, man. What is going on?"

Mike looked up to see Ryan staring at him, paperwork in hand. He sighed. "Nothing. Is that the paperwork for the Camry?"

"Yeah. It's all set." He handed the paperwork to Mike.

"Thanks."

Ryan stood staring at Mike for another minute, then shook his head and returned to the garage. Mike looked at the paperwork, made some notes in the computer, then hung it in a clear folder on a peg behind the desk. He shouldn't be down. Business was going well, life was going well, and he had made up with Jennifer. Kind of. He was at least giving it another shot. But he wasn't exactly feeling confident.

They had seen each other twice in the last week, and he could tell Jennifer had been trying to get back in his good graces. She had been complimentary, and supportive, and positive. But it was as if she were trying too hard. It didn't feel natural, comfortable. It felt forced. And, considering how wishy washy he had been about her in the beginning anyway, was "forced" the kind of relationship he wanted? Was it what Jennifer wanted? He kept waiting for the other shoe to drop, so not only were their interactions slightly awkward, but he felt on edge, uneasy. No wonder he'd been so grumpy at work. Not that he would tell the guys any of this.

Mike had good friends. They were fun to hang out with, and he knew they had his back if he ever needed support. But when it came to feelings and relationships, he just didn't feel comfortable opening up to any of them. And he hadn't really ever been in a position to need someone to talk to about his feelings. Except with Addy. But then, Addy had been the person he talked to about them. They had worked through it together, even if it hadn't ended up the way he wanted. He couldn't do that with Jen. So who could he talk to?

The thought occurred to him that maybe he could reach out to Addy. He had never been so comfortable with someone before, so able to open up. But that would be beyond awkward. Discuss a current love interest with a previous love interest? No way. So who could he talk to?

Maybe Maggie, queen of the lonely hearts, could help him. It was worth a shot. And if he didn't end up having the guts to talk to her, at least he could get a decent meal and a great piece of pie. He decided to pay her a visit that night. He would have to make it later than usual, though. She was usually busy when he closed the shop. And that was not conducive to a heart-to-heart conversation. Decision made, he turned his focus to the customer coming in the door. At least work helped keep his mind off his relationship troubles.

When he walked into the diner at nine that night, he looked around for Maggie. To his dismay she didn't seem to be around. He saw Jordan, the new kid working for her, wiping down tables on one end. And he saw Richard, her new partner, coming out of the kitchen area. Richard smiled and greeted him.

"Hello, there, Mike. What can I do for you?"

Should he act like he was just there for pie? He hadn't been able to wait so long for dinner, but pie was always welcome. Or should he ask for Maggie? "What have you got left for pie?"

Richard took a peek in the case at one end of the counter. "Let's see. A couple slices of apple, lemon meringue, and one slice of blueberry."

"I'll have an apple."

"Coming right up." Richard scooped a slice onto a plate and brought it over. "Here you are."

"Thanks."

"No problem." Richard hesitated before moving on. "Anything else I can get you? Coffee? Water?"

"Coffee would be great." It wasn't as if he would be getting much sleep that night anyway.

Richard poured a cup of coffee, but still he hesitated.

Mike gazed up at him, feeling somewhat self-conscious.

"I – " Richard began, then shook his head. "You seem to have something on your mind. And it could be my imagination, but it looked like you came in here wanting more than pie. Is there anything I can help you with?"

Mike sighed and put down his fork. "I guess I'm just a hot mess today. I was actually hoping to see Maggie tonight. I had something I wanted to run by her."

"Ah. It's her night off, but I could give her a call if it's important."

"No, it's okay. I don't want to bother her on her night off."

"To be honest, you might be doing her a favor. I get the impression that she's struggling with floating around in a quiet house by herself. I'll be right back."

"Maggie moved out?"

Richard nodded. "Yup. Bought the house about a month or so ago, officially moved in last week. She was so excited, but... I don't know how to put it. Her eyes seem to have lost some of their twinkle."

"Poor Maggie."

"Yeah. I'm sure it will just take time. It's quite an adjustment." He stepped into the back room, and Mike took a bite of pie. Jordan came over, put up a hand in greeting, asked if he needed anything, and, when Mike assured him he was fine, went into the back room, too.

A moment later Jordan came out wearing his coat. "Have a good night."

"You too," Mike replied. What was taking Richard so long?

Mike had just polished off the last bite of pie when Richard finally emerged. "Sorry for the delay. Maggie would love to help. She was just wondering if she should come back in, or if she should invite you to her new house."

"Oh no, I don't want her to go to any trouble. It's fine. I'll just catch up with her another time."

"She thought you might say something like that. She'll be here in five minutes. Her house is right around the corner."

Mike felt horrible. He had just come in for a little advice, and now he was inconveniencing Maggie and making her come out in the cold. He just should have stayed home. Instead he sipped his coffee and waited.

Maggie came in a few minutes later, complaining about the wind but with a smile on her face. "Hello, Mike! How are you today?"

"I'm doing okay, Maggie. How are you? I'm sorry to make you come out in the cold."

Maggie waved away his concerns. "No trouble at all. I was a bit at loose ends myself."

"Richard said you bought a house. Congratulations. I guess it's been a while since I've seen you."

Maggie settled onto a stool beside him. "Thank you. It has been a while. To be honest, I'm having mixed feelings about the house." She sighed. "It's just so darn quiet!"

Mike grinned, happy to be focusing on someone else. "I imagine it would be, especially when you're used to the hustle and bustle of the diner."

Maggie shook her head. "You live alone, don't you?"

Mike nodded. "Yeah. I have for a while."

"How do you bear it?"

Mike shrugged. "You get used to it after a while. Sometimes it's nice to have a place to yourself, where you don't have to worry about anyone else and can do things the way you want." He sighed. "And sometimes you put something on TV for background noise and wish you had someone to be with." He gave Maggie a sad half-smile.

Maggie patted his hand. "And that's what brought you out here to me, isn't it?"

"Hey, you've said yourself you take care of the lonely hearts in town." He attempted a real smile.

Maggie laughed. "I guess I do. So," she said, slapping both hands on the counter. "What can I do for you?"

"I was hoping for some advice, but I have no idea where to begin. I guess it's like you were just saying, though. I live alone. And sometimes my house gets really lonely. I had really thought I would be settled by now, married, kids, the whole bit."

"You want me to play matchmaker?"

Mike laughed. "No, not that." He sobered. "I've been seeing someone, and she's great. I think. Maybe. I just... When we first met there was no spark, you know? I didn't really feel a connection. But I'm not getting any younger, and I thought that maybe over time it would grow. I thought that if we could develop a good foundation, that love would come with time. And we were getting there. I was thinking maybe we could have a future after all. And then she got really upset and judge-y about something to do with my shop, and I saw a side to her that I really didn't like. She apologized. Took a while, but she did. But ever since then I just get this feeling, you know? Like I'm expecting her to flip out again, or I'm preparing myself for when she disappoints me again. Things are awkward and tense, and I don't know what to do."

Richard had brought Maggie a cup of coffee while Mike had been talking, and she took a sip now. "Oh, Mike. As much as I would love to help you, I don't know what to say. My love life has been mostly non-existent since high school. Running the diner took up my whole life. I do understand what it's like to be lonely, to want someone to spend your life with. But it sounds like being with her is making you feel even lonelier, if that makes any sense."

Mike nodded. "I definitely don't feel comfortable around her anymore. I'm not sure I ever really did."

"Before the situation you mentioned happened, how did you feel around her? Aside from looking at the future, how were you in the present?"

"In theory, she's everything I would look for in a woman. She's smart, and pretty, and confident. She looks out for the little guy, and we seemed to want the same things out of life."

"But?"

Mike sighed. "But... I guess I always got the impression that I wasn't good enough, like I had to impress her. I think she looked down a bit at what I do for a living. She's a lawyer."

Maggie nodded. "And if that incident hadn't happened, would you have been content going on as you were?"

Mike thought for a minute. "I don't know. I thought I was. But talking about it and thinking about it, I don't think I was really happy then, either."

"Then, there you go. Maybe what happened just pushed your negative emotions to the forefront, so you could really confront them."

"You are a wise woman, Maggie."

Maggie laughed. "Hardly. I just know how to look at things from different perspectives. One of the perks of working with people for so long, I suspect." She smiled at Mike. "You are a wonderful man, Mike. And I know someone will appreciate you for who you are. If this woman is not the one for you, then let her go. She will find her own path. You deserve to feel happy and comfortable with someone."

"Thanks. I guess..." He sighed again. "I just get tired of waiting, you know?"

"I know. Believe me, I do know. But you are still young. You have time. Unlike me, you are not too old to find happiness."

Richard had made his way back over, wiping down counters. "You are not old, Maggie," he insisted.

"Oh, Richard. You're just saying that because if I was old, you would have to admit you were, too." She grinned at him.

He grinned back. "You're only as old as you feel."

"Then I must be a hundred."

"And I must be thirty. There's still lots of life in me yet."

Mike watched their interaction. The twinkle that Richard had said she lost seemed to have returned, at least when she was looking at Richard. He smiled to himself. Maybe Maggie would find her own happy ending, after all. But in the meantime, he had to face facts with Jennifer. No sense dragging things out.

"Oh!" Maggie suddenly turned back toward him. "Guess who I heard from?"

Mike shrugged.

"Addy! She is doing well and wanted to let me know that she took my suggestion to heart."

"Your suggestion?" What was Maggie talking about?

"When she came for Christmas. She and I had a bit of a heart-to-heart, too. And now she's thinking of starting her own business."

"Doing what?" Mike couldn't help it. His heart had skipped a beat as soon as Maggie had mentioned Addy.

"The kind of thing she's been doing in that job of hers, painting or something. She had lots of ideas to make it even better, but apparently there isn't much potential where she is. So she's thinking of starting something herself."

"That's great." Mike's heart sank a bit. If she was starting a business, that meant she would be getting even more settled where she was. That tied up that loose end, he supposed. Still, as long as she was happy.

Maggie didn't miss the cloud that had passed over his face. She patted his hand. "Don't worry, Mike. Everything will work out as it's meant to."

Chapter 36

April

Maggie slipped her feet into her slippers and stood up. The sun wasn't quite up, but she was on morning shift, and she had to get moving. This had proven to be the hardest part of moving out: getting ready in time to get to the diner before opening. At least the mornings weren't quite as frigid as they had been. Definitely still cold, but there was hope that spring was on its way.

As she moved about getting ready for her day, Maggie mused that things were getting easier overall. She was finding new routines and getting used to the stillness. Sometimes she even looked forward to it, especially after a particularly busy shift at the diner. It was nice to be able to step away from it all, breathe deeply, and relax. There had always been an underlying current when she lived at the diner, the feeling that she would be called into action at any moment. Here she was able to truly unwind, and, once she got the hang of it, she found she liked it. She was going to need some hobbies, though, to pass the time. She had never been much of a TV watcher, and, while the radio was great for background noise, it didn't help her fill the empty hours. She was looking forward to being able to work outside, but until the weather got warmer, she didn't venture out often.

So far she had been spending her time baking, reading, and making puzzles. On one of her days off, when she had had a full day of nothingness stretching out ahead of her, she had made it over to the town library, where she was shown books and puzzles she could borrow, plus a list of programs they had scheduled. She hadn't been brave enough yet to try any of the programs, but she had taken advantage of the books and puzzles. One of these days maybe she would make her way to the non-fiction section, to explore the gardening and crafting books, and see if there was anything else that appealed to her. She hadn't quite left her comfort zone yet, but she was tiptoeing to the edge.

One other way she had been spending her time was emailing back and forth with Addy. Since Addy's initial email, they had opened up to each other on any number of topics. Addy was starting to feel like the daughter she had never had. It was nice to have someone come to you for advice, but also nice to be able to express your own thoughts and have an honest conversation about them. It was a shame Addy didn't live closer, though that was a topic Maggie was considering bringing up in her next message. Addy's business plans were progressing nicely, and she was learning more every day to prepare. But she still hadn't decided where to start this business of hers. Maggie wanted to shout from the roof: Pine Valley! Come back to Pine Valley! But she didn't think Addy would take kindly to that. So she had tried to be subtle, bringing up as often as she dared how there was a lack of entertainment options in town, how she was looking for more hobbies and others were likely in the same situation, and how Pine Valley was growing but needed more young blood. Perhaps this evening she would be a bit more blunt about it. She was just afraid of scaring Addy away.

Morning routine complete, Maggie put on her shoes and coat, locked the door behind her, and made her way over to the diner. She had considered getting a car, but it didn't seem necessary. The diner was so close, and she could use the exercise. She had gotten a rolling cart for when she went grocery shopping, and she liked being able to greet people as she walked along the sidewalk. Yes, it had been tricky in the winter, when the sidewalks could get icy, but the truly treacherous moments were few and far between. So on days when she thought her walk could get precarious, she put special grips on her shoes and carried a jug of ice melt with her. She must have been a sight walking to work like that, but better safe than sorry.

Maggie unlocked the diner door and pulled it open. It had taken her a while to get used to the diner being dark. How many years had it been open all day and night? But there was a small light they left on over the counter, and she liked to think that the diner was getting a well-deserved rest on the nights they closed. It had been a loyal companion, and now it needed a break, too.

She flipped on all the lights as she passed, then put her coat away before starting coffee and warming up the oven. Though she often left the baking to the others, sometimes even ordering specialty pastries from a bakery in the next town over, this morning she had decided to make her popular cinnamon rolls. She had started some of the prep work the day before, so this morning she mostly just needed to roll and bake. They were, after all, celebrating. Today they were knocking down the wall.

Coming up with the plans for the party room had taken longer than anticipated. Then there was clearing out the space, getting the permits, working out the financial bit, and finally getting everything scheduled. Yesterday the electricity had been re-routed, freeing up the one questionable area on the wall. And today, the opening would be made.

She and Richard had decided to build a doorway rather than an open archway. They determined that would give them more options. For live entertainment, they could prop the doors open, letting the music flow freely. For more private functions, they could close the doors as needed. But the doors would be mostly glass, making the room seem like part of the diner. More expensive, yes, but important to keep the community feel they were going for. Maggie could hardly wait to start scheduling events. She only hoped construction would go smoothly.

She had just slipped the cinnamon rolls into the oven when Jordan arrived.

"Good morning, Miss Maggie," he said, making his way to the back room. "Something smells really good in here."

She smiled at him. "Cinnamon rolls. They'll be ready soon, and you can be my taste tester. It's been a while since I've made them."

Jordan grinned. "I'd be happy to. Have to make sure they're good enough for the customers, after all."

"Absolutely." Maggie wiped down the workspace, then went to the dining area to pour herself a cup of coffee. She poured one for Jordan, too, adding plenty of cream and sugar, just as he liked it. She handed it to him as he joined her. "So how are things going, Jordan?"

Jordan nodded. "Thanks. They're going pretty well. Can't complain."

"That's great. I'm glad to hear it."

"I'm going to be getting an apartment soon."

"Really? That's wonderful."

"Yeah. A place in town is opening up next month, so I've put in an application. After this week, I'll have enough for the security deposit and first month's rent. I've been saving up."

"I am so glad to hear that."

"I wouldn't be here if it weren't for you, Miss Maggie. I will never be able to thank you enough."

Maggie rested a hand on his shoulder. "Jordan, it has been my pleasure. You are an amazing young man. I wish nothing but the best for you."

Jordan ducked his head, taking a sip of coffee to hide his embarrassment.

"I suppose we should get ready to open up." She grabbed an apron that was folded under the counter, tied it around her waist, then moved to the front of the diner, turned on the open sign, and unlocked the door. Two of her regulars, retired men who got together almost every morning, were walking up the path. "Perfect timing, gentlemen," she said, holding the door open for them. "Come on in."

The town had adjusted to the diner's new hours with relative ease. The general consensus seemed to be that they were just happy she wasn't closing. And the more she had considered it, the more she realized that opening all night during the week had affected her more than the town. Customers in the middle of the night had been few and far between. It made sense to only stay open late on the weekends, when she had a much higher chance of seeing someone. Or *they* had a higher chance. She was still getting used to that.

Mick and his crew showed up around ten o'clock. Though it would have been fun to simply attack the wall with hammers, the dust and debris that would have resulted would have been much too disruptive to the diner. And closing wasn't an option as far as Maggie was concerned. So they were taking a slightly less exciting approach, using small saws to cut out the opening on both sides. Still dusty – and they had closed that section of the diner as a precaution – but far less disruptive.

The construction was a great conversation piece, and Maggie found business increased somewhat over the next couple of days, as people in town stopped in to check on the progress. Everyone she spoke to seemed excited about the prospects of entertainment and a space available to rent. Maggie practically rubbed her hands in anticipation. Who would have thought this time last year that she would be this excited about the diner? It was amazing what a few months could do.

Subtle, Maggie, Addy thought, rereading Maggie's latest email. *Really subtle.* The only thing less subtle would have been a neon sign flashing "Move to Pine Valley!" in giant letters. Addy sighed and pushed her laptop away. She had picked up on Maggie's other hints. It would have been hard not to. But something was holding her back. She just couldn't put her finger on it. Was it the potential awkwardness with Mike? Maybe. But he had said at Christmas he was seeing someone. He seemed to be fine. Was it simply the dread of having to move again? That was likely part of it. Or maybe it was her insistence that she was a city girl and needed to live somewhere full of people and options. She might have hit the nail on the head with that one.

She had grown up in a city. It was what she was used to, where she was comfortable. The only flaw with that reasoning was the fact that despite living somewhere "full of people and options," she hadn't taken advantage of any of it. Over the last several months she had stuck to her adopted neighborhood for the most part, venturing out only to volunteer and attend classes. She had found she liked being able to walk everywhere, greet the few people who had become familiar to her, and stay home when she didn't have places to be. Was it her insecurity that made her want to stick to the familiar? Or was she really a small-town girl at heart?

She had to figure it out. Though technically she still had time – almost five months until her lease ran out, longer if she chose to renew – she felt a sense of urgency that made her uncomfortable. She didn't like not knowing. She wanted to know where she was going, what she was doing, what the future held. Unreasonable, maybe, but she felt better being able to plan, to know that she was prepared for what was coming. Maybe it was a result of so many years of relying on other people to tell her what to do, what to say, how to act. She didn't want to wait for other people to make decisions for her. She wanted to feel in control.

Maybe that was the problem: Maggie wanted her to move to Pine Valley, so she was rebelling against it. Maggie, who had become a mother figure to her, who she had started to rely on for advice and feedback. Addy didn't want to listen to her mother, even if that mother wasn't actually her mother and really did have good intentions.

Addy felt like screaming. What a tangled-up mess. Frustrated with herself and the entire situation, Addy closed her laptop and stood up. She needed to talk to someone.

Kate was at the kitchen table, doing something on her own laptop. She looked up when Addy approached. "Hey."

"Hey." Addy fell into the chair across from Kate. She knew Kate wasn't working. It was Sunday, and Kate never worked on Sundays. That made her feel slightly better about disturbing her.

After a moment, Kate clicked a button on her computer and closed it. "Looks like you have a lot on your mind. Gab session or ice cream?"

"Maybe a little of both."

With a curt nod, Kate stood up and went to the freezer. After grabbing two pints of ice cream and a couple of spoons, she went back to the living space. "Couch might be more comfortable."

They went to the living room area, where Kate handed Addy a carton of ice cream and a spoon. Opening her own, she looked at Addy. "Okay, spill."

Addy took a deep breath. "I don't know where to start." She opened her ice cream carton and ate a spoonful.

"Well, is your current crisis guy-related, business-related, or general life-related?"

"Not really guy-related, though possibly guy-adjacent. More a combination of business and life."

"Okay. You still thinking of starting your own business? Or is that part of the crisis?"

"Still planning on that. Not sure where to start it, though. That's what sparked the current crisis, though it's spiraled a bit."

"Got it. Okay. So what are your options?"

Addy took another spoonful of ice cream and thought a moment. "I've been considering other areas of Boston, or checking out other cities that are not too far away. Springfield, or Providence or something."

"Just cities?"

Addy sighed. "That had been the thought. Not set in stone, but..."

"Part of the crisis?"

Addy nodded. "I told you about Pine Valley, right?"

Kate nodded. Addy remembered telling her bits and pieces about it, car breaking down and going back for Christmas, a little bit about Mike.

"There's a diner there, the one where I spent Christmas, and I've been emailing the owner back and forth. She's become a friend, a bit of a mentor."

"Okay. And she wants you to move to Pine Valley."

"How did you guess?"

"Just connected the dots. But you're set on a city, not a tiny town in the middle of nowhere."

"Well, it's not that tiny. When I went back at Christmas, I drove around a bit to look at the lights. It's bigger than I remembered, but, yes, it is still a small town."

"And you have no interest in moving there."

Addy sighed again. "I don't know."

"Have you made a pros and cons list? That sometimes helps me."

Addy shook her head. "No. I guess I could try that."

They sat in silence for a moment, eating their ice cream.

"Okay," Kate finally said, pointing at Addy with her spoon. "You remember a while back when we talked about why you were unhappy, and we started with why you decided to move to Boston?"

"Vaguely."

"Do you remember why you moved to Boston?"

Addy couldn't remember what she had told Kate. And since she hadn't had a concrete reason for moving to Boston, she shrugged.

"You told me that you basically picked Boston because you had a rough idea of where it was. And you wanted to live in a city so you could be around a bunch of people and lose yourself. And you were miserable because deep down that wasn't actually what you wanted. You wanted to find yourself, not lose yourself."

"Okay." It sounded familiar. And, unfortunately, it sounded like her.

"I'm glad you've been happier these past couple of months. And I know it's because you've been actually connecting with your true self, not trying to hide or do what's expected of you. So I'll ask again: why are you so set on starting your business in a city?"

Addy felt tears welling in her eyes, but she blinked them back and sniffed. "Well, wouldn't a city be better for business? There would be more traffic, a bigger potential audience. I want my business to be successful."

"Of course you do. But a city isn't the only place you could be successful. Sometimes, despite having more people, a city can be harder to make it in. There's more competition. And they're expensive, so you'd have to make sure the people who are there have the money to spend at your business, especially since your business wouldn't be a necessity like food or something. Not to mention the higher rent and other expenses."

Addy didn't have anything to add, so she stayed silent, absorbing what Kate was saying.

"Let me ask you this: are there businesses in small towns?"

Addy looked up. "Of course."

"And are they successful?"

Addy shrugged. "I would guess so. It seemed like all of the businesses in Pine Valley had been there forever."

"Okay then. So obviously a business can succeed in a town, too, not just a city."

"I know. I just…" She sighed. She thought back to Maggie's not-so-subtle hints, about the lack of entertainment in Pine Valley, the need for more hobbies for people to do, the growing town. Would there be a market for her business there? And was that really what was holding her back? Her crisis hadn't been brought on by a fear for her business's viability. It had been emotional.

Kate had been leaning back against the sofa arm, polishing off her ice cream, while Addy was thinking. "I think you've been working too hard. And focusing too much on this business thing and the future and all that. We should go out and do something fun, get your mind off it."

"It's Sunday."

"So what? There's still fun stuff we could do on Sunday. Though I don't think I would want to go clubbing or anything when I have work in the morning. Let me do a little digging and see what I can find."

"Okay." Addy worked on her own ice cream while Kate went to retrieve her computer. She appreciated Kate more than she could say. While they had gone out on occasion, catching entertainment at the local cafe or going shopping, they had also stayed in frequently, ordering takeout and watching a movie. And Kate had been supportive, a great source of advice and ideas, a very helpful sounding board. Kate had been a good friend. "I'm going to miss you when I move."

Kate looked up to meet Addy's gaze. "Right back at you." She smiled, then looked back down at her laptop. After some clicking and tapping, she looked back up. "Okay, there are a couple of singers at local clubs, an art gallery opening, or we could head to the movies and check out that new romantic comedy."

Addy thought for a moment. She really needed to get her mind off things, and she could use a good laugh. "Let's go with the movie."

"Sounds like a plan. Next showing is in an hour and a half. Think we could make it?"

Chapter 37

Mike thought back to what Maggie had said about living alone as he wandered from room to room, aimlessly searching for something he couldn't identify. He felt bored, lost, lonely. The shop was closed, his friends were all off doing other things, and he hadn't found someone new since he had broken things off with Jennifer.

He needed to get out of this house.

Grabbing his jacket and keys, Mike stepped outside and locked his front door. He had no idea where to go, but at least if he was walking he would be getting some exercise. And it would feel like he was doing something, even if he was just wandering aimlessly.

His house was at least a couple of miles from the center of town, and not really close to anything other than more houses. It was a quiet, residential neighborhood, with big backyards and trees lining the sidewalks. A good place to raise a family. That had been his thought process when he had decided he should settle down. His business had been doing well, and he wanted to put down roots, not keep dumping his money on rent. He had gotten a great deal on the house. It had needed updating and cosmetic work, and doing the renovations himself had been ideal for keeping his mind off the fact that he would be living alone, with no real prospects for a life partner to share it with. That had been five years ago. And he was no closer to settling down now than he had been then.

Mike sighed and shoved his hands in his pockets, veering toward the center of town. At least there he had a chance to see other people. Not many businesses were open on Sundays, but he could swing by the grocery store and pretend he needed things for dinner. Or grab a coffee at the cafe.

It was a beautiful early spring day. Trees were starting to bud, and he could hear children laughing and playing in yards as he walked past. He ignored the pang in his gut. He had to accept that a family might not be in the cards for him. Maybe it was time he came up with a backup plan. Maybe having something else to focus on would keep him from feeling so hopeless.

Mike tried to brainstorm as he walked. What were his options?

He had found purpose when he opened his business. It gave him something to do, and a decent paycheck, but it was also a way to meet the needs of the town while using his mechanical and problem-solving skills. He did not regret starting his business, and he had no intention of walking away. So he needed something to either fill the hours he wasn't at the shop, or something to help ease the loneliness he felt. Or both.

Filling the hours could be as easy as finding another hobby or project to keep himself busy. Cooking didn't take up too much time, and sports were dependent on weather and other people. He had been into woodworking when he was younger. Maybe he should pick that back up. He would have to get some tools and chunks of wood, but that was a possibility. Would he tackle carving small items, or making big stuff like furniture? Probably small items. He didn't have the room for more furniture. He would start small and see where it got him.

Okay. Good. He was getting somewhere. He was feeling better already. It might not ease the hole in his heart, but at least it would give him something productive to do. He had a feeling figuring out the loneliness part would take longer.

As he approached the center of town, he took in the sights that had been part of his life since he was a kid. Some things had stayed the same, and some things had changed. Overall, though, it remained the same welcoming small town he had grown up in. He loved it here.

It occurred to him that he hadn't seen the hole in the wall at the diner yet. Deciding to head there first, he made his way around the corner and across the street. If the diner started bringing in live entertainment, that would be something to occupy his time, too. The local bar sometimes had musicians come in, but he couldn't hit the bar all the time. And a little variety would be nice. He wondered what they had in mind.

Pulling open the front door, Mike stepped into the brightly-lit space. His eyes immediately made his way to the large doorway now visible at the far left of the back wall. "Wow." He walked over to the opening, still blocked off by caution tape.

Maggie joined him a moment later, chuckling softly as she approached. "Come to see the hole?"

Mike nodded. "Had to. It's been the talk of the town."

"This town needs better things to do with its time."

"That's where you come in, right?" He turned to face Maggie, grinning. "I hear you're going to offer entertainment."

Maggie nodded slowly. "That is part of the plan. And the space will be available for groups and parties. We may do some special events."

"It will be great when you have your holiday party."

"Yes, the extra space will come in handy. This past year got a little tight."

They both stared at the empty room past the doorway. Maggie had left lights on, likely to alleviate some of her visitors' curiosity. It looked like they were still working on finishing up the space, but it would be great when they were done.

"So what's the plan for the room? How will it be set up?"

"Well," Maggie said, gesturing as she spoke. "Here to the left, we're thinking of having a raised platform in the corner. It can be a makeshift stage if we get musicians or poets or whatnot, but in the corner it will be mostly out of the way otherwise. We'll be getting more tables and chairs to set up around the room. These will be different than the other ones in the dining room, though, because we want them to be foldable. We're going to be making a storage room over on the right, past the bathroom. That way if we want to make a large empty space, for dancing or something, we can just fold up the tables and chairs and tuck them away. There's the bathroom, of course, which will be getting a bit of updating. And that door on the end leads to the back room and kitchen, so we can have a server bring food and drinks right through there."

Mike nodded. "Sounds good. I can't wait to see it when it's done."

Maggie sighed. "We still have a bit of work to do. The construction part of it should be done within a week or so. Just the storage room needs to be built, and the doors installed. Then the bathroom remodeling. We'll be giving the regular bathrooms a face-lift at the same time, so that will take a little longer. And we need to order the furniture. We saved that for last because we don't really have a place to put it until the storage closet is completed."

"You've got it all figured out."

"Mostly. Costing a pretty penny, though."

"I think it will be worth it. I bet traffic will go up. And if you charge admission for the events, that will help recoup the costs, too."

"I don't think we'll be charging admission, but I suppose it depends on the event. We haven't worked out those details yet. But we do expect to see more people, and we're working on a catering menu for parties and such."

"That's great."

Mike ordered a cup of coffee to go and continued on his walk around the town center, drinking his coffee as he went. He was vaguely heading toward the grocery store, but he wasn't in a rush, so he took the long way around, past the library then turning the opposite way and heading toward the medical center, the motel, more houses and small businesses. He was definitely getting his steps in today. But more importantly he was killing time that otherwise would have been spent at home. This week, he decided, he would head to the closest place to find woodworking supplies.

"I've been thinking about your situation," Kate said to Addy a few days later after dinner.

"My situation?"

"Yeah, your where-to-have-your-business situation. Your friend wants you to go to that little town, and you seem determined to be in a city. Maybe what you need is a road trip. Scope out some possible locations and see if they feel right to you. That way you can make an educated decision."

"Hmm." Addy sat and pondered for a minute. "So you mean I shouldn't just point to a place on a map and uproot my life again?" She grinned.

Kate smiled back. "A little research is usually a good thing."

"It's not a bad idea."

"I've been known to have a few good ones."

"I have a few days off next week."

"There you go, then. Great timing."

So Addy spent the rest of the evening working out a path for her road trip. It would be a bit of a loop, heading south toward Providence, then west into Connecticut, north toward Springfield, then finally back east toward Boston. She would only have a few days, so she would have to be selective about where she stopped. That meant more research.

Her research was pretty helpful when it came to typical rent, demographics of the different areas, and other businesses in the vicinity. But when it came to foot traffic, Addy found that difficult to really get a feel for online. That would have to be done in person. All the more reason to follow Kate's suggestion. She was also finding that the cost of rent varied drastically, sometimes in a relatively small area, which meant she would have to explore the areas a bit and see what would best suit her needs.

If she was honest with herself, she had to admit that she was a bit nervous. When she left D.C. she was fueled by righteous indignation, and determination to change her life. Sure, she had been nervous, and insecure, and a bit lost from an emotional standpoint. But she knew she was making the right decision. Now she dreaded the thought of moving again, but, more importantly, she was anxious about starting over again, not knowing anyone again. Was that a good enough reason to move to Pine Valley? Or was she just being insecure? Maybe this road trip would give her some clues as to how best to proceed. It was worth a shot.

Mike didn't get around to going out for woodworking tools until Thursday. The shop had been busy, and he had just wanted to crash when he got home. But Thursday he was able to sneak out of work a little early, and he decided to see what he could find.

Plenty of craft stores carried a small selection of woodworking tools, and he likely would have been fine with a basic starter set. But he found a store that specialized in woodworking, and he decided to take the trip. It was a little farther than he intended to drive, but it was a beautiful day, and he rolled his window down and cruised along, wind ruffling his hair. He felt at peace for the first time in a while.

The store was larger than he had anticipated, with rows of unfinished wood and simple furniture toward the back and aisles of everything from carving tools to stain and paint filling the rest of the space. It was a little overwhelming, but he had time to spare, so he strolled through the aisles, looking for inspiration and refreshing his memory on how it all worked. He didn't want to bite off more than he could chew, but the store was a little bit of a drive, and he didn't want to have to come back every couple of days, so he needed enough supplies to last him a while.

An associate from the store was able to guide him toward some starter sets, and Mike selected knives, chisels, and a couple of simple kits. He found himself more drawn to carving and whittling than to full-on project construction, so he selected things accordingly. Then he headed over to the wood aisles, which overwhelmed him all over again. Since he was just doing this for fun, though, he selected a variety of woods based on how they felt and looked. He figured he would learn about their durability and temperaments just fine as he worked with them. He would just have to keep track of which was which. Picking up a small hand saw to be able to cut the pieces down, he decided he had done enough damage to his wallet and headed toward the register.

As he headed to his car after checking out, a sign across the street caught his attention. The building housed an organization of some kind. It looked to be Big Brothers Big Sisters. And in one window was a big sign that read "Mentors Wanted." *Hmm.*

After unloading his purchases into his car, Mike wandered closer. The building looked to be closed for the day, but there was a phone number and a website, and Mike jotted a note in his phone to look into it later. He wondered what mentoring entailed.

By the time he got home, he decided it was too late to get started on the woodworking, so he heated up some leftovers from the night before and settled with his laptop in the living room. He wanted to learn more about this mentoring thing. From what he could recall about mentoring, it involved helping kids, being a role model and supporting them. He could do that. It would be like being a parent without being a parent, a bit of a sample. He had always thought he would be a good dad. And since it looked like that wouldn't be happening any time soon, maybe this would be the next best thing.

Mike spent the next hour learning all he could about being a mentor, then submitting an interest form. It looked like the process would take a while. They had to vet him a bit, make sure he would be a good fit, and learn more about him to match him with a child. He was excited but also a little nervous. What if they didn't want him? What if the kid hated him? He tried to talk himself down a bit. He could do this. It would be fine. What was meant to be would be and all that.

Regardless of the end result, Mike felt positive about taking a step. He could make a difference in the life of a child, even if he wasn't in a relationship. He could be a role model, a parent-like figure. And if this opportunity didn't work out, he could try other places. Maybe the school or library or something would have ways for him to work with kids on a volunteer basis.

By the time he headed to bed, Mike had a smile on his face. Yes, this was a good thing.

Chapter 38

Addy wished she had a more reliable car. She hoped it would survive the mini road trip. She did not want a repeat of what had happened in October. So she resolved to drive as little as possible, rely on walking or public transportation when it was practical. That would also give her a different perspective, she reasoned. It would be more research into the areas she was considering.

Though it made her nervous, Addy opted to take back roads rather than stick to the highway. While she was focusing on certain cities, it didn't hurt to check out the towns on the way. So she ate each meal in a different town, taking the time to walk around and scope out the surrounding businesses and residential areas a bit. The weather was perfect for a stroll, and she felt she had to give each town an opportunity to win her over. Pine Valley wasn't the only small town in New England, and there were larger towns, too. Even if she decided not to be in a city, that didn't mean she had to go to Pine Valley. She had options.

Kate seemed to think that Addy would feel it in her gut when she found the right place, that the right town or city would call to her. Addy was trying to take a more practical approach, and she had come armed with her research to make an educated decision. But she had to acknowledge that while she drove through many charming – and not-so-charming – towns, nothing felt quite right.

She decided to find a hotel just outside Providence, then take a bus into downtown. That would help her avoid the potential traffic nightmare of driving into the heart of the city, plus she could check out public transportation and the surrounding area.

Providence seemed nice. Modern but historic, busy but welcoming. Addy walked around for a bit, checking out the mall and other commercial areas. There seemed to be lots of opportunity here, plenty of people, nice areas to walk around. A good selection of specialty shops and restaurants that her business could fit into. She explored, getting a feeling for the vibe of the city, before stopping for dinner at a burger bar. After dinner, she hopped on a bus and headed back to her hotel. She wasn't looking for nightlife, especially not by herself. Maybe next time.

When she was back in her hotel room, she pulled out her laptop and did a little more research on Providence. As with many cities, rent would not be cheap for a commercial property, especially if she wanted to be in the heart of the city. Outskirts were a little less, but the decreased visibility could affect her prospects, especially in the beginning. She made some notes in an online document about the towns she had seen earlier in the day and her impressions of Providence, then got in her pajamas and settled in with a movie. She was asleep by ten.

The drive from Providence into Connecticut the next morning was peaceful. Addy came across many small towns and plenty of picturesque scenery. She felt her body relax, the tension from her predicament fading. Though Addy felt energized being in the heart of a city, she had to acknowledge that the tranquility of these rural areas held its own appeal. Would the lively pulse of the city continue to invigorate her? Or would she long for stillness after a while? Would peace and quiet continue to soothe her soul? Or would she long for excitement? Maybe she should go with one of the larger towns. Surely those would be the best of both worlds, right?

Maybe she was just putting too much pressure on herself. No one said she had to have all the answers. She could take her time. Or she could change her mind in a few years and head down a different path. A year ago she had no idea what she wanted to do, and now she was demanding that she have all the answers. No wonder she felt torn and stressed.

She felt butterflies as she approached Pine Valley. She hadn't told Maggie she was coming. She wanted to see how she felt without intervention first. And as she pulled into the parking lot beside the diner, she got her answer.

Addy had never seen Pine Valley in the spring. The now-familiar sights looked lush and green, full of life and hope and promise. And as she stepped out of her car, she felt it in her gut. She was home.

Addy felt tears welling in her eyes, and before she could help it, they were spilling down her cheeks. She collapsed onto a bench by the side of the road, unable to stop the downpour. All the pressure of her past life, the strain and worry of a new beginning, the anxiety of feeling lost and confused – it all poured out of her, falling in teardrops on the grass by her feet.

That was how Mike found her.

She saw his feet stop in front of her, though she didn't know who it was. When the feet turned, and she felt him sit next to her, she sniffed and scooted away a few inches before gazing up at the person who had invaded her personal space. When she met Mike's gaze and saw the concern and affection in his eyes, the tears began anew.

He put his arms around her, and she leaned into him, letting him comfort her. He stroked her hair, not saying anything, offering her strength and support. After a while the tears subsided, but still they sat, silent, watching the cars and people go by.

When Addy finally pulled away, she felt cold, and she tucked her jacket more closely around her. Had she imagined the sense of serenity that had fallen over her? She took a deep breath, closed her eyes, and absorbed the whoosh sound of the traffic, the scent of coffee coming from the cafe across the street, the bacon and fries seeping from the diner. It definitely wasn't the city. But something about this little town spoke to her. It welcomed her, embraced her, and made her feel like she belonged. She hadn't imagined that.

Addy opened her eyes and turned to face Mike. "Hey," she said after a moment.

"Hey." He gave her a lopsided grin. "What are you doing here?"

"Do you mean in Pine Valley? Or sitting on this bench balling my eyes out?" She attempted a smile.

"Both, I guess." His expression softened. "Are you okay?"

She nodded. "I think I'm actually more okay than I've ever been."

He stared at her a moment, then nodded, too. "Yeah, I think you are." They stared at each for another moment before he cleared his throat. "So, why are you here?"

Addy looked around the bustling town center and sighed. "Scouting out a location for my new business."

Mike's eyebrows shot up. "You're starting a business? Here?"

Addy shrugged and turned back to face Mike. "Thinking about it. What do you think?"

"I...uh...give me a minute to process."

She grinned at him, watching the range of emotions flashing over his face.

"So why were you crying, then?"

Addy's grin faded. "Because I was lost and confused and stressed and over-whelmed and torn and miserable. And then suddenly I wasn't. I guess all those feeling had to go somewhere."

Mike cocked his head to one side and looked at her, his eyes flitting over her face. "And now?"

Addy took a deep breath. "Now I feel suspiciously hopeful."

Mike took one of Addy's hands in his own. "I'm glad I decided to go for a walk today."

"What *are* you doing walking around town on a Wednesday morning?"

Mike shrugged. "Needed a little fresh air and used running out of office sup-plies as an excuse. I can honestly say you were the last person I expected to run into. Especially sitting on a bench in tears."

"Thanks for joining me. I wasn't expecting that, either." She released Mike's hands and placed both hands on her thighs, then took another deep breath and stood up. "But now, I think I have to go see Maggie and tell her she was right."

"About what?"

"About Pine Valley."

Epilogue

The grand opening for The Art Spot took place in October, on the one-year anniversary of Addy's first visit to Pine Valley. Addy was a bundle of nerves. She had poured her heart and soul into this space, transforming what had once been a clothing store into a blend of learning space, retail shelving, and creative haven. She knew Maggie had been telling everyone about the grand opening, and there had been an article in the town newspaper about it, too. Of course that didn't mean she would see anyone, but she hoped at least someone would show.

For her opening weekend, she was offering special deals on after school programs, parties, and select items to paint. She had decided to also stock assorted art supplies that customers could purchase and use on their own, figuring this would help fill a gap in the town's retail offerings while also providing another source of income for her, and some of those items were on sale, too.

But her favorite part of the shop was actually something that brought her no money at all and would end up costing her. She had decided to mount a canvas on one wall, with a picture drawn on it in pencil, that visitors could help paint. It would be a community art project, with the end result being auctioned off for charity. She had set up stools in front of the canvas, and a cart with paints, brushes, and a rinsing cup. A sign invited guests to participate. She hoped some people in town would participate. She would feel a bit awkward doing it all herself.

Addy had decided on a nine o'clock opening time, and at about a quarter of, as she was setting out refreshments, Mike arrived. He knocked on the door, and she let him in, grateful to have him by her side. He had been an invaluable support to her over the past few months, offering suggestions and business guidance, or just a friendly ear. They hadn't discussed resuming their relationship, but the possibility was there. She supposed only time would tell.

Maggie arrived shortly thereafter, oohing and aahing over everything. She had seen bits and pieces of the store's renovation but hadn't yet seen the final product. She walked over to the white canvas hanging on the wall. After a moment, she nodded. "I like it."

Addy grinned and released a breath she hadn't realized she'd been holding. "Would you like to be the first to paint a section?"

Maggie hesitated. "I'm not much of an artist."

"That's okay. The idea is to just share a little piece of yourself, work together to create a piece of art."

After a moment, Maggie agreed. She picked up a brush and opened the jar of blue paint. The picture Addy had drawn was a bouquet of flowers, and Maggie colored in the petals of one flower. "There."

"Perfect." Maggie placed the brush in the rinsing cup, and Addy checked her watch. "Oh! It's time!"

Walking over to the front door, Addy unlocked it and pushed it open. To her surprise, a small group of people was waiting on the sidewalk in front of the shop. "Hello! Welcome." She ushered them in, inviting them out of the chilly morning air. They spread out, grabbing mini doughnuts and pastries from the refreshment table, picking up flyers and brochures, and perusing the shelves of offerings. A couple of women approached the canvas and, after figuring out its purpose, added bits of red and purple to the picture. Addy's stomach flipped in excitement. It was working. It was actually working.

More people came in, and the space filled with chatter and laughter. Addy answered questions, helped customers pick out items, and even set up a family to paint pottery pieces. Visitors came and left, seemingly happy with the new addition to town. By the time she closed the doors nearly ten hours later, she was exhausted but excited. She had scheduled a birthday party, a holiday party, and a scout troop event. She had sold an assortment of art supplies, with many of the customers commenting on how nice it would be to get these things locally now. Several of the visitors had decided to paint pottery, and the canvas on the wall was nearly halfway completed. Some of the artists had even added shadows and texture, giving the canvas less of a paint-by-numbers feel. It was coming along beautifully.

Mike had come and gone during the day, checking on his own business in between making sure Addy had food, didn't run out of anything, and sat down for at least a little while. When he showed up shortly before closing time, she greeted him with a grin.

"I take it you're happy with how it went."

"It went so much better than I anticipated. The advertising worked, and every-one was so friendly, and look!" She walked over to the canvas wall and gestured. "It's looking amazing!"

Mike grinned back at her and moved over to place one arm around her shoulders, pulling her close to his side. "I'm glad it went well."

They turned to look at the store, now somewhat disheveled and with slightly empty shelves in places. "I am not cleaning up tonight," Addy said with a sigh. "I am so ready to crash."

"Not surprising. Why don't you lock up and cash out, and I'll clean up the food and trash. We can work on some of the clean-up tonight, then the rest can wait for the morning."

"Sounds like a plan." She walked toward the front door, flipped the open sign to closed and locked the deadbolt. With a deep breath she gazed out at the street in front of her. The town was winding down for the evening. Silence had fallen, a stillness she had grown to appreciate.

"What are you looking at?" Mike asked, coming over to stand behind her.

"Nothing. Just the town."

"I'm glad you came back."

Addy turned to face him. "Me, too."